The Conversion

Also by Joseph Olshan

The Conversion

Joseph Olshan

ST. MARTIN'S PRESS

NEW YORK

This is a work of fiction. All of the characters, organizations, and events portrayed in this novel are either products of the author's imagination or are used fictitiously.

www.stmartins.com

Book design by Jonathan Bennett

Library of Congress Cataloging-in-Publication Data

Olshan, Joseph.
    The conversion / Joseph Olshan. — 1st ed.
      p. cm.
    ISBN-13: 978-0-312-37391-7
    ISBN-10: 0-312-37391-0
    1. Americans—France—Fiction.   2. Novelists—Fiction.   3. Self-actualization (Psychology)—Fiction.   I. Title.

PS3565.L8237C66 2008
813'.54—dc22

                                                   2007044345

First Edition: April 2008

10 9 8 7 6 5 4 3 2 1

For Anne B. Adams and Francesca Duranti

~

"I never made him do anything in my life but once, when I made him burn up a bad book. That's all!" At her. "That's all!" Paul broke into an irrepressible laugh; it lasted only a second, but it drew her eyes to him. His own met them, but not long enough to help him to understand her; unless it were a step towards this that he felt sure on the instant that the burnt book (the way she alluded to it!) was one of her husband's finest things.

—HENRY JAMES, "The Lesson of the Master"

Part One

One

~

WHEN ED AND I WENT TO STAY at the Auberge Bi-rague, we certainly never expected to meet up with anyone either of us knew. Our habit was to take breakfast in the café and sit near a window that opened onto a flower box overflowing with nasturtiums already wilting in the sultry air. One morning several days after we arrived, a woman in a short-sleeved black shirt and beige linen pants entered the café and sat down several tables away from us. I noticed Ed watching her with laserlike curiosity. "My God!" he gushed to me in a whisper. "I *know* this lady." She turned out to be Marina Vezzoli, an Italian writer he'd met at a literary festival in Chile. He got up and approached her, shoulders canted forward like a primary-school student cowering before his teacher. Extending his hand, he said, "Hello, Marina, Edward Cannon. We met in Santiago. At the festival."

She was around sixty, quite trim with tawny shoulder-length hair veined with gray. Her eyes were pale and thoughtful as she looked at him with puzzled reserve. But soon her face kindled with recognition. "Ah, of course," she said. "Forgive me. What are you doing in France?"

Ed explained that he had lived in Paris for ten years, that he'd just sold his apartment right across the street from the Auberge Birague, and that he and I were staying at the hotel for a couple of weeks before he left for America to begin a tenured teaching job at New York University. At this point Marina Vezzoli shot me a look of bemused curiosity. And then, for some odd reason, Ed launched into Italian.

After listening to a few awkwardly constructed sentences, Marina leaned forward, patted him gently on the hand, and said, "Why don't you speak in English, my friend? It would be easier on both of us." I winced for Ed. His Midwestern charm was usually able to warm even the chilliest reception. As famous as he was, he was unaccustomed to having his own pretentiousness pointed out to him. Clearly stung, he straightened his six-foot-two frame, nervously raked his fingers through his longish, thick dirty-blond hair. He was fifty-nine years old, and if you'd seen him at a distance you might have mistaken him for an aging, slightly paunchy surfer. He returned to our table, flustered and embarrassed.

Genuinely bewildered, I said to him sotto voce, "Why did you . . . switch to Italian like that?"

"I don't know why. Now I feel like an idiot."

"Well, don't worry. It's not *that* critical."

"Something is wrong here, Russell," Ed warned me. "She acts as though she barely remembers me, but believe me, she does. We sat next to each other at dinner, as a matter of fact." They'd spoken at length; he remembered one fascinating conversation in which Marina Vezzoli assured him that Henry James didn't really understand Italians. And then a few years after Santiago, Ed had served on a panel in Saint Paul de Vence discussing two Italian writers, one of whom came up and introduced himself as a friend of hers. "Now she treats me like a stranger," he grumbled.

"Whose ego is as big as Mount Vesuvius." I glanced over at the woman now perusing the *Corriere della Sera* while sipping a glass of freshly pressed grapefruit juice.

Ed went on with a bit more restraint. "Besides, I've told you all about her. She's the one who wrote that wonderful novel that was made into the film we saw. The one called *Conversion*." He leaned back in his chair.

"Oh," I said. "So that's who she is."

As though perceiving that Ed and I wanted to gossip about her, the woman took a last bite of her toast, carefully folded her newspaper, and pushed back from the table. Nodding cordially at us, she left the breakfast room. I remember Ed watching her exit with an expression of pure reverence.

Our room at the Auberge Birague was decorated in blond Swedish furniture; it had tall glass doors that opened onto a balcony. Late in the night on the day we encountered Marina Vezzoli, I woke up to a terrible pounding, to the smell of sweaty bodies, to the alarming realization that there were other people in the room besides us. Two men wearing black ski masks pulled down to their lips had burst in from the terrace. One of them held what looked like some sort of semiautomatic weapon. The other pulled out a long, bowed knife, the sort that might fillet a large fish. When I saw the first glint of the rifle's muzzle, when I heard the menacing click of the magazine, I was paralyzed by one desperate hope: that the gun and the man who held it would somehow just melt into fantasy and that I wouldn't have to die right there. "Stay where you are!" the gunman garbled in foreign-sounding French. As if we'd dare to counter them.

"Your money! Your passports! Where!" snarled the other one with the knife.

I managed to tell him and he opened drawers, quickly scrabbling through the contents. He turned back to me and took several steps closer, waving his dagger. "They're not!"

"I have them," said Ed, who was leaning up in bed on his elbows, looking typically angry at something not to his liking. It was as though he hadn't even registered the threat of the weapons.

From here on it all blurs, the order of things. I don't know if it was right then when one of them actually protested, "Wait, shit! Two men. *It's two men,*" before Ed recklessly jumped out of bed. Standing there in a T-shirt and skimpy underwear, he started screaming in English, "Get out of here, you monkeys! Go fuck up somebody else!" There was a quick tirade in a language other than French, but then they actually listened to him. They turned and rushed back to the balcony and clambered out whatever way they had come in.

Ed and I sat on our twin beds in quiet disbelief, staring at the doors opening onto the slate mansard roofs of the place des Vosges. The curtains billowed as if in the lingering spirit of such an outrageous intrusion. "Are you insane?" I finally shouted at him. "They could've killed us!"

Collapsing onto the bed, Ed, looking befuddled, admitted, "I can't believe what I said."

"You called them monkeys. And they weren't even black!"

"By the way, that language they broke into, that was Albanian."

"So what! They still could've understood English."

He stared at me, blinking. "Of course, you're right, Russell. But you should know me by now. What happens when I get angry."

"Ed, you told them to fuck off," I reminded him.

This most eloquent of poets, who could also be profoundly vulgar, actually laughed. And then I did, too—comic relief it must have been. It suddenly seemed as though the bizarre incident had never even occurred. The apoplectic yelling had attracted no attention, no knock on the door, nobody calling up from the lobby. The hotel had remained absolutely still. Could no one have heard the commotion?

"We've got to call down and tell them what happened," I insisted.

"Okay, but wait a minute." Ed swept the hair out of his eyes and peered at me. He was breathless. "You heard them say 'two men,' right?

I told him I had.

"They weren't expecting to find *us*."

I didn't answer, trying to figure out why this might be significant.

"Don't you get it, Russell? They were expecting a man in bed with his wife."

"If that's true, then we're doubly lucky they didn't shoot us, the wrong people."

"No, Russell. If they were hired or politically motivated, if they'd have done something to us, then they would've failed their purpose."

"All the more reason to let them know downstairs."

Ed looked distressed. "I don't want to," he insisted. "I just can't deal with anything more tonight. They'll insist on calling the police, who will want to take reports. We'll be up all night." He hesitated. "They're gone; they're probably halfway across Paris by now. We can let the hotel know in the morning." He paused again, seeming bewildered.

"What is it, do you think you recognize something about them?" I asked.

"No, no, it's not that," he replied. He got up and went into the bathroom and left the door ajar. "Not at all." He remained there in complete stillness and finally I asked him if anything was wrong. When he didn't answer, I walked over and found him staring at himself in the mirror. His eyes finally met mine. "Nothing's wrong, I'm just getting some Xanax." He reached for his shaving kit, opened a plastic cylinder, and took out a one-milligram pill that he divided equally and gave half to me.

I awoke the next morning from a very deep sleep. The room was profoundly quiet. Ed's face looked unnaturally pale. I climbed out of my bed and went over to check. I ventured to feel his forehead. It was chill to my touch, winter cold; he no longer seemed to be breathing. This was as shocking to me as the appearance of that semiautomatic rifle just hours before. "It can't be!" I said aloud. "He can't possibly . . ." I told myself, cradling him in my arms like a child. I swept my fingers through his hair and softly whispered, "No, no, no," as though my gentle reproach could make him breathe again.

Two

~

NEARLY A YEAR EARLIER, a mutual friend had mentioned to Ed that I was spending six months in the 18th arrondissement on an apartment swap and encouraged him to contact me. He called on a Sunday afternoon in early August, assuming that I'd drop everything I was doing to meet "the renowned poet" for a drink. But I couldn't meet him that particular afternoon, and when he asked why, I recklessly divulged that I had a date with a married man. Ed kept pressing for details until I described how Michel's wife sprinkled Chanel into the washing machine when she did his laundry and how the faintest whiff of Faubourg Saint-Honoré boutiques and haute couture came off his neck when I climbed aboard his black BMW and we rode the arrondissements, leaning into the corners, rocketing our way out of the city toward the Périphérique, and beyond that, a rush of woodlands on the way to Versailles. Frenchmen tend to be compact and slight; Michel, however, was half German, tall and broad with wide shoulders and a lean, taut belly that I clutched as we rode. When the weather is so hot and blistering, two guys in tank tops on a black BMW motorcycle is probably not so abnormal a sight in Paris. I suppose there might have been something unusual about our intimate configuration, in the way I rested my hands proprietarily on his narrow hips when the motorcycle coasted to a halt in traffic. People would often stare at us both in admiration and disdain.

"He sounds delicious," Ed had said to me. "I'll look forward to meeting him, too."

"Unfortunately, you won't be able to. He's in the closet. Being quite married," I explained.

"You certainly look smitten," Ed commented the day we finally did meet at a café off Saint Germain. It was another sweltering evening and the scantily yet always tastefully clad patrons were facing the street, sipping tall cocktails in the shade of contiguous umbrellas, and despite the weather, managing to look cool and composed. Out of place, I'd shown up sweaty and conspicuous in a heavy leather motorcycle jacket; Michel and I had just returned to Paris from riding out to Chartres.

"Just overheated," I replied, shrugging off the jacket.

Looking me up and down, Ed frowned. "You're really perspiring. Couldn't you have bothered to change?"

I apologized; if I'd gone back to my apartment in the 18th, I'd have been late meeting him here on the Left Bank. Hesitating a moment, I finally slumped into the chair opposite him.

"You reek, too," he complained.

This was getting annoying. "Maybe we should meet some other time, then," I said, making a move to get up.

Ed flinched and I could see a flicker of anger freezing his

expression. "No, stay," he insisted. "Have a drink. What will it be?" Flipping his hair away from his forehead, he continued to stare at me intently. His eyes were a startling, deep sea blue, and, I remarked to myself, darker than Michel's. He pointed to his own drink. "How about Campari?"

"Fine."

He flagged the waiter's attention, gave the order in perfect French, and then gently asked about my own command of the language.

Less annoyed now, I managed to tell him my French was, at best, mediocre. Although I did have Italian. "Which actually helps me understand the Parisians."

"How much longer are you here?"

"Another six weeks."

"So you'll try and improve it, won't you?" he asked. "You won't be like those Americans who come here thinking that English is so universally spoken—"

"Believe it or not, you're the first person I've spoken English to at length for weeks." I neglected to tell him that Michel spoke pretty good English, a language in which we conversed almost exclusively.

My first impression of Ed was that he looked exceptionally well for a man in his late fifties. His body was meaty and yet well proportioned on his six-foot-two frame. He had a broad and florid fullness to his face, lively eyes, and, of course, his bleached-out surfer's hair. He asked how I'd gotten to know Italian, and I explained that I was first-generation Jewish-American; that my father had been born in Ferrara and, beyond that, in college I'd majored in my ancestral language.

Ed considered this for a moment. "Todaro," he said to me

with the proper accent on the first syllable. "That's really not a Jewish-Italian name."

"How do *you* know?" I asked, secretly impressed.

"Jewish-Italian names are pretty recognizable. They're often the names of cities. If your name, for example, had been *Ferrara* . . ." He broke off.

I explained that the family name was once Todà and that my great-grandfather had changed it—perhaps out of some kind of silly snobbism—well before Mussolini assimilated Hitler's racial laws. But my mother's family did indeed come from Ferrara.

"Do you know that Giorgio Bassani came from there?" Ed asked.

I explained that, in fact, the writer and I happened to be second cousins.

"Oh really? Fantastic! So then you knew him."

"Actually we never met. But of course I've read everything he's written."

"Ah, but what a shame. I'm sorry you never did." Ed began drumming his fingers on the crisp linen napkin that lay before him on the table. I noticed how thick and strong his hands were and thought they looked more like the hands of a dockworker than those of a poet. He went on. "I was lucky enough to spend some time with Bassani . . . twice in Rome. We had dinner together. He was a great man. Unfortunately, the Italian literary world destroyed him. He died miserable. His English was excellent, however. He would have been able to read *your* work."

I looked at him.

"Our mutual friend gave me a copy of your novella. I admired it," he said in a measured tone. "It made me curious to meet you. I'd like to talk to you about it sometime. Perhaps when we're better acquainted."

"No time like the present," I said, and Ed waved me off and said he wanted to wait until at least the next time we got together.

I figured Ed was merely being polite and hadn't really appreciated what he'd read. The manuscript, itself, had been consistently rejected until it found a home in a literary quarterly out of Oregon.

"So how old are you anyway?" he asked.

I told him that I was thirty-one.

"Ah, nice and young. You have your whole life ahead of you. Your whole career."

I pointed out that by the time Ed was my age, he'd already published a few books and was well-known. "I mean, you're probably one of those impossibly successful people. Who started high and never looked back. Who never even had a failure."

Ed laughed. *"Que tu est naïf!* There's nobody like this. Even the most successful people have failures, although from the outside it might seem to the contrary. And of course there is always the strong temptation to perpetuate the notion of wild success. As for me, I've known failure. In fact, I've been living with failure for a decade."

"What do you mean?" I asked with skepticism.

Ed claimed to have been working on a memoir for what seemed like forever. He'd spent much of the last ten years wrestling with it day after day. "And it's still basically a piece of shit."

"Oh, you're just being hard on yourself," I told him.

He grimaced. "I wish that were so. If anything, I'm too easy on myself."

For a moment I tried to imagine this sort of internal struggle. "Well, what do your peers, your editors say?"

He smiled tightly. "Nobody's seen it. I wouldn't dare show a single word of it to anybody."

In the silence that followed, Ed leaned back in his chair, catching the late-afternoon sun on his broad face. I had a feeling that he drank a lot more than he should. "But enough about me. Are you working on anything?"

I told him no, that I'd basically spent the last three years freelancing for Fortune 500 companies, translating business Italian into business English, and that I was currently doing a large job for IBM. However, I'd also translated the odd poem, and one novel for a small press in Louisiana.

Holding his drink up to the light, inspecting it as though it were some kind of multifaceted jewel, Ed said, "Your novella really should be translated into Italian." He now locked eyes with me. "It'd be a delight for you. I *love* reading the Italian editions of my poetry."

He sounded faintly obnoxious, but I'd soon discover that this sort of bluster was more self-protective than arrogant. Unfortunately, the thrill of meeting him had begun to evaporate. Slowly I was being engulfed by the familiar, plummeting sense of despondency over the small rations of time that I was spending with Michel Soyer; the fact was I'd become fatally hooked on a married man.

Then, as though reading my thoughts, Ed surprised me with the gentlest of gestures. Grazing my chin with two of his fingers, he said, "You *have* to pick yourself up, Russell."

Thinking that he was referring to my stalled literary career, I said, "Hey, maybe I'm just not meant to be a luminary like you."

"No, no, I mean I can tell that you're sad . . . about your lover. So let me forewarn you: You probably have a lot of heartbreak ahead of you in your life."

I was affronted. Heartbreak? From whom? Not from *him*. "Why do you say that?"

His arrogance was gone. "Because I believe that human nature has a tendency to choose misery over happiness. That's why we all keep repeating the same mistakes."

And so he had divined the nature of my attachment to the married Frenchman and perhaps even sympathized. Ed's last comment would plague me for months.

A week after our meeting at the café, without even realizing it, I passed Ed's apartment building on the rue Birague. I was making my monthly pilgrimage to the Museé Victor Hugo at the far corner of the place des Vosges. The museum was my own private shrine to literature. I'd wander through the scantily attended drawing rooms, eyeing the relics of the great novelist's life, his collection of landscapes and portraits, his thousands of books. At various times during my visit I'd stop strolling, shut my eyes, and start praying for the inspiration to begin writing again.

I'd always been impressed by the fact that Hugo wrote standing up. I liked to linger at the entrance of the room where his tall, simply designed desk was on display. I'd imagine him dipping pen to inkwell and scribbling *Les Misérables*, which, after Balzac's *Cousin Bette*, was my favorite nineteenth-century French novel. I remember that particular summer afternoon I was feeling distressed at how preoccupied I'd become with Michel. It was this discomfort that had brought me to seek solace at the museum.

From the very beginning Michel had made it quite clear that he was deeply entrenched in married life and that his sex life with men was and would always be strictly recreational. He'd even warned me that if and when his wife found out about our affair, he'd be bound to break it off without any deliberation. When somebody boldly shows their cards in this way, when everything seems so straightforward, it's almost easier to deceive yourself. One might think, for example, "Okay, I can clearly see that this is a bad situation and I'd be a damned fool to get too caught up in it." But then, I painfully discovered that, paradoxically, such candor on the part of your lover can also be disarming.

I mistakenly thought I'd be able to see trouble coming long before it arrived. I certainly tried to keep Michel's unavailability in mind every time we got together. But I found that with each session of lovemaking, my resolve to protect myself unraveled just a little bit more. Eventually I fell into that unwanted state of longing for someone to whom you're profoundly attracted but who will never be able to give you what you want. But you hang on anyway. Nothing is more painfully absurd than when lust dupes you into believing it's destiny.

Standing before Victor Hugo's mahogany *secrétaire*, I thought to myself that if I only could begin another writing project, this just might prove to be the antidote to my quixotic attraction to Michel. I reckoned that starting even a short story would give me a focus, a purpose that would have as much power to distract me as a new lover might. Then I impulsively reached beyond the silk cordon that forbade entry into the room and grabbed a leg of Victor Hugo's desk. The wood was wonderfully smooth and cool to the touch, and I closed my eyes for a moment and prayed for inspiration, even for deliverance from my romantic obsession. The next thing I knew, a hand grabbed my shoulder. A guard in vermillion uniform had appeared out of nowhere. "Touching, that is not allowed here, *sir!*" he told me imperiously. "You will have to leave now." Hand clamped to my arm, he escorted me out of the museum into the place des Vosges, where, in the gauzy, summer light, Parisians were sunning themselves in the formal gardens, eating their sensibly small tidy lunches.

In some corner of my soul I believed that my prayers to the ghost of Victor Hugo eventually would be answered; and they actually would be, but not in the way I'd wanted. That very evening Michel called me with an atypical invitation: to ride with him to Aix-en-Provence, something like a six-hour trip on the back of his motorcycle. "We'll stay a few days," he said in his characteristically unflappable manner. And yet his deep baritone voice always seemed to carry an undercurrent of seduction. "Then maybe go on to Nice. See how we feel," he said. "What do you think?"

"What about Laurence?"

"She'll be going to the house in Brittany with the children. Why do you ask?"

Why did I ask? Simply because ever since I'd known him, Michel always dutifully accompanied his wife and children to their house in Brittany. And so I boldly inquired how he'd managed to wrangle the time away from his family. There was a pause, as though Michel had not anticipated such scrutiny of his generous invitation. "I like to go on long rides. Once or twice a year I take off for five days. And this time I thought to myself: Why not have the company of a sexy American boy?"

He arrived at my place in the 18th early the next morning. He'd told me to bring only what I wore, an extra pair of dress pants, and the necessary toiletries. Although at six feet tall, two inches taller than I am (and ultimately, two inches shorter than Ed), we wore the same size button-down shirts and T-shirts.

Michel liked me to wear his clothing, mainly because it was always beautifully laundered (and mine never was), but also because it was a fetish for him. In particular he liked me to borrow his very brief French underwear; he hated what he called my "unsexy American boxer shorts." When we lay down together, he'd pull his underwear halfway down my thighs and with an evil grin tell me how "slutty" they looked. This part went on in English; his enunciation of the two *t*'s in *slutty* was charmingly erotic.

The first morning of our excursion, when I climbed aboard the BMW, knowing that he'd carefully packed the saddlebags for two (and, I imagined, with the clothes that he wanted me to wear), I started to get hard thinking about it. We began to weave through the North African 18th arrondissement, passing street vendors hawking roasted corn, Arabs mingling in their djellabas. I tightened my knees around his legs and remarked to myself how good our bodies felt in this sort of motorcycle tandem.

Although Michel's height and bulk made him seem more like an American, his face had a refined, carved look that could not belie his Germanic ancestry. At the same time, his almost-too-prominent features were softened by the ringlets of light brown hair that highlighted his gray eyes. Sometimes when I'd had a few drinks, or when I was annoyed with him, I found his face too sharp-featured, too angular to be called handsome, and when he made me furious I thought he looked like a rodent.

Our relationship was primarily an inspired, romanticized sex life whose reverberations were deceptively profound. A sex life characterized by a lot of sultry chatter about the sorts of things we did and what we might do in the future. Until I met Michel I never realized that previous erotic episodes could be talked about to heighten the mood of the present; until I met Michel I never realized that remaining partially dressed during the act could be incredibly arousing. He certainly broadened my appreciation of the male body, from the obvious pull of his form-fitting T-shirts to the suggestion of contours through well-cut business suits. On the rare occasion that we went out for dinner, he would supervise my dressing and always insisted I wear a crisp button-down shirt and a tie. There was nothing sexier than taking off another man's tie, he used to say. It didn't take me long to realize that the more layers Michel had to go through to get to the core experience of the unadorned body, the more turned on he became. Which was why he was a big fan of leather—arm bands and chaps—and of flimsy G-strings. He liked adding these accoutrements to the mix as much as he liked to talk about what we'd do in bed. Once I even dared to question him if he made love to his wife in a similar fashion, and he looked at me as though I were insane, as though he expected me to just assume he made love to his wife as chastely as possible. Or that he no longer made love to her at all.

It was a glorious excursion blessed by arid, cloudless weather; the wind blasting our faces on the motorways was as dry as dust. The temperature spiked during the day but always ended up in chill. It took two days to get to Aix. We arose early every morning and had enormous breakfasts of baguettes and local cheeses and huge cerulean bowls of café au lait. We avoided the superhighway and found our way along secondary roads, stopping for hour-and-a-half lunches of hard salamis and cornichons and bottles of Burgundy. We spent so much time on the motorcycle that the vibrations from having ridden that many hours stayed with me long after we dismounted.

We had sex at least twice a day—usually at the hotel. However, on one occasion we managed to do it in a secluded grove of poplar trees that Michel staked out before pulling off the main road. He'd brought a vinyl tarp that rolled up tightly and commanded very little space. Wrapped inside the tarp was a bottle of lubricant that came in the shape of a medium-sized dildo. He spread the tarp in the shade and we went at it like two beasts. I must add that during our entire time away, he was effusively affectionate and seemed incredibly content, although I did notice a few moments when he became worryingly withdrawn.

We rode back into the city in late afternoon of the fourth day—glorious Paris luxuriating in a scarf of sunny amber; so many vibrant fruits were perfectly arranged in oak bins, grand monuments casting languorous shadows, well-heeled Parisians crowding the narrow, smoky cafés and strolling the Seine arm in arm. There was a pervading smell of fermenting yeast and the slow, simmering scent of cognac sauce. Hugging Michel around his taut stomach, resting my chin on his shoulder, I found myself bitterly regretting that in a just a few moments I'd be alone. And, indeed, in a month's time, my apartment swap would be over. I found myself wishing some other opportunity for work would present itself before I'd have to hoof it back to my cheap one-bedroom flat in Brooklyn in an out-of-the-way place called Gravesend.

As we drew within a few blocks of my apartment, the sadness

of having to part with Michel overwhelmed me. After all, I'd never before had him to myself for four days straight. It was a luxury I felt I could easily get used to and even began fantasizing that Michel's feelings for me would become so urgent and undeniable that he'd be forced to leave Laurence. I got myself worked up into such a state of absurd hope that I felt tears smarting in my eyes and had to fight off the urge to weep. For I instinctively knew I could never show this desperate side of myself, that it would portend disaster. Instead, I promised myself a swim at the fifty-meter pool at the Forum des Halles. I'd do laps, look at all the attractive Parisian men, maybe even get some attention, and somehow make myself feel better.

When we finally arrived at my building, Michel parked the motorcycle next to one of those green, octagonal newspaper kiosks. The swarthy North African man who sold roasted corn there recognized me, nodded, and smiled. But I didn't really pay much attention to him then because I was fighting to keep my composure. I hastily grabbed my toiletry bag and my dress pants and was preparing to say good-bye when Michel hit the motorcycle's kill switch and said to me, "Russell, I need a word."

"About what?" Sensing something wrong, my whole lovesick body went on pulsing alert.

His gaze was steady and without expression. "Well . . . honestly Laurence finds out about our relationship."

The terrifying feeling of free fall began. "She *did?* But did you tell her?"

"Of course I don't tell her!"

"Then how?"

He heaved a great sigh in the way the French do and exhaled

through tightened lips. I was so light-headed and frantic that the subsequent words came to me piecemeal, as though we were in a wind tunnel. Apparently, the previous week while he and I were having coffee in out-of-the-way Saint Germain-en-Laye, a friend of his wife also happened to be there, unbeknownst to Michel. We'd been seen holding hands and nuzzling each other.

I heard him saying quite distinctly, "And so when Laurence asks me, I don't deny it." Not quite comfortable with English, Michel had an annoying tendency to cling to the present and future tense, whose narrow dimensions somehow made his news sound even more harrowing and irreversible.

"Well, you said you would never deny it," I replied automatically in a breathless voice.

He merely shrugged. "She has told me to stop it. And as you know, and as we discuss, I must do as she asks."

"But . . . the last four days?" I sputtered. "What have they been *about?* Why did you go away with me when you knew *this* was going to happen?"

Michel said, "Well, she knows I will be with you. I tell her I want to be. And she let me go, but only if I will speak to you at the end."

"So you've known about it the whole time?"

He nodded.

"That's . . . really lousy." I began to stutter. "You at least could have told me first!"

Michel's expression was at once compassionate and, I couldn't help noticing, slightly impatient. Later on, after replaying the scene thousands of times, I began wondering if that moment of slight irritation was actually the sign that, although my sexual power seemed to equal his, he was actually realizing that I was still a lot younger and greener than he was, in short a liability. An enormous leaf came feathering down from a tree and brushed his face and he closed his eyes self-protectively. At that moment he looked so vulnerable. Had I wanted to, I could've easily punched him and knocked him to the ground. When he spoke again, it was with more patience. "Would you really want to know, Russell?"

Of course. Why wouldn't I?

He shook his head resolutely. "If you know, I doubt you will have gone with me. And if you know and still decide to go with me, you would never enjoy yourself." He smiled forlornly. "At least we can say that we have these four wonderful days. Not true?"

Now I think to myself: Who else but a Frenchman would be able to pull off a breakup with such disarming diplomacy? But of course, at the time I still felt monstrously mistreated.

"Well then, if I have no say in this, then what *can* I say?"

"Nothing but good-bye, Russell," he replied with great courtesy, offering me a handshake instead of a kiss. Quite a contrast to perhaps six hours earlier when he was begging me for sex.

I was so furious with Michel at that moment I couldn't speak. Although the compulsion to attack him and hurt him openly grew stronger by the second, it ended up scaring me into a state of inertia. All I could do was watch him lope over to his BMW and mount it. With a flick of his wrist, the motor ignited and his motorcycle launched down my street, its chrome tailpipe transmitting a sad flash of acknowledgment in the dusk of a late-summer city.

Watching him ride out of my life was so incredibly painful. There was no delayed reaction, no numbness or shock. The tearing sensation that is so clichéd was stunning. And somehow in the midst of it, I happened to notice an elderly woman, in a kimono, her thick mascaraed eyes staring down at me from her apartment window, a cigarette between her fingers. She observed the obvious signs of a *chagrin d'amour* with what I imagined to be the recognition of someone who'd perhaps lived through it many times herself. She reminded me of a wise old Colette peering down into the street like a patron saint.

I sank into a fuguelike depression, the sort in which your appetite dries up and there is a perpetual coppery taste in your mouth. I slept very badly, my dreams frenzied and feverish and always of operatic length. I'd wake up in the middle of some outlandish scenario in which Michel was playing most of the parts—male and female—and marvel at the insane dimensions of my imagination and then, like a psychic prisoner, tumble back into the same nightmare.

I will say, however, that Paris comforted me: the precise contours of its formal gardens à la française; the rapturous, musky scent of its towering linden trees; winding streets bulging with shops whose eclectic displays inspired fabrics with brilliant color and texture; fresh flowers that seemed to have been cut only moments before in some vast, sun-dappled field. All of it brought brief moments of solace.

One week into this terrible interlude, Ed called me out of the blue. He sounded genuinely surprised to learn of my *chagrin d'amour* and immediately invited me to dinner. By our third engagement he'd already begun lobbying for me to stay on in Paris—with him at his apartment on the rue Birague. Until he'd mentioned the tantalizing idea I'd been consoling myself with the thought of getting far away from Michel and France, of returning to America. And now I can admit to myself that I let Ed convince me to stay on because I still held out some stupid glimmer of hope: Michel would miss our relationship so much that, despite his promise to his wife, he'd come back to me.

Three

~

I N AN HOUR WE SHALL CROSS INTO ITALY. And I believe that will make you feel better," says Marina Vezzoli,
the Italian writer Ed and I met in the café. A day after his
death, she'd contacted me, extended her condolences, and offered to let me stay in her family's villa in Tuscany while I sorted
things out.

I look out at the taupe-colored landscape of moldering stone
farmhouses, gnarled olive trees, and espaliered grape vines. "Beyond the border we'll stop for a *panino*," she suggests. "You've
eaten nothing since this morning."

"No, grazie, non ho fame." I find myself answering in Italian,
then regretting the switch, hoping she won't admonish me to
speak English the way she did Ed.

She nods respectfully and I vaguely realize: Of course she
won't correct me. Not at a time like this. She's knows what I've
dealt with during the last few days in the wake of Ed's fatal
heart attack. I've eaten very little and have hardly slept. "May I
ask you something?" Marina now says.

"*D'ai,*" I answer.

This triggers her to lapse into Italian. "You didn't go back to America with the body—"

"I couldn't afford to, knowing I had to come back for the inquest."

"Nevertheless. I just don't get a sense that you are in love with this man."

Or the way Ed used to say it, "You can't love me the way I want to be loved," something that continues to pester me. I explain that for me, but unfortunately not for him, the relationship had been more of a friendship. And if Ed hadn't died perhaps it might have been only a matter of months before our closeness was wrenched apart by this inequality of feeling. In light of this, Ed's dearest friends had always treated me with caution, even contempt, as though I were some kind of literary hanger-on.

"First of all, not every relationship is sexual," Marina observes. "And second, it's absurd, this idea you're a hanger-on." She signals to change lanes. "Didn't you tell me that besides your translations to earn your living, you've done some serious work?"

"Yes, that's right." I'd told her that I'd translated some poetry and one novel for a small press.

"I've also been informed that you published a novella somewhere, too," she presses.

In a literary journal out of Oregon, I tell her, but then ask point-blank how she found this out.

"I have a friend who works in Intelligence. When I mentioned to him that I invite you to the villa, he insisted on having a look into your life—before I would bring you to my house. Let's just say he did some digging."

How strange, I think. I wonder why Marina would do such a thing.

"So what is this novella about, anyway?" she persists.

I briefly describe the story line, which is based on an incident in my childhood where I witnessed the drowning of a young child and, in my way, felt responsible.

Marina listens with interest and finally says, "But now, if you've published something such as this, you deserve to be called a writer. You are among *us*. Only time—and not the critics—will anoint the writer whose work will last."

Her glance is shrewd, her eyes glacially pale. I know Marina is being earnest; she hardly seems the sort of person who'd indulge in flattery. I want to tell her that I feel as though my small *succès d'estime* is a fluke of nature, that the need to make a living has propelled me far away from the conviction that I have any sort of literary vocation.

Beyond this, I am hardly surprised to learn that she has her contacts in Italian Intelligence. Ed had told me that Marina's father, an anti-fascist, had been a famous politician who'd helped craft post–World War II Italy's constitution, that his death had been observed all over the country, and that, for a while, Marina herself had bent to the pressure of following in his footsteps and briefly served as the mayor of Genoa before returning to her childhood home in Tuscany.

And yet her manner and appearance strike me to be more Scandinavian than Italian, even down to her tasteful yet simple dress, which is neither ultra chic nor expensive. She seems to prefer tweed jackets and corduroy pants with snug twinset sweaters that are often much brighter in color than the rest of her ensemble.

Marina now asks me how I met Ed, and I explain that a mutual friend had introduced us and how, when my affair with the Frenchman ended, he'd been mysteriously waiting in the wings and had helped me through that difficult time.

"I understand now. Say no more," Marina murmurs. She brakes the car in anticipation of the last toll station that remains before Italy begins. She pulls up to the booth, smiling at the boyish sentry patiently waiting for her payment, then realizes she hasn't even prepared it and begins rummaging through her purse saying, *"Désolée . . . désolée,"* eliciting his smile of indulgence. Once she finds her euros, pays the toll, and we are speeding along again, she sighs and continues in Italian, "The last few days . . . hard to believe when you actually think about it."

A thumbnail flash of the brutal intrusion, the faces in fury, but at what? The dull gleaming gun. And the evil sun, the long, scabrous knife, the clammy fear gripping once again. "I just wish I could . . . well, just take in what's happened," I say. "It all still seems so absurd."

"You're in shock," she reminds me. "Of course you are. Now, I must confess to you how bad I feel because the last time I spoke to your friend, I made him feel his Italian was inadequate."

"Luckily, he was a Francophile," I find myself saying. For the first time since our journey began, we both laugh.

This bit of shared irreverence seems to dismantle the facade of strict decorum that we've been maintaining. The highway is crossing a divide that affords a commanding view of the Mediterranean, whose tourmaline depths, now more than a thousand feet below us, pitch and roll beneath the glaring sunlight. The heat wave plaguing Paris also afflicts the South of

France; with the warm dry air blasting me in the face, I look out over the water and dream of a cooling swim.

"I do remember that your friend worked very hard at being charming," Marina remarks at last.

"He didn't think his charm worked very well on you."

"Nonsense! I just couldn't place him at first."

"Apparently you had long conversations."

"So what? Not everybody is blessed with immediate recall. I wasn't expecting to see him. But he obviously demanded instant recognition because of his celebrity." Hearing Ed spoken of in the past tense gives me a terrible jolt, and a buzzing, windy silence follows the remark. "I don't know about you, Russell, but I must say I never feel completely at ease around people for whom charm and suavity are second nature. I admit that I am utterly fascinated by them, but that's where it ends for me."

"But charm isn't ever second nature. It comes at great expense. Always," I say just as I spy ahead of us a checkpoint where cars are being randomly stopped and searched by men in military fatigues. In travel between one European Union country and another, this border searching seems superfluous, a throwback to another era before the European community became economically linked. However, in light of the recent Middle East conflicts and the various terrorist bombings in Europe, the "instant checkpoint" is becoming more frequent. On certain days the Italian authorities set up random roadblocks and do unannounced inspections and searches. "What a mess!" Marina exclaims, and then suddenly pulls the car hard to the right and steers for a man wearing a splendid khaki uniform. More prepared this time, she rolls down her window, reaches deftly into her purse, and pulls out a green laminated photo I.D. The official scrutinizes it, then smiles at her flirtatiously and waves us through in a lackadaisical manner.

I wait for Marina to explain why we have been so effortlessly conducted into her country while the rest of the motorists have been detained at checkpoint. But the silence endures. So finally I ask.

"I do this drive so much that they've given me a badge. Not for privilege, but rather to just make it simpler when they do these checkpoints. Only because I often go to France on government business."

I ask what sort and she says, "A cultural emissary of sorts. I am often invited. The French like the fact that I was once a politician." As though to avoid further discussion of her ambassadorial role, she tells me, "Now, this is the part of the drive, from Ventimiglia to Tuscany, that I detest. Because of people like him." She gestures at the rearview mirror. I turn around to find that an aggressive motorist has driven up to what seems to be only a few feet of the rear of Marina's car, insistently flashing his lights. This is typical behavior of drivers who streak along in the left lane and muscle slower motorists to the right. But Marina is already in the right lane, so there's nowhere she can go. "My God, this is madness! What do you want?" she demands. "Does he want me to drive off the road?" she asks me.

The car finally pulls up alongside us. The long-haired driver peers at us through reflective sunglasses and then races ahead. Out of my window, a sign for Ventimiglia proves that hundreds of kilometers behind us is the city of Paris, where I've just spent a year and a half, and hundreds of kilometers ahead of us in Tuscany is Marina's famous residence, which is called the Villa Guidi.

Crossing into Liguria, we follow a series of high overpasses and tunnels carved into the mountainside. "You don't have so many tunnels in America," Marina remarks to me. "They cost a fortune. That's why our motorways charge such high tolls." We descend along the coast, passing Genoa and La Spezia and the Gulf of Venus, where Shelley's boat went down on the way from Livorno to Lerici. As I begin to think about untimely deaths, I wish that Ed had woken up before his heart attack, that he'd said something to me, given me a few words, however trivial, to hold on to. The last thing he told me before the sedative took hold and induced him to sleep was, "I feel funny, Russell."

We finally turn inland right before the beach town of Viareggio, where Puccini spent his last days, and soon are heading in the direction of Florence. Partway to that Tuscan city, we quit the *autostrada* and only moments later arrive at a pair of tall iron gates. A long driveway lined with linden trees leads to an enormous villa with ocher-colored walls, a terra-cotta hip roof, and surrounding hedgerows of oleander and hydrangea. "At last!" Marina exclaims, and exits the car to be hysterically greeted by a pack of six dogs.

"Russell was absolutely fine until Italy. Now he sleeps all the time."

"Doesn't that make sense?" asks a man. "Think about it. Held at gunpoint, wakes up to find his lover dead of a heart attack."

"Wasn't a lover. Really more of friend."

"Oh, come on, Marina, you know what I'm saying."

"I'm merely explaining the facts to you."

"You've made them quite clear. Nevertheless—"

"If he doesn't get up tomorrow like a normal person, I'm going to yank him out of bed and make him walk with me."

Their voices fade as their conversation migrates to another part of the villa. Who could this other person be?

What is this fatigue that has endured for these last ten days? I've been sleeping in eighteen-hour increments, my sleep fevered with nightmare. The scenes are mostly Parisian, late-night excursions through a city of dark splendor in which I am on my way to collect Ed's ashes from a crematorium. And as I try to find my way through a warren of streets, I'm carrying a burden of depression, the yoke of a man who has always been single and solitary, *célibataire*, as the French say. In these dreams I feel so dejected by the death of my friend that I thrash and flail and often wake up with my head at the foot of my bed.

Now it's late at night and a throaty chanteuse is singing American hit songs from the seventies and eighties: "You are the sunshine of my life"; "I want to make it with you." I smell attar of roses and deep spice. Once again, there seem to be intruders in my room, and I cry out.

"*Ma è una camera privata* (But this is a bedroom)," a woman exclaims to her companion, who says, "*Ah, scusi, Signore. Non lo sapevamo* (We didn't know)."

"Didn't you see the do-not-disturb sign on my bedroom door?" I shout at them.

"We were looking for a place to make love," the man admits candidly.

These straggling guests have ventured where they don't belong. On the way here from France, Marina explained that although there were many grander villas in Tuscany, Villa Guidi's common rooms are extraordinarily large, which makes it prized for weddings and corporate functions. She rents it out and conducts a bustling business. During my stay there already have been two large and raucous affairs. Lying there, listening to the din of voices and the cover tunes, the revelry in full swing, I somehow manage to fall asleep again.

And awaken, but now to the sounds of a chain saw. I've cycled back into daylight, but it's hard to know precisely what time it is. The villa is hunkered down for siesta, and my wooden shutters, opened by the housekeeper very early in the morning, are closed once again around noon to ward off the late-summer heat. I've been staring up at the high coffered ceiling of carved circles and hexagons and now get out of bed and throw open the shuttered window. The sky is an untarnished azure, the lawns stretching toward the tall stone walls surrounding the property are freshly mown, and Marina's young, angelic-looking Polish groundskeeper is hacking away at the limbs of a fallen tree. There is a smell of freshly sawed wood and burning fires. Intent on staying awake, I keep the shutters open and instinctively move to the densely packed bookshelves lining an entire wall. I find literature in five languages including poetry, biographies and political texts. I notice the short novels of Mario Soldati and my favorite Italian novel of all time, *La Coscienza di Zeno*, by Italo Svevo. Then I discover an entire shelf filled with editions of the *Bibliothèque de la Pléiade*.

Pléiade books are printed by the great French publisher, Gallimard, leather-bound volumes decorated with gold leaf, onion-thin pages that I consider to be the most beautiful mass-produced books in the world. The volumes are dedicated to the "stars" of world literature, showcasing in the splendor of high production values a renowned author's greatest works. Owning a library full of Pléiade editions is something that I've always dreamed of, despite the fact that my French still lags substantially behind my Italian. Michel had quite the collection.

I tentatively approach the sacred volumes. I crack a few, setting off flares of dust and a delicious crunching of leather spines and parchment: a sort of literary chiropractic. Here are some of my favorite authors: Musil, Voltaire, Lautréamont, Baudelaire, Rousseau, Sartre, Proust, and even Faulkner and Sinclair Lewis. The Pléiade is proof, I tell myself, that when the author dies, his words continue a life of their own. I used to dream of literary life after death for myself until I learned that it was possible that one's work could be completely ignored; then I began to say to myself, "What does it matter, anyway?"

But of course things mattered greatly when it came to the literary legacy of somebody like Edward. I remember how, shortly after the police came and took his body away, I went to the folder that contained the last sequence of poems he'd been working on, many of which I had typed for him. With shaking hands, I rifled through the printed pages, as precious as sheets of gold, reading about the watery reflection of Venice seen from the window of his room in the Palazzo Barbaro.

Among the Pléiade in the bookshelf I notice a very broad, very old book on European judicial theory. And then it suddenly occurs to me: I have a court date in Paris.

In a panic, I throw my clothes on, scrub my teeth, and rush out into an enormous dining room with a gray-and-white marble floor. Staring at me are two huge portraits done in oil: a man in nineteenth-century military regalia with a diagonal sash across his chest, and a woman decked out in a ball gown ruffling with tulle. At the end of the room are a suite of six pairs of

French doors, and just beyond them I spot Marina sitting outside on a loggia half as long as a football field. Showing a lot of
leg in a short floral skirt, she is holding a glass of white wine
and chatting with another woman, more or less the same age,
dressed in tennis whites. I rush toward them barefoot, and Marina no sooner says, "Oh my God, look. The ghost has arisen?"
than my abrupt arrival triggers the pack of her six dogs lying
at her feet. A single bark trips off a yapping chorus and soon I
am surrounded by howling, hackled mongrels of various sizes.
"Basta," says Marina in a low throaty voice. *"Zitti! Tutti."* The
dogs continue barking compulsively and she then begins to
question them like children, asking them whatever do they
want and what they are on about.

"What day is today?" I ask.

"The twenty-fourth of August."

"I knew it!" I cry. "I was supposed to be in Paris yesterday.
I've missed the inquest!" The dogs, startled by my tone of voice,
begin a reprise of barking backed with a lot less conviction, and
this time Marina doesn't even bother to silence them.

"All taken care of. Wait a moment. First, meet my sister-in-
law. Daniela."

"I'm sorry. How do you do?" I say in English.

"Well, and waiting for my afternoon *partita,*" the woman answers coquettishly.

Marina now tells Daniela in Italian that she needs to speak to
me privately and suggests they begin their card game a bit later
on. Daniela gives a shrug of disappointment and pushes her
rhomboid-shaped sunglasses down over her eyes like a race-car
driver. Showing off her English, she says, "Glad to have met you
finally," before loping across the loggia.

Once we are alone, Marina informs me that she'd consulted a physician who'd told her that my sleeping for most of the day was a symptom of shock over Ed's sudden death and advised her that I shouldn't travel back to Paris. "And so I had to get a Parisian friend of mine involved—a lawyer who went to court on your behalf and told them that you were not well." She went on to say the Parisian medical examiner had come to the conclusion that Ed's heart attack had occurred a few hours after the men broke into our room. No prosecutable link could be found between his death and their intrusion.

"So they're not going to investigate?" I ask.

"Well, of course they will still try to find these men. They must. Otherwise other people could be killed. But now you've already given the police a statement, correct?"

I tell her I had.

"So you've done your part. And you're free." Marina flips her hand in a whimsical manner and smiles at me. "You can return to America, although you're certainly welcome to stay here at the villa until you're feeling better."

I collapse in the cane chair opposite her, keenly feeling the loss of Ed, remembering how, after I had called down to the front desk, a doctor not much older than I arrived at our room barefoot and in silk pajamas. Obviously a hotel guest who had been summoned from his room, the physician had taken one glance at Ed, felt his pulse, and murmured, "He's gone." Then he turned to me and asked how *I* was.

"What difference does that make?" I recall snapping at him.

"Your friend is obviously dead," he replied with typical French evenhandedness. "There's unfortunately nothing more I can do for him. But you, you're still alive."

Marina, meanwhile, has been looking at me with great concern. "Do you realize that you've been sleeping almost continuously for days on end?"

The words no sooner leave her mouth than the urge to crawl back into bed seizes me. I nod and tell her I can't help it.

"Understood. But you must try to not sleep so much now," she scolds gently. "Go for walks, take a trip into the city. Walking there takes only a half hour. Make yourself do things. And as I said, stay here for as long as you like."

"You've been very kind to me."

"Who wouldn't be kind? Perhaps I have some reason to be kind," she says mildly with a smile.

"Oh?"

"We'll discuss it on our stroll."

It occurs to me that Marina seems far too sophisticated to entertain the idea of perhaps having an affair with a younger man clearly wired toward members of his own sex, not to mention the fact that I am dealing with the emotional fallout over Ed's death. But neither does she seem particularly maternal. Besides, hadn't she just introduced me to her sister-in-law? "I had no idea you were married," I say in English.

She laughs and responds, "We didn't discuss it," gazing at me with disarming directness. "You sound disappointed. As though you were hoping to court me."

" 'Court you' is a very antiquated phrase."

Marina ignores my comment and returns to Italian. "Anyway, I am married, but not to her brother."

"You divorced him?"

"Not exactly. We were already separated when he—her brother—died very unfortunately. In an automobile accident."

I murmur that this must've been very tough and she solemnly nods her head in agreement. "Yes, it was. Terribly. And now I am married for the third time," she admits quietly.

I stare at her, fascinated. "So then where's your husband?"

It's her turn to look surprised. "What do you mean, where is my husband? He's here at the villa."

Feeling awkward, I say, "Why haven't I met him?"

"Well, you've been asleep."

"But shouldn't I?"

"I suppose you should. But actually he's a recluse. He stays in his room mostly. My Carla brings him all his meals. Have you noticed all those books in your room?" she asks. "In fact, the room used to belong to Stefano. But when I began renting the villa out for weddings, he moved to the part of the house that would be the farthest away from all the public activity. He mostly just stays put, reads and writes his articles. At night sometimes, if you stand in the middle of the *salone,* you can hear the pitter-patter of his old typewriter, the one he's always used, dating back to his days as the chief cultural critic with the *Corriere.*

"Anyway," she goes on, "you have two phone calls. One is from that very aggressive Annie Calhoun."

"Did you actually meet her in Paris?" I ask.

"We introduced ourselves at the hotel."

"She's Ed's literary executrix," I explain.

"I figured as much. She called—it was a few days ago—and was asking about a certain manuscript of your late friend."

I groan and then inquire about the other call.

A puzzled yet somehow amused look shades Marina's face. "A Madame Michel Soyer."

I involuntarily pitch forward in my chair, my head reeling.

"What's wrong?" she asks.

I explain that she's married to Michel, my ex whom I haven't seen in over a year. Why on earth would she be contacting *me?* "How could she have found me *here?*"

"With ease, my friend, with such incredible ease, you have no idea. As one would guess, the death of the decorated American poet has been reported. And you, as his companion, are mentioned, obviously." She begins counting with her fingers "It was in *Le Monde,* here in *La Stampa, Corriere della Sera, Il Gazzettino,* and even in our local paper, *Il Tirreno,* where they reprinted . . . I guess it was the last poem that he ever published."

" 'Venice Sinking by Degrees'?" I ask.

"Yes, the very one. It's really quite graceful, even in translation. It gives a very unusual glimpse of a city that has been written to death. I must say, the images of decay are remarkable. Down to the descriptions of the algae in the water and the barnacles on the boatslips."

The poem had actually been written about a trip that we took, Ed and I, when we stayed in the Palazzo Albrizzi, a private residence owned by a Venetian nobleman. Besides the barnacles and the algae, Ed melodiously describes the enormous hanging glass lanterns in the palazzo's entryway. The poem seems to be about the dying of energy and ardor but it's actually—he admitted as much—about the fact that I'd been unable to return his aroused affections in such a romantic setting.

"Anyway," Marina goes on, "this woman who called you here surely saw the articles and rang up the hotel. And probably made the concierge think she knew you well enough to get information."

Another wave of fatigue, the urge to recoil from Ed's dying and these people trying to contact me who clearly want something. I suppose my eyelids begin fluttering because Marina barks at me, "Don't fall asleep again! I'll make you a coffee. For God's sake, you need to do things. Get your mind off of this. I know, go make your phone calls. The names and numbers are written down in the kitchen. Then get on some proper shoes and we'll go for our walk."

One of the dogs understands the word *passeggiata,* and the frenzied barking begins again. Marina silences them, amused.

She gets up and leaves the loggia, whose stone balustrades are so old they seem to be crumbling or dissolving. To the left of me, over a walled Tuscan city just a few kilometers away, rise the blue peaks of the Apuan Alps.

Reluctant to get into a conversation with Ed's overly zealous executrix, I linger on the loggia. I gaze up thirty-five feet at high arches, frescoed with trompe l'oeil to look more architecturally ornate and gilded, and then toward the far wall. Here are beautifully executed though slightly pockmarked frescoes of a pastoral scene: sheep and their shepherds, a snaking river, the unmistakable gold-and-olive-colored Tuscan hills, tall cypress spires.

There is a blue slip of paper next to the kitchen telephone with Marina's scrawl:

For Russell:
1. Annie Calhoun   001 212 777 4145
2. Madame Soyer   0033 42 71 65 86

Suddenly fearing bad news about Michel, I decide to call Madame Soyer first.

To my great disappointment I get an answering machine with a bilingual message in French and English. I hang up, and as I am standing there contemplating my next move, Marina's housekeeper, Carla, comes into the kitchen. A stout woman of late middle age with dark copper hair and a practically lineless face, Carla has been kind enough to bring me a few meals in my room: carbonara that she claims is made from the eggs produced by her chickens; pasta complemented by the villa's fresh tomatoes and mint; plates of prosciutto; wedges of Tuscan pecorino with clusters of Sicilian grapes.

Carla speaks a blurred, truncated Tuscan dialect that is a challenge for me to understand. However, a few days ago I overheard her telling a workman, "No, no, you can't go in there now. He's sleeping. Sleeps all the time. Like a crazy." An insult perhaps, but somehow this struck me as uproariously funny and I started to laugh, so much so that Carla opened the door and said, "What, what is it? What is so amusing, *so* suddenly?"

"I'm not a crazy," I said, still chuckling.

"God in heaven forgive me," she'd replied. And then commanded me to go and stroll the garden. "Would be the cure of you," she'd said gruffly. At the time I didn't listen to her.

Now she greets me brusquely and, putting her stout muscle behind it, begins wiping down a lazy Susan built in the middle of a round highly varnished wooden kitchen table. To me a lazy Susan is a very middle-American convenience, and I wonder what such a suburban contraption is doing in a fifteenth-century Tuscan villa. On the counter a slab of prosciutto nestles in a delicatessen meat slicer. Eyeing it, Carla asks if I'd like some. When I politely decline she mutters something unintelligible to herself and begins to mop the terrazzo floor. She merely pretends to be disgruntled and disagreeable; I will soon learn she is completely devoted to Marina, and even more devoted to Marina's mysteriously reclusive husband.

Annie Calhoun, the literary executrix, picks up after the first ring and actually hesitates before agreeing to have the charges reversed to her. She claims to have gone to the New York University–subsidized apartment where Ed had sent all of his belongings, has successfully found all the writing files in his computer, sorted through his papers, which are all relatively well organized, but has not yet located the manuscript of "the memoir," which she'd unsuccessfully searched for among all the papers he'd had with him in the Parisian hotel.

Annie Calhoun had known Ed for more than thirty years. An essayist of sorts, very early in her career she landed a tenured job at a small New England college; according to Ed, she went on to publish very little, virtually nothing during the last two decades. Annie is the sort of person who would think nothing of badgering the Cathedral of Saint John the Divine into postponing an afternoon concert in order to book Ed's funeral, something she boasted about having done when we first met after he had died. I just happen to know that Ed had seriously considered transferring the responsibility of his estate to somebody whom he felt was more emotionally stable, somebody less petty and volatile than Annie Calhoun. But I guess now that's a moot point.

During our first meeting at the hotel, I'd tried to explain that the French authorities had ordered me back to Paris in ten days' time to be a respondent in a formal inquest. I told Annie I had very little money in reserve, certainly not enough to stay on in France for another ten days. My only choice would be to use the one-way ticket that I'd bought to go home to America and then borrow money to return to France when it was necessary.

"So why do *I* have to be concerned with this?" Annie had asked in a voice hoarse from traveling all night and from smoking unfiltered cigarettes.

Hesitating a moment, I said, "If I had any resources at all I wouldn't even bring it up."

"So then you're asking *me* for the money?"

"I was actually hoping . . . well, that the estate might help pay, being that Ed is at the center of all this."

Annie is a tall, long-limbed woman with shoulder-length iron-gray hair and a shrewd, sculpted face whose smile pulls her lips up asymmetrically to the left. That day she was dressed in thin charcoal-gray slacks and a black cotton V-neck shirt that revealed a throat covered with liver spots. "I'll look into it, Russell, okay? In the meantime, I have a lot to deal with here."

So summarily brushed off, I found myself remembering all of Ed's complaints about Annie, including that she leaned on him far too much while expecting him to do the same. There, in the hotel lobby, I'd noticed that we were attracting attention from the traumatized staff, who, instead of accepting the idea that riffraff could so easily infiltrate their establishment, had already convinced themselves that we'd hired a street hustler and that Ed had died perhaps after pulling an all-nighter of recreational sex. In light of these assumptions they were making it quite clear that they were eager for me to depart.

Now, standing in Marina's kitchen, hoping to stave off a conversation about Ed's memoir, I ask Annie if she's managed to locate copies of the last sequence of poems that he'd been working on.

"The ones about the Palazzo Barbaro?" she asks, referring to the famous residence in Venice that had attracted a cluster of well-known American poets during the sixties and seventies, Ed among them.

"Yes."

"As I said, I have everything *except* 'the manuscript.' There is where I believe you come in," she says pointedly.

Obviously, the discussion can no longer be stalled.

As he had explained when we first met up at the Left Bank café, for the last ten years Ed had been struggling with his memoir, which ran some three hundred pages. Many of his friends—Annie in particular—had kindly offered to read it and give suggestions and, hopefully, encouragement. But Ed kept his own counsel. He tortured himself with the idea that it was an irremediable failure. In the year I spent with him I'd noticed that he seemed to agonize a lot less over his poems, which he either massaged and filigreed to a state of impeccability, or simply destroyed before they saw the light of day—all in all, a very cut-and-dried attitude. And yet I thought that some of his throw-away efforts were perfectly good attempts that would have been gratefully published by any number of top-tier magazines. He was a self-flagellating perfectionist of a poet who understandably had much more difficulty writing straight, narrative prose.

As it happens, I'm familiar with a good swatch of the manuscript—according to Ed, besides himself, the only person in the world who is. At his wit's end one afternoon, he'd asked if he might read a section aloud to me. He told me that he was willing to take this leap of faith because I'd managed to publish a novella. When Ed read to me for the first time I offered both genuine encouragement and, according to him, provocative suggestions. Soon he began showing me what he felt were some of the manuscript's more problematic sections. And I agreed with him, they *were* problematic: they were long-winded, meandering accounts of where he'd been when he'd written certain poems, as well as pages upon pages of descriptive writing that neither told a story nor illuminated any persons or events—in short, thousands of words of lapidary travelogue. There were also long, somewhat embarrassing rants on his loneliness, his inability to remain in a relationship for more than a few years. My ongoing advice to him was simply to streamline the memoir as much as possible.

Finally, after having won his trust the hard way, I'd only recently begun working with him on what I felt was the most promising and powerful ninety-page section of the book with the idea of his publishing it either as an excerpt or disguising the characters and some of the events and bringing it out as a novella. Ed actually approved of my edits but made me swear to absolute secrecy about our collaboration. And although he would have been loath to admit it, this surreptitious engagement had become the central pillar of our relationship.

I now tell Annie, "If the manuscript isn't at NYU, I have no idea where a copy could be. Have you checked the mail in the Berkshires?" Ed had planned to spend the last few weeks of the summer at the house he rented every year in Massachusetts.

Annie claims to have already contacted the post office there. They'd found nothing. But now comes a salvo that she clearly has been waiting to deliver. "I found a yellow Post-It in the trunk full of his papers that says in his handwriting . . . Here, let me read it to you directly: 'The manuscript is in Russell's computer.'"

Busted, yes, but not in the way she thinks. Before I came over to Paris for the apartment swap I'd bought a new laptop and was using my old laptop case to carry books and papers. Several months ago Ed had asked to borrow this older case to carry around the typescript of *his* manuscript, which he'd written partly in longhand and partly on a typewriter. He'd jocosely taken to calling the contents of the carrying case "Russell's computer." He distrusted computers and used them only to store the final versions of his poems for the purpose of printing copies to send along to various magazines and publishers. My response to Annie manages to be the actual truth, although it conceals a lie. "That was his plan all along. To input the entire manuscript on my laptop. But he never got around to it."

"Why don't I believe this?" she says after a short pause.

"You don't trust me. But then again why should you?" I hazard to say.

Just then a ringing phone startles me and I realize I'm standing next to a very compact-looking fax machine that begins to groan electronically as it prints out a thermal curl of paper. I can't help but read the communication, a wedding confirmation. I resume, "Let me ask you this. When you do finally locate the manuscript, are you planning to publish it?"

"That's hard to know. I have to see what form it's in."

"Even though you know he wasn't ready to bring it out?"

"I know that he certainly complained about it a lot."

I remind Annie that Ed had plainly told both her—and me—that he would never publish his memoir until he got it absolutely right, that he was greatly dissatisfied with it at the time of his death.

"Certainly. But then there are the critics and the scholars and the students of his work, not to mention his readers to consider."

I hear somebody coming into the kitchen and turn to see Marina carrying two empty wineglasses, which she places quietly in the sink. I hold up a finger and make a lugubrious face. "*La strega letteraria*," I whisper in Italian. "The literary witch." Marina rolls her eyes and leaves.

Annie resumes, "Russell, I will ask you once again if you've found any part of this manuscript."

"I'm sorry, but I haven't," I say, which is a lie.

Shortly after Ed died, before Annie found and read the papers he had left in the hotel room, I removed his manuscript from my old computer bag, sandwiched it among my own belongings, and replaced it with a pile of mail that I'd been carrying around for him. I did this because I believed that Ed would not want the book published in its present form and knew that if Annie found it, she would take it back to his publishers in New York. As soon as Annie had finishing going through Ed's papers, I'd put the manuscript of his memoir back in my old computer bag and brought it with me to Italy.

Ed was so paranoid about his work-in-progress that he always kept it hidden and either read parts of it aloud to me or gave me small excerpts for written commentary. I never saw the piles of pages in their entirety until after he died. And so, I reason, if the work was so vital to him, wouldn't he have made a copy of it as he did all his poetry, even the material he ended up destroying? Surely this must mean that he had no intention of allowing the memoir to leave his hands until he was completely finished with it. If this is true, how can I possibly give it up now?

Four

~

HOLDING A WALKING STICK, Marina and the dogs are waiting for me out on the loggia. I quickly relay to her the gist of my conversation with Annie. Surely Marina will want to know if I actually have the manuscript, and I am prepared to unburden myself completely. I'm surprised when she merely remarks, "That impossible woman! This is exactly why I destroy all the drafts of my books as well as the notes I take. I do not like this idea of scholarship trying to take unfinished work and separating good ideas from the chaff. I like it even less—I despise it, in fact—when a writer's private life is discussed and dissected in a biography. Their work fine, but what they did in bed, what for?" She bangs her stick on the ground as though to emphasize her point. "Now, are you ready to walk?"

A steep grassy slope descends to a lily pond, and the dogs, bounding ahead of us, leap into the water. They emerge shaking and jubilant, trying to rub up against Marina, who shoos them away. Even when her bare legs end up covered with mud splatters that look like slugs, she doesn't seem to mind so terribly much. Having watched the dogs piling into her wing of the villa at night, I now ask if she allows them on the bed. "Oh, yes," she says. "They go wherever they please."

"So they all sleep with you?"

"They quarrel over me, actually," she says, as if pleased by the idea. "There isn't room enough for six dogs. The bigger one there"—she gestures to a tall and sturdy black-and-white dog with a splotch of discolored pigment over one eye—"although he is *capo*, he usually lets the others sleep with me and takes the floor. Primo is the wise one. He dominates but he is fair. We call him *Il Papa*, Primo. After the Pope." She goes on to say her room clears out when a bitch in the neighborhood goes into heat. "Then I only have two girls with me." She bends down to pat what looks like an Australian shepherd cross. "Isn't that right, Suzy?"

Marina reminds me a bit of an English aristocrat who favors her pets over other human beings and shows them an infinite patience. "So none of the male dogs is fixed?"

She says, bridling, "We don't believe in this. In Italy you don't cut a male and deprive him of his sex life. You've been here enough times. You should know this by now."

"Ah, but then you'll spay the females? Isn't that sexist?"

Marina refuses to rise to the bait. "It's a bit more complicated. Females will give birth to puppies who could be neglected and starve to death. A terrible cruelty. Besides, my girls, although they are fixed, can still make love. And they do. And have always done. There have been many, many dogs at the Villa Guidi, ever since I was a small child. And the bitches, no matter if they were fixed or not, were always making love."

We've been following the tall meandering stone wall that

seems to be in very good condition; Marina claims it was built in the sixteenth century and has never been restored. With dogs racing back and forth, we stroll along a row of tall, impressive linden trees until we intersect the property's long gravel driveway and its sweeping front lawns.

"You describe this wall in your novel about World War II, don't you?" I say. She nods and I tell her, "I've only seen the film version."

Marina turns to me and points to a large cave on the far side of the lawn that seems to be some kind of underground entrance. "That's where a Jewish family came and went to their hiding place."

"But it's a pretty obvious entry."

"Now it is. But during the war there was lots of undergrowth and they could slip in and out undetected."

As we near the entrance to the hiding place, Marina describes how the villa, where she also lived as a child, was seized by the Nazis and used as a command post. Her father, a famous antifascist, was forced to go into hiding in the Apennines, leaving his wife and five-year-old daughter. The Germans overran the main living areas and the upstairs trompe l'oeil ballroom, forcing the fatherless family to move into what had once been servants' apartments at the basement level. "Because I was raised by a German nanny and spoke the language perfectly, I was called upon to be the middleman between the Nazis and my mother," Marina tells me. "They sent messages back and forth through me. For example, my mother would complain about how the house was being treated. The commandant would try to show her some respect. He'd promise that his men would be more careful, but he never was true to his word. They continued to disregard the house." She smiles. "Then, can you imagine, the commandant used to tell me what a perfect German child I'd make and what a shame it was that I was born the daughter of an anti-fascist.

"But the story has an even more interesting angle. Close family friends of my parents—a Jewish scientist, Signor Stellini, and his family—went into seclusion in a maze of burrows inside the lower walls. This hiding place was put there when the villa was constructed during the fifteenth century. So they lived on the other side of the walls from us in the basement and my mother provided food and water to them. At night, after the Germans got done with their drinking and their singing in the upstairs ballroom, the Stellinis came out from behind the walls and played rubbers of bridge with my mother.

"Then one night one of the guards saw the youngest of the Stellini boys going into this very entryway that we stand facing, and after that there was a great deal of suspicion. The commandant started asking my mother about the goings-on down where we were living, whereas up until then they could have hardly cared less about it. The Stellinis realized they should be afraid, and my mother managed to relocate them to a nearby convent, which also had underground chambers. They were wonderfully looked after by an order of Carmelite nuns—so much so, in fact, that they eventually converted to Catholicism."

A squirrel suddenly darts out from a thicket near the secret entrance and the dogs give it a frenzied chase.

"This conversion," I say, "isn't it how you got the title of your book?"

Marina nods.

"So are any of these converts still alive?"

"They all died, except for one of the daughters, who still lives in town. She's actually a good friend of mine. She comes to the villa to play bridge."

"Does she ever visit her old haunts?"

"We don't speak of them. She acts as though that time of her life never happened."

We begin walking again while I digest this idea of somebody refusing to revisit a childhood memory. "Well, surely she read your novel."

Marina looks doubtful. "Honestly, I don't think she ever did. But then, why should she? She lived it. She doesn't have to read about it."

"Yes, but surely there are differences. It's a novel, after all. Unless you're saying it's more memoir."

"It's *not* memoir. It's autobiographical fiction, as are all my books. Just for the record, I don't believe in writing memoirs unless either they're cautionary tales or the author has what I would call a Nabokovian power of recall. Otherwise the details are usually made up. So the book may as well be a novel."

Then something occurs to me. Perhaps the Stellinis' religious conversion was a delusional state brought on by the belief that if the past was erased from their memory, then it would never have existed.

We begin to loop backward toward the villa's facade that, from where we stand, looks like a tall ocher-colored square cake with its characteristically Tuscan terra-cotta roof. I hear a slam and notice on one of the upper floors Carla opening the shutters to welcome the cooling air. A favorite phrase of Italian wafts over me— *spalancare le persiane*, to throw open shutters. The wonderful mystery of another language is how certain words and phrases take on a kind of exotic resonance and even a concision that might be impossible to rival in the native tongue. In this case, the verb, *spalancare*, describes one action that in English is expressed by two: *throw open*. The other word, *persiane*, intimates the Middle Eastern origin of a *shutter* (rather than something Venetian), bringing an alien flavor to something that otherwise appears to be rather ordinary. A translator must always be aware that certain phrases and ideas do not always find easy equivalents in other tongues; they can be like two religions based on similar principles but that have flourished under the organization of different regimes. Some words simply cannot be converted. They are devoutly untranslatable.

"I almost converted. Recently," I suddenly find myself admitting to Marina.

She stops in her tracks and looks horrified. "Really, and what possessed you?"

Momentarily affronted, I say, "Well, your friends did."

"But they had a concrete reason. They converted to save themselves. So they could act the part if and when the Nazis came."

"But they never went back to Judaism."

"Well, first of all, they brainwashed themselves into believing they were Catholics. And second, they gave me the impression that had they decided to convert back to Judaism they wouldn't have been so easily welcomed back by their Jewish brethren." She scrutinizes me. "So what's your reason for wanting to convert?"

"Love . . . pure and simple. I was under its influence."

She grins. "Ah. Of course."

"I might even have gone through with it if it hadn't been for my father, who threatened to disinherit me."

She laughs. "Good for your father, to threaten you like this. Not that I suggest his punishment would have been deserved. Rather, good that he stopped you from doing something foolish. Correct me if I'm wrong, but it's through your mother that you're related to Giorgio Bassani?"

I nod.

"Who wrote about a family of Italians who were deported to the death camps and died because they were Jewish. But leaving this aside, I happen to believe that if you're born into a religion you should stick with it. Since fundamentally most organized religions are one and the same. It's the *fundamentalists* who are trying to make us believe otherwise."

Marina gently taps my shin with her walking stick. "So, now tell me how did love nearly bring you to conversion?"

And so I tell her about my relationship with an Episcopal priest from Argentina whom I'd met at the gym in lower Manhattan and who convinced me to start attending Trinity Church. How I used to approach the altar with the rest of the communicants and rather than taking the wafer, crossed my arms and received a blessing from James, my lover, who made the sign of the cross on my forehead. The first time I received his blessing, it left me in a jittery elation. At first I assumed it was merely the thrill of being touched publicly by the man who made love to me in private, but then I began to wonder if the experience itself might be divine. I found myself lamenting that Judaism had no equivalent of Holy Communion and made the mistake of mentioning this to James.

One Sunday, while I was kneeling in the Communion line, instead of making the sign of a blessing on my forehead as he usually did for those who were not Episcopal, James deftly slipped the wafer into my mouth. Taking me with the sacrament as he took me with his body. The host dissolving on my tongue tasted of exhilaration but also undeniably of bitter shame. I made a move to get up from the rail, to avoid drinking holy wine from its chalice. A scorching look from James told me I must remain, and soon I had my sip, committing my second sacrilege.

An hour later we were in bed together. And he was whispering something in my ear, though I couldn't quite make out what he was saying. Or so I told myself at the time. When we were through and lying there, James began to insist that I take the necessary instruction to make an Episcopalian conversion.

"I'm not ready to," I told him. "I need to consider something like this for a while. It's a big step."

"But in a way you already have converted," he said. "You had the sacrament."

"You forced me."

"You opened your mouth, you took it willingly. Like a little fish," he said with a devilish smile. His liquid dark Latino eyes fixed me in a fervent stare. I said no more. I knew he was unused to being opposed.

I describe to Marina how James lived a half a block from Trinity Church in an apartment that overlooked the crater where the World Trade Center used to be. How many of the buildings damaged in the disaster were palled in long black drapery, slated to be dismantled. How the neighborhood reminded me of a city under military siege: blown-out windows longing to be fixed; streets blocked off to traffic so that work crews could dig deep into the earth to repair ruptures and clot the steam devils. How rats, disturbed from their nests, ran amok in the fallen girders and broken pavements. How, on the day the airplanes rammed into the skyscrapers, James walked the streets, wading among the stricken, holding trembling hands, and blessing the dead. He strolled through the deserted Financial District in a black coat that draped to his ankles, his clerical collar gleaming white against his swarthy throat. He resembled some kind of mystical figure who one could imagine climbing off horseback to walk down Wall Street. What I don't tell Marina is how he didn't like to use condoms when we fucked and acted as though there was nothing to worry about.

Then somebody my father knew happened to see me in church and reported back to him. I got a call asking why I was attending Episcopal Mass. I tried to tell my father that I was a truth seeker, that I would embrace whatever religion that could get me to a more spiritual place. "A spiritual place, huh?" my father shrieked at me. "If you convert, Russell, say good-bye to your inheritance. See how spiritual you feel then! Obviously, you don't get it. You don't understand how so many of these Episcopalians sitting next to you in church secretly hate the Jews."

"Our relationship depends upon your religious conversion," James told me, upping the ante.

But then the conflict unraveled when a man approached me at the gym. Dark wavy hair, celadon eyes, he was a few years younger than I. He was one of the most beautiful men I'd ever seen, and my first impression of him was that he bloomed with vitality. He spoke to me directly and seemed terribly nervous, claiming once to have been the priest's lover. I told him that James had never mentioned him.

"I didn't think he would," the man said and went on to explain that several weeks after James mysteriously severed their relationship, he, the ex-lover, came down with a terrible flulike illness: high fever, rapid weight loss, and an outbreak of herpes. He was bedridden for two weeks and finally dragged himself to see a doctor who diagnosed an HIV infection. James had been the only person he'd slept with for six months.

"Didn't you take the proper precautions?" I asked him, knowing that I hadn't myself.

He claimed to have been fastidiously careful.

"Then how could it have happened?" I pressed him.

The young man's doctor surmised that there could have only been one way. One morning before leaving to serve Mass, James came into the bedroom and told his lover that his closely cropped beard was irritating to his face and ordered him to shave. James had obviously just finished using the razor himself. His lover was nervous and cut himself while shaving; the doctor suggested that there could have been fresh traces of James's blood on the blade, allowing the virus to be passed.

Shortly after the breakup, when the younger man called to announce that he had sero-converted, James thanked him for sharing the news and got off the phone quickly.

Marina is understandably sobered by my story. "This is very sad," she says. "I didn't know the disease could be passed this way."

"Neither did I."

"Poor young man. But with these drugs available he can still live a long time. Not true?"

I sigh and say that one can only hope.

"But now, when he found you at this gym, he was feeling okay, he was doing better, wasn't he?"

"He looked remarkable. Like a god. You'd never know."

I try to explain to Marina the paradox of sero-conversion. That often in the early months, in the early years of infection, the men who carry the virus bloom with robust health. I suppose you could call this a kind of feverish beauty, the final attainment of physical perfection before the gradual decline.

She is visibly stirred by what I've just told her. Her pale eyes give the impression that she is deep in thought. At last she says, "Like one of my roses so perfect and seemingly so alive right before the petals begin to droop and drop. You do make it sound mysterious, Russell."

"I guess it is kind of mysterious."

"You might consider writing about it someday."

It's been so long since I've done any writing, and although I've not mentioned it, Marina seems to be aware. In the throes of Michel I eventually stopped trying to set things down on paper. Then, living with Ed, it was easier to focus on his work instead. Writing about the priest, how would I even approach it? I wonder aloud.

Marina raises her right hand, as though to swear by her words. "If you'd only begin, it would become an act of discovery."

Her attention is suddenly distracted by something she sees at the villa. "Ah," she says. "There's Stefano. We're getting a rare view of him." I can just barely make out a man dressed in a bathrobe with long, straggly gray hair standing at a downstairs window at the far right corner of the building. "He is taking a break." Gazing toward her husband, Marina breaks into a fond, beatific smile.

Stefano is staring back at us inquisitively but makes no gesture of salutation. A moment later he has vanished.

Marina suddenly seems to grow agitated. I can see her inadvertently chewing the inside of her cheek. I wait to see how this change of mood will manifest itself. Taking a deep breath, she continues, "Stefano writes many things that are unpopular. He has a remarkable intelligence that can take a premise and argue all its different angles with marvelous conviction. Even though he has written novels as I have, this sort of persuasive facility may actually be his strongest suit. He would never admit to this, by the way," she informs me with a pinched smile. She suddenly appears uncertain, and now I'm sure something is bothering her. "He has, for example, written about the problems of Muslims who are living in Italy. And because of his articles he has made many enemies."

I'm remembering the roadblock near Ventimiglia, which, according to Marina, was established to help screen for foreign terrorists who might be entering Italy. At the time Marina had mentioned that, unfortunately, people of darker complexions tended to be stopped more often; in fact, many became detainees because it was discovered that they were entering without visas. "Does Stefano think they should not be allowed to wear religious garb in schools?"

"Good God, no. He has written more about how we can protect ourselves from . . . shall we call them 'home-grown terrorists.' "

"This is what you wanted to talk to me about," I fill in.

She nods. "Precisely." A cacophony of church bells in the nearby city intercedes for a few moments. Finally, Marina says, "About the men who broke into your hotel room."

"What about them?" I say, feeling a sudden chill. When I inwardly replay the strange nocturnal episode, the invasion takes on the quality of heat waves visibly waffling into the air above a blistering roadway, the surrealist memory of men leaping through the French doors, of waking to their acrid smell and their jerky fumblings and their gruff orders, to the outrageous semiautomatic gun and the gutting knife. To Ed's reckless outrage and then the intruders' sudden inexplicable disappearance.

"I know this might sound very strange to you, maybe even James Bondian," Marina continues. "However, my friend who works in the Italian intelligence office believes they might have been looking for *my* room."

"*Your* room?"

She shrugs. "That is correct."

"To attack *you?*"

"Not me. *Stefano.*"

Stefano was to have accompanied her to Paris, to see a certain exhibition of medieval manuscripts at the Museum of the City of Paris. He hadn't left the villa in ten years and made the mistake of writing about breaking his self-imposed incarceration in one of his newspaper essays, divulging his traveling plans. Shortly before they were to leave, Marina received a call from this friend in Intelligence who warned that information had been received about a possible assassination attempt against Stefano.

"I first thought it was ridiculous. Why would they bother to assassinate an ailing older man who writes a newspaper column?"

"Because lots of people read it and might be influenced," I say.

"I will tell you there are far more important and powerful people to hit than my Stefano."

Of course Marina would want to assume this.

"The problem is that my friend in Intelligence admits that his own sources aren't as reliable as he'd like them to be. But he still said we shouldn't take chances. So that is why Stefano stayed home while I went to Paris by myself.

"Anyway, I changed my reservation at the very last moment from a double to a single room. And then I learned what happened in *your* room. So . . . here we have Ed and Stefano, two well-known writers who easily might have been confused with each other, possibly by whoever informed the men which room it was. So if they were actually looking for Stefano, once they realized they were in the wrong room, they probably just fled."

"I think they *fled* because Ed went crazy on them," I say in English. "Totally bananas. It threw them, I think."

"So you're suggesting his foolish behavior was what saved your lives?"

I explain how it's been proven that being daring and aggressive during an attack can put the aggressor off guard.

Marina dismisses this with, "Just as likely they could've been provoked to kill both of you."

"Possible," I agree. "Thank God they didn't. I just assumed they were only after money and passports."

"Money and passports are valuable to people who want to commit terrorist acts."

"Yes, but commit terrorist acts to obtain them?" I ask her.

"Why not? Of course you'd rather believe that a gun pointed at your head was being used to commit a robbery rather than to kill you," Marina tells me. "And who wouldn't?"

"Did I tell you that while it was happening, they momentarily switched from French to another language—Ed claimed it was Albanian. I reported this to the police, but frankly I never understood how he was able to recognize that language."

Marina explains that Albanian has been influenced by Latin words and that the Arbëreshë dialect is spoken widely in Italy.

"But I know more Latin-based languages than Ed did, and I didn't recognize any words." I go on to say that the switch in language involved approximately four short sentences that were quick and garbled.

"I see," Marina murmurs. "And what about the comment you said they made . . . something about 'two men.'"

Homosexuality is a shock to many people, I remind her. And it's anathema to many religions, certainly to Islam. That still doesn't tell us very much.

I go on to point out what was to me the most significant development surrounding the incident. One of the policemen who'd questioned me mentioned that the hotel had had some trouble with robberies in the past; in fact, our room lent easy access from several adjacent buildings and had been broken into repeatedly. (Of course, the management had avoided mentioning this.) Standing at the large balcony windows, the point of entry, the policeman indicated two roofs of neighboring buildings. So, as much as one could wonder if the intruders were Italian Albanians looking for Stefano, one could also theorize that we were chosen merely because our balcony was vulnerable. "Ed was the only one of us who felt they might have been looking for somebody else. But you also have to know that Ed was one big drama queen."

Marina now laughs and slaps her thighs. "I think you'd make a good detective, actually."

I remind her that in my thorough questioning by the Parisian authorities, I'd been forced to examine and re-examine what happened in great detail.

"Of course you did."

I am just now realizing that Marina's invitation for me to stay at the villa, all her zealous efforts to troubleshoot my obligations to the French courts, make a bit more sense. If she hadn't wondered whether the intruders might have been looking for her room, would her generosity have been less forthcoming? In one way, I am relieved; now her gestures don't seem so lofty and altruistic. Surely, her belief that the men were out to assassinate her husband instead of Ed is what she wanted to discuss.

"So you really think Stefano is in danger?" I ask.

"I'm actually waiting for news from my friend, more conclusive news. I could tell you that for the last twenty years, many such threats have been thrown around by one disgruntled group of people or another and have come to nothing. But, as you well know, the terrorists of today are adamant and organized. They have certainly killed many people who have gone in opposition to them."

I take all this in for a moment, and then tell Marina another idea that has been revolving around my brain: that now, after all has been said and done, Ed probably would have approved of his own death. It was a better way to go than suffering some long, withering illness.

"Who's to say that would have happened?" Marina asks.

And I now explain that Ed had also been infected with HIV and had lived with the virus for years.

Marina nods and says, "Oh, I see. Poor man," she mutters.

We arrive at a series of five front steps that ascend to delicate French doors with mullioned glass panes, doors leading directly into the downstairs *salone*. The villa doesn't have a formal entrance per se but rather a ponderous, beautifully carved wooden door at the side that is controlled by an electric lock. This small entrance in the front is hardly grand. Marina sits down on the worn stone steps and tilts her face to the sun. I am looking across the valley halfway up a mountain where, surrounded by towering, mature cypresses, sits another residence of substantial proportions. Pointing to it, Marina says, "That, by the way, is the convent where Puccini's sister lived. The one on which he based *Suor Angelica*. You could take a hike there." I tell her that I might just do that.

Several moments pass and, somewhere in the distance, the dogs begin to bay in earnest. Marina finally gets up and walks toward the French doors. Then something stops her and she turns around. "And you?" she says. "Do *you* have that virus, too?" Blunt as usual.

Five

~

ANOTHER NIGHTMARE. I'm on the balcony at the Parisian hotel, or maybe it's on scaffolding looking in on the crime scene, before losing balance and free-falling. The final impact of the pavement is a rude shock, and my breathing is blocked by blood gurgling up into my throat. I awaken once again with my head at the foot of the bed, my face in the pair of socks that I left there, smelling the sweat of my own feet.

It's three o'clock in the morning, and lying here I remember having similar nightmares when, at the age of fourteen, I read for the first time Giorgio Bassani's bildungsroman, *The Garden of the Finzi-Continis*. It's one thing to read a novel about a wealthy Jewish family who are deported to the concentration camps during World War II; it's another thing entirely to read about a family that is actually your own. The author's first cousin, my mother, was born into much more modest circumstances, and yet her father, my grandfather, was prescient enough to get his branch of the family out of Ferrara before the Nazis invaded. My mother came to America at the age of five and remembers little of her early life in that wealthy Italian city with high walls. She completely abandoned her native language while growing up and, when I was a child, rarely made reference to how our Italian relatives were herded into trains and transported to the death camps of Poland and Germany. The only thing she'd ever discussed in any great detail was the guilt of my grandfather, who managed to survive the Holocaust while losing most of his family. My grandfather died of a heart attack shortly after I was born.

My mother once told me that my grandfather had an explosive temper and went into unbridled rages—I suppose much in the way Ed did—often over smaller, insignificant events or circumstances. I used to warn Ed that one of these fits might trigger a heart attack, but he never listened to me. I'll admit there is part of me that worries that I stayed with him for the wrong reasons—not because I was in love with him (as it perhaps should have been), but rather because I so profoundly admired his mind and his writing. In light of this, I easily could have become his good friend instead of his live-in companion. But knowing I was short on money and badly wounded over Michel, he encouraged me to come and stay at the rue Birague, perhaps hoping that from the height of my esteem for him I'd fall in love. I believe he hoped for this against the odds that I probably would be unavailable to anyone for a long time. And so, I ended up causing great pain to a vain man who'd been used to charming and sleeping with lots of attractive people. Ironically, the poet who could write beautifully about desire and the nuances of love just couldn't accept the fact that I continued to be obsessed with somebody else.

Again and again, I find myself involuntarily reliving that last night in Paris, the menacing men cloaking their identity in paramilitary garb, men who, when they entered the room, shifted my life into a strange gear, a third world nightmare of arms and hijackings and blithe murder without any sort of conscience. But then I remind myself that these intrusions underwritten by violence occur in America all the time, often without reason or for some spurious psychological motive.

And then of course, his heart attack. If only I could've known the attack was happening to him when it did, been awake when it struck. For then at least I could've knelt down, reassuring him that everything would be fine, all the silly platitudes that you murmur to people who are dying. Yeah, I know they call death during sleep a blessing, but I also hate the idea of going out without even realizing it: going to sleep intending to wake up fully restored and never waking up again. It just reinforces the idea of the finality of death. As scary as it might seem, I think I'd want to know it if I was going to die.

I may be dreaming again, but now there seems to be some kind of distant commotion going on, doors slamming and a woman shrieking. I sit up in bed and try to listen for further reports. I hear nothing and yet I get the distinct feeling that something outside my own head is actually wrong. And then I start worrying and switch on the night-table lamp. Exactly what I feared: I don't see my old computer bag with Ed's manuscript hanging where I'd left it in an open closet. Then I remember with a groan that yesterday Carla had kicked me out of the room in order to clean the bathroom and change the sheets. Did she move it? And if she did, where did she put it?

I jump out of bed. I never want to find anything in my life as much as I want to find "Russell's computer," as Ed called his

72 ~   *Joseph Olshan*

book. I begin scouring the room. Five fanatical minutes elapse
before I finally locate it hanging from the inner knob of the bathroom door—a very odd place to have left it. In fact, I don't remember having done so. My heart hammering in my chest, I
grab the shoulder strap and transport the bag to my bedside. The
zipper is partially open and I see, peeking out of the side, the hybrid of manuscript pages: sheets of bond typed manually and
yellow-lined paper filled with his tiny, hardly legible handwriting. Ironically, Ed's actual handwriting bears more resemblance
to the electronic diagram of a heartbeat than to something ortho-
graphic.

Since Ed's death, the only thing I've done with his manuscript is organize it between typewritten and handwritten
pages, shuffling to make them into a neat stack and reading the
odd paragraph here and there. When Ed died he was considering some revisions I'd suggested. I begin flipping through the
manuscript until I locate my favorite ninety-page section that is
earmarked with a metal clamp. In this part Ed discusses a three-
year teaching stint at Dartmouth College, as well as an affair
he'd had with one of his most promising students, a fair-haired
lad who came from a Boston Brahmin family and who was terribly torn up over his love for his renowned professor. The relationship ended abruptly when the student fell off a five-story
building and smashed his skull on a driveway. At the autopsy,
the young man's blood alcohol level indicated that he was drunk
when he fell.

The death was devastating to Ed (then in his late thirties),
who descended into a two-year-long depression in which he
wrote absolutely nothing. This phase was followed by a steady
period of manic production when he managed to compose his

most famous poem, entitled "The Deer," which was published in *The New Yorker* and which, at one hundred and fifty stanzas, became the longest poem the magazine had ever printed. Many critics compared the poem to "In Memoriam," Tennyson's paean to Arthur Hallam, with whom the poet was secretly in love and who died tragically of fever in Vienna. "The Deer" became the title poem in a collection that went on to win the National Book Award.

I skip to the last seventy pages, material I've never seen; until now I've never had the entire manuscript in my possession. The first thing out of character that I notice is how the paragraphs keep getting shorter and shorter, until sometimes they are no more than one sentence in length. The writing itself seems more rough-hewn than earlier sections and clearly has not been so meticulously groomed. Curious, I read a few sentences and then stop abruptly. I've stumbled upon a rant: Ed ranting about me.

He complains of all the obvious things: that I am not as emotionally involved with him as he'd like me to be; that I am not physically attracted to him; and that I'm still obsessed with Michel Soyer. This so-called lingering obsession, he goes on to say, was easier for him to accept early on but became more and more difficult as the months elapsed, for clearly I have continued to be preoccupied by what happened between me and the Frenchman. Of course it would. But then his complaints get stronger. He comes out and calls me elusive, he calls me remote. He even complains how unfair it is that I have sexual self-confidence as well as "some" literary ability (that is how he phrases it). Any intellectual worth his salt, he says, should be plagued with self-doubt about his power to attract others. Russell should be insecure about his body, his sheer physicality.

It's the yin and yang of high-mindedness, he writes. But I certainly never got a sense that Ed was insecure about his sexual power or his ability to attract. By his own admission, plenty of people, both men and women, had fallen in love with him during his lifetime.

Even more worrisome is his concern that I was with him because I wanted to draft off his success as a famous writer, that I probably wouldn't be around if I didn't think he could help my career. He claims that I treat him generally well but believes that basically I am indifferent to him. This is so untrue and so unkind. I adored Ed as one adores a close friend; I was anything but indifferent to him. However, I know that believing the worst as he did must have been terribly painful for him. It's certainly excruciating for me to read.

Ed concludes his assessment of me by saying that although I have some talent, I probably will never get very far in my writing career. "He's so possessed by his passion for his Frenchman, he'd do anything. He'd give his life over to love. That's why he'll never write anything good."

The most recently written words of a dead man, even though I know they were written in jealous anger, truly sting. I gather together the loose leaves of the manuscript and stow them once again in my old computer bag. It is one thing to sense that you've made somebody miserable; it's another thing entirely to read about it conclusively from their point of view and to know that they never really believed in you.

We'd certainly had discussions, Ed and I, about what I planned to do with my writing career, what I was conjuring up. He seemed surprised that I didn't have a long list of subjects that I wanted to tackle. And yet I always felt that he was curious, not so much because he thought I *should* be working on something, anything, but rather because he wanted his companion, whomever he might be, to be engaged in something that could be discussed in mixed company, in short how his light might be refracted in the person closest to him. But then, too, he had to be the star, so my lack of conviction, my uncertainty about what came next, might have suited him on some level as well.

I felt stymied; my novella was basically a fictional autobiography of a drowning I witnessed at the age of six. The experience itself had been so tramatic, all the details of the terrible time were easily available to me. I wrote the first draft in a great heat, and what I put down didn't really need much modification before I arrived at the final version. But I suspected this was a fluke; indeed, it was the only thing I'd ever written that I hadn't obsessively rewritten. Moreover, while I was putting the final touches on the manuscript I fell in love with somebody and grew so distracted that it took me several months to finally finish my work. When I explained all of this to Ed, he ran with it, claiming he'd never let anyone stand in the way of his writing. He boasted that he'd worked every single day of his adult life, except for the two years when he was, by his own admission, "catatonically depressed" over the death of his student lover.

My heart is beating rapidly; I can feel it flip-flopping around in my chest. To distract myself, I approach Stefano's bookshelf and automatically begin removing one Pléiade edition after another. I page through the lovely printed sheets that seem to be offering me a purchase on wisdom and clarity, but in light of my state of mind, the French seems particularly dense and hard to comprehend. If only I could find a way to start writing again.

I glance over at Ed's manuscript and now feel myself un-healthily drawn back to it, as strong as the urge to scrape my fingernails across an itching rash. I have to know just how miserable I made him and can't help but begin reading again, specifically about what happened in October, a month or so after I started living at his apartment.

Ed describes a particular evening when he'd escorted a rich unmarried woman of a certain age to a dinner party and how I met him afterward at a bridge that connects the Right Bank to the Ile Saint-Louis. This particular bridge is known as a cruising area; before Ed arrived, I was overtly propositioned by two old trolls. It was a chilly evening, and there were sprites of damp breezes pirouetting off the Seine. Finally I saw him rounding a corner, walking at a brisk pace. He was holding a tightly rolled-up copy of a newspaper. Upon reaching me, he held up *France Soir* and said nervously, "There's something here I'd like you to see." He led me over to the nearest street lamp, which arched above us with a long swanlike neck. He was dressed in a dark pinstripe Italian suit that, like many of his clothes, was beyond his means but which had been bought impulsively in the midst of a snowballing credit-card debt. The suit had an admirable, slimming effect.

Exfoliating the onion-thin newsprint pages, he showed me what at first appeared to be a typical gossipy article about a haute couture benefit on the avenue Victor Hugo, then zeroed in on a sentence. "And there was Madame Michel Soyer, whom we haven't seen much of in the wake of her separation from her dashing husband, the president of Jeunesse Fabrique."

Shocked, I reread the sentence, flummoxed by the word *separation*. In light of everything Michel had told me apropos his secure marriage, that nothing would ever induce him and Laurence to separate, I imagined it might have been somehow easier to read his obituary.

Pointing to the article, Ed said, "Is this the Michel you've been talking about?" He turned to me. "I thought when you first mentioned him something was familiar. When I read the article I realized that I actually knew him." Ed tightly refolded the newspaper and with a smug grin said, "In fact, I have my own little *histoire* with him."

I cringed. "Meaning?"

"Meaning we had a little *flingee* ten or twelve years ago when I was in my late forties. Still in my prime." He laughed self-deprecatingly.

I looked at Ed in bewilderment; this *was* certainly a bizarre coincidence. He completely misinterpreted my expression. "What's so surprising about that?"

"Nothing at all," I shot back. "I just assumed he was strictly into younger guys."

"I suppose that's true enough, most of the time at least." Ed tucked the newspaper under one arm and looked at me shrewdly. "But then knowing him the way I do, I could also say that *I'm* surprised that the two of you had an affair."

"How so?"

"Being that he normally has a yen for slim, smooth Arab boys. Whereas you're a brick shithouse Ashkenazi Jew with a furry chest."

Insecure now, I said, "I guess he has more than one type."

"The point is, Russell . . ." Ed faltered for a moment. "This guy has been around for a while. He's officially in the closet, but I've seen him out at some of the bars. And his penchant for *les*

Arabes precedes him. His is one of those very common situations here where the wife knows what goes on, turns a blind eye, and yet keeps him on a very long leash. He gets to do what he wants. And believe me, he likes to slum it, to mix with types he'd never come in contact with socially. The more exotic the better. You probably don't even know this, but he's said to have a taste for transvestites and transsexuals."

I did actually know this but didn't immediately reveal it. Indeed, before he got involved with me, Michel had been spending time with a very beautiful Moroccan transsexual.

Ed rubbed his forehead with one of his big, weathered-looking hands and went on, "This particular kind of *divertissement* is something that these upper-crust French queens adore. If Michel were straight, he'd probably be paying for high-class hookers."

"Well, he's bisexual," I countered.

"No, Russell. Not bisexual. Queer. Queer as a three-dollar bill. Trust me. *Je connais mes clients*," he said.

"That's a cute expression," I said mockingly.

"There's no equivalent in English. So exacting, so imperious, so mocking. Leave it to the French."

"Anyway, you can't presume what somebody's sexuality is unless you're inside their head or under their skin."

"Ah, but I can if I don't fundamentally believe in bisexuality," Ed said. "I think people will certainly try different things, different relationships if you will, but their gut, their visceral passion is either for one or the other. Don't get me wrong. Gay men marry women all the time and make excellent husbands. And why not? You can care about somebody very deeply, you can love them, live with them for your entire life and be relatively content. But at least in the very beginning, if there isn't the visceral yearning that, if not fed, will make you come completely unhinged, then there isn't really a sexual bond to begin with.

"If you ask me, you were damn lucky to get away from Michel Soyer when you did," Ed went on. "One could move the heavens, but cravings aside, there is too much that prevents him from leaving his wealthy *femme*."

"But he did, according to this!" I cried, indicating the newspaper.

Ed made a dismissive gesture. "Oh, please. That's just Gallic gossip. I don't believe it for a second."

"If you think that, then why did you show it to me?"

Ed looked at me shrewdly. "Because you read this paper and might have seen it for yourself."

In short, a preemptive move, I remember thinking to myself at the time. Ed wanted to make sure I distrusted the article's implication; for if not, then my hope engine, constantly idling, would launch into forward gear.

And so I came back with, "Isn't it said that gossip is more often true than not?"

Ignoring this, Ed continued, "These rags are desperate for rich people's dish. He probably went to a few functions alone and they noticed and *forced* their own conclusions . . . down their readers' throats, as it were. Trust me, he's not separated. He's still living in his high-class digs on the avenue Foch."

I felt a sudden chill. "I don't remember telling you he lived on the avenue Foch."

"Darling, people—and certainly I—know where this lothario lives!" Ed waved his hand at me dismissively. "Remember, I had him myself! The apartments over there are so enormous that he and his wife could actually *be* separated and still live together and hardly see each other. Beyond this, many French couples I know spend substantial time apart, even have separate residences, but are not considered *separated*. So, in the end, there is no reason for your Michel Soyer ever to leave his wife. He has so much rope that he probably will never hang himself. So it's good that you're not with him anymore."

Obviously not what I wanted to hear. And yet I also knew that by now Ed had invested heavily against the possibility of Michel Soyer's ever being available again. I fell glumly silent, but finally thought of something. "Well, then, if he had so much rope, so much freedom, why did she force him to leave me?"

Ed shook his head just as a lashing of wind came in off the river and tousled his hair. He combed it back into place with his fingers and was delicate when he replied, "Well, that's what *he* told you. But who knows the real truth? I mean, did you ever consider somebody else might have just come into his life and usurped you, exactly the way you did the Moroccan trans?"

How did Ed know that Michel had left the Moroccan for me? I was afraid to learn, to consider that he might have asked one of his many influential friends to do some digging. Or done his own, for that matter, through my personal papers and notes. Ed seemed to know quite a lot about Michel, and though he certainly was making a valid point, I found this disconcerting.

But yes, in moments of sadness and despair I'd wondered just this, if somebody else had come along and captured Michel's attention, then chalked up my worrying to a sort of desperate self-pity. After all, Michel had seemed utterly sincere when he told me about the family friend spying on us in Saint Germain-en-Laye and his wife's finding out and insisting that he end things with me. I'd also reasoned that if he'd met another guy—especially if the relationship was relatively new—this person would never have tolerated his going away with me for those four remarkable days in the South of France. Beyond this, during that brief holiday, I'd sensed urgency to Michel's lovemaking, which made me conclude later on that he was losing me against his will. Conversely, had there already been another man in the equation, surely, out of obvious conflict Michel would have held some part of himself in reserve—and I would've sensed that immediately in tactile ways. I kept all this to myself, however; I didn't want Ed to try to refute any of it. If my reasoning was specious, for the moment, I chose not to be the wiser.

Ed and I began strolling along the Seine, idly looking at the illuminated river churning over itself. A passing pleasure barge blared schmaltzy organ riffs. Suddenly Ed stopped and turned to me. Lighted by a nearby lamp, his disheveled hair looked radiant and youthful. "Were you safe with him?" he asked pointblank. It wasn't the first time he'd quizzed me for specific details about my sex life with Michel.

"Of course," I said.

"You're such a liar," he accused quietly.

I shrugged. "Don't believe me."

Shaking his head, Ed started walking again and I followed him for a half block or so. Then he stopped and drew close to me. "Look at me, bucko!" I could smell the wine on his breath. His eyes were bloodshot; he'd clearly had a lot to drink. "I'll never forget the way you looked that first day I met you in the café. Completely taken over by him."

"So?"

"You'd have done anything that guy wanted."

"That's not true." I tried to sound measured rather than un-nerved by his accusation.

"You're deluding yourself." His voice cracked as he began walking again, more briskly this time. With his back to me he said, "That one's been around the block a few times. I just hope, for your sake, that you've taken those precautions you claim."

The memoir's description of that evening stops precisely with Ed's last remark. And here precisely is where memoir ends and my memory takes over.

The following afternoon I knocked on the door of his study. Ed was staring out the window at an alder tree whose leaves had turned a deep vermillion, the sort of natural brilliance that I imagine to be impossible to re-create on a palette or in a dye. There was a blank piece of white paper lying on his blotter and a troika of pencils sharpened to needle point.

"How is it going?" I forced myself to ask.

He shook his head and said, "It's not."

"Well, I'm going to stop in at the Marmottan and then take a little stroll in the Bois."

He slowly swiveled around, looked at me over his reading glasses, and, sounding inattentive, said, "Well, have fun. Don't pick up anybody in the park."

I went instead to the American Hospital in Neuilly for an HIV test. The nurse who attended me spoke with an Iowa twang, chattered about missing prairie life as her needle dipped deep into my elbow and sucked a dark red spurt into a glass tube. Floating above her prattle in a state of anxiety, I watched the sample accumulate with slight surface foam and realized it

matched the color of the dying alder leaves. Then I shut my eyes
for a moment and prayed for some mystical totem, a determi-
nant as to whether or not I'd been infected by Michel, who, like
many men, was perhaps a lot more promiscuous than he'd have
liked me to believe. And then came an almost synesthetic recall
of the last few problematic days I'd spent with James, the Episcopal priest, the harrowing conversation with his former lover,
the betrayal of a liar, and the dread of infection. I once again
damned myself for taking such risks, creating this present state
of intolerable anxiety.

After my blood was whisked away to a lab, I took the Métro
a few stops and got off at the Champs-Elysées. The street was
bustling with squadrons of schoolchildren bumbling into one
another with their Day-Glo backpacks, as well as with throngs
of conspicuously foreign-looking tourists—groups of Japanese
and waddling, overweight Americans. The moody slant of sunlight at this time of day seemed peculiarly autumnal. Finally entering the quieter 16th arrondissement, I turned down Michel's
street, the august avenue Foch.

It's a broad boulevard that has for centuries been an enclave of
wealthy, entitled Parisians. Lined with impressive buildings and
brownstones that house both apartments and embassies, the avenue Foch has a sliver of park in its median with footpaths on either side. As I walked I remembered Gertrude Stein once lived
here in a rambling apartment. I remembered that in the first
volume of *Remembrance of Things Past*, Swann and Odette spend
afternoons riding down a similar avenue in a private *calèche*. On
one of these jaunts Swann comes to the stunning realization that
he has somehow fallen deeply in love with "the wrong woman"
who had never pleased him and who wasn't remotely his social

equal. It occurs to me now that neither was I Michel Soyer's social equal. Beyond this, I'd also been his lover, which would have made me completely unacceptable within his particular 16th arrondissement milieu.

Strolling purposely along, I calculated that Madame Soyer, having two young daughters, would most likely be at home around five-thirty in the afternoon. I passed several impeccably dressed prostitutes who were curvaceous to an almost scoliotic degree. I knew them by their sauntering gait, but also because avenue Foch is famous for its high-class hookers. They were joined by trickles of veiled Middle Eastern ladies making excursions from their flats to and from the various Arab embassies, fluttering along the boulevard in their burkas like tremulous moths. Just as I arrived at Michel's building, a soignée woman who looked like Anita Ekberg in *La Dolce Vita* opened the door of a black Maserati, sat down on the passenger side, and smoothly, almost robotically rotated her hips to elegantly situate her legs in the tight confines of the sports car. Her calves, covered with flesh-tone nylons, were perfect. She caught my eye and, throwing me a saucy smile, looked down at her legs as though she knew how sexy they were, and then, once again, leered at me. The second glance alerted me that she was surely a prostitute. (Michel had told me that the well-heeled ones were often seen motoring up and down the boulevard in luxury cars.) Then, into the driver's side climbed a swarthy older man with silver-flecked hair that was unctuously brilliantined. They began squabbling loudly and she threatened to put his testicles in a sling. The argument seemed to be about another woman.

This was actually my second visit to Michel's apartment. When we were first involved he'd made it quite clear that this apartment and his life were off-limits to me. But then one day we were talking about Victor Hugo, and Michel mentioned owning a Pléiade edition of *Les Misérables*. Delighting in the astonished look on my face, he informed me that he owned more than fifty Pléiade editions. "I'd love to see them sometime if that's ever possible," I told him.

Hesitating thoughtfully, he then replied, "I know I say that I never bring you to my apartment." The lovely cleft in his chin deepened as it often did when he was pondering something. "But I can trust you. I know you will appreciate my collection of books."

He seemed to take our common passion for Pléiade as a mystical sign that he could bend the rules and bring me here to the avenue Foch on a weekend Laurence and their daughters would be at their country house in Brittany. It was an unspoken given that we would never make love in his apartment.

My visit occurred at nighttime. Nearly all the rooms were kept in gloom; it was as though Michel had wanted me to see as little of the apartment as possible. However, I could see glimmers of elaborate decor: lacquered furniture, large canvases with gilded frames whose period and subject matter were sealed off from me by what seemed to be a deliberate blinkering of indoor light. I caught sight of a marble tabletop and a silk brocaded room divider that looked Chinese and attempted to more intimately divide an apartment of truly cavernous proportions. I hadn't been able to see much, but what I saw seemed heavy-handed; in short, very impressive but a bit too formal for my liking.

"This place is like a football stadium," I remember telling him, implying that the overall feeling of the apartment was rather impersonal. "It must swallow up a family of four."

Michel had laughed but missed the subtle meaning of my remark, as he often did when we spoke in English, which we did
most of the time. "It's true. The flat is way too big for all of us.
But it is in my family for over a hundred years. My parents own
it. And we will bring them back when they are too old to be on
their own."

I remember being struck by the fact that he sounded like a
happily married man committed to his spouse for years in the
future. Listen to what he is saying, I chided myself. Take this in,
and don't be fooled. I was suddenly aware of the poisonous nature of sexual attraction and felt Michel had made a grave mistake by bringing me here. How I would have hated to be the
unsuspecting wife at a country house in Brittany.

He must've undergone a simultaneous attack of conscience
because, in the midst of leading me through the apartment, he
turned to me and admitted, "I feel guilty now."

No shit, I'd wanted to say. But then like an idiot, I put my
hands on his broad shoulders, feeling how tense they were. "I
am, too," I said. "But listen to me, Michel. You have nothing to
worry about. I won't compromise you. I swear on everything
that's sacred that when this ends, however it ends, I won't show
up here or try to contact your wife. And when it comes to us not
seeing each other anymore, I'll just go back to America."

He hugged me in gratitude. I pressed my hands against the
broad back of his neck and then, in provocation, he pressed his
pelvis against mine.

The hypocrite now stood in front a twelve-story building with gargantuan windows. Oddly, until this very moment, I'd felt full of
urgent purpose rather than apprehension. But now I was petrified.

Not petrified so much of seeing *him*; somehow I just figured he wouldn't be at home at five-thirty in the afternoon—if, indeed, Ed was right and he was still living with his family. Rather I was frightened of being summarily turned away by his wife, of learning or seeing something that would cause a lasting disturbance. I didn't even consider the most likely scenario: that my showing up unannounced would provoke outrage as well as the assumption that I'd turned into some kind of married-man stalker. And yet I knew I would be obsessed with *France Soir*'s assertion that Michel and his wife were separated until I learned the real truth.

Unfortunately, I didn't know the code required to be tapped into the numbered entry pad and was forced to wait until a diminutive elderly woman dressed at the height of chic left the building. Luckily she was having trouble with the mullioned inner door, for once I helped her swing it open, her muttered inquiry, "Whom are you looking for?" was halfhearted. *"Livraison,"* I told her. Delivery.

After studying a brass console of tenants' names until I found SOYER, I pressed a buzzer and walked up a grand winding staircase to the third level. There, in the hallway, I spied a fortyish woman dressed in a tweedy tailored suit peering at me through oblong eyeglasses. "May I be of help?" she said.

"Madame Soyer?" I approached more slowly. She was certainly pretty but in a shrewish, hard-bitten way.

"Who are you?"

"I'm a friend of your husband's." Then I decided it was best to say, "Michel."

"Oh?" she said, hesitating, clearly taken aback. And then, imperiously, "I am *not* Madame Soyer. I'm afraid you will have to try some other time, preferably by telephone."

There was probably a look of disbelief on my face. The woman shook her head at what she no doubt construed as shocking social impertinence and turned to walk back into the apartment.

"Who is *there*, Martha?

"All taken care of, Laurie."

Now I knew the woman hadn't lied to me, that she was *not* Madame Soyer. A moment later a slender younger woman ventured out into the hallway. At first glance I easily could have mistaken her for one of Michel's teenaged daughters. Seeing me standing there, her curiosity getting the better of her, she gravitated toward me. "I am Madame Soyer," she said. "How may I help you?" Her French sounded slightly foreign.

Laurence—or Laurie, as the other woman had called her—turned out to be a rather plain woman with a trim figure who appeared to be in her mid-thirties, perhaps ten years younger than Michel, with a pale complexion and dark half circles under her large chestnut-brown eyes. I apologized for coming unannounced. Terribly nervous now, my French faltered. "But I had to see you," I managed to say. "I was once a friend of your husband's."

"I was trying to tell you this," the other woman scoffed at her.

"No!" Laurence refused to be influenced. "Who are you?" she asked me.

"My name is Russell Todaro," I said quietly.

She put her hand over her mouth and silently gasped. He'd told her my name.

"I will go in now," the other woman said haughtily and stalked back into the apartment with a tommy-gun clicking of high heels.

Laurence, in the meantime, was blushing deeply, her small, delicate mouth contorted with anger. For a moment she peered down at the tiled floor of the enormous landing, then jerked her head in what seemed to be sharp annoyance. "For Christ's sake!" she said in English. "Why did you come here?"

I was flabbergasted. "You're American!"

She recovered herself somewhat. "You didn't know?" she said stiffly and now was able to meet my eyes.

"Not a clue," I said, feeling suddenly worse. A tendril of guilt began to weave itself into my keyed-up state. "Michel never mentioned it. I figured you were some kind of French aristocrat."

This actually made her laugh. "Oh, please."

"I'm serious."

She looked at me shrewdly. "Okay, if that's true, then here's your free lesson about the French aristocracy. If I were his *French* aristocratic wife, this conversation would last thirty seconds tops. You'd be told that it was only because I allowed it that you'd ever had anything to do with my husband. Then I would have reminded you that it's totally against the rules for you to show up at my apartment. I would have said good-bye and closed the door quietly.

"Whereas in America, you'd get cursed out and have the door slammed in your face," she added with grim humor, unable to suppress a sardonic smile.

"I'm sorry to come here unannounced," I repeated. "But you know it's quite over between us."

"If you were that sorry, you wouldn't have shown up. Especially because you promised him you'd never do it."

"I know I did. And I guess I felt I didn't have a choice. Because I had to find out if something I read in the paper was true."

She sighed as though having expected to hear just this and glanced toward a large clear window at the far end of the hallway. From there you could see the fringe of the tree line in the Bois du Bologne, where I'd told Ed I was going to stroll. "You also could've called and at least spared me showing up here. If you'd called, I would've told you what you read is a lie."

"Well, then, believe it or not, I'm actually relieved. My good friend assured me that the paper was exaggerating."

Madame Soyer looked skeptical. "Relieved?"

"Yes, relieved. Because he told me that he'd never leave you and the children. And if that's why he couldn't be with me, then I'd want him to live and do as he said."

Laurence's face softened. "That's very naive. How old are you, anyway?"

"Thirty-one."

"That's what I figured."

I didn't like being patronized. "How old are *you?*"

"Thirty-nine."

"You look younger."

She grimaced. "Is Michel the first man you've ever . . . loved?" She pronounced the word at last.

I found myself wanting to be candid. "Yes and no," I said. "No, he's not the first man I've been involved with and thought I loved, but yes, I suppose, to this degree."

A look of sympathy telegraphed itself across her face and then she shook her head and suggested, "Why don't you come in for a bit."

"Are you sure?"

"Yes, I'm sure. Either that or leave." She swiveled around and began walking back into the apartment.

Here I was now, breaking my sacred promise to Michel and following his wife into their apartment. And thinking: No wonder Michel's English was decent, his *frigging* wife is an *American*. Why hadn't he told me, dammit? But then, noticing that her baggy jeans and white chenille T-shirt were the spousal equivalent of his very understated daily uniform of faded jeans, scuffed boots, white T-shirts, and a cheapo diver's watch, I realized precisely why. In carrying on his affair with me, Michel had probably felt a chivalric duty to give his lover scant information about his wife and children. He knew me well enough to realize that I'd be dangerously intrigued by the fact that his wife was another American.

Now, during daytime, I could see a wider range of furnishings, how there were many more antiques, including an extensive collection of overly gilded Venetian furniture: several pieces including a highboy and an armoire painted a bright robin's-egg blue. The polished mahogany floors were covered with Aubusson rugs, overlooked by the unsettling gazes of eighteenth- and nineteenth-century portraiture: Michel's male ancestors, many of whom reminded me of stern magistrates. I still found the apartment to be somewhat fusty.

Madame Soyer led me into Michel's library, where I'd once feasted on his collection of Pléiade with the green and gold-leaf spines in a heady aroma of leather, where I'd rifled through his Baudelaire and Zola and Gide and with great delight discovered many writers of other nationalities: Goethe, George Eliot, Halldór Laxness, and Cervantes. As I sat down opposite her I remembered Michel telling me he had begun collecting Pleiéde editions when he'd received a gift from his mother of *Les Misérables*. It was this very Pléiade that he'd actually insisted on giving me, against my protest of it having been the first volume of his collection and therefore commanding sentimental value. I remember how he frowned and nervously ran his fingers through his coarse brown curls, how the cleft in his chin pinched with what I hoped was fondness, even love. How he'd explained, "Mother gave it to me because I asked for it, not because she thought I would want it. That's a big difference. Besides, you love these books," he'd gone on. "And it would give me a lot of pleasure knowing you will have one."

"But Laurence might notice it missing."

Michel had smiled at some private recognition. "More important, do you think you can read it?"

I never got a chance to tell him how my Italian helped me with the French.

Now I tried to avoid glancing at the Pléiade but couldn't help noticing them, at least peripherally. I took a deep breath. Being in Michel's study when he was at such a remove from my life was upsetting.

"You've been in this room before," said Madame Soyer.

"He told you."

"He told me enough. Obviously, I don't want to know everything," she said meekly but with pain in her voice.

"I'm sure he explained the only reason why I came to the apartment was to see these." I pointed to the Pléiade on the bookshelf. "Nothing else went on."

"Yes, that's what he said."

Laurence had assumed what I felt was an interrogative pose with her legs crossed and a slim elbow resting on one of her knees. She had a way of maneuvering the dark, straight hair away from her face that I thought was decidedly European. It occurs to me now that if she hadn't made a point to speak to me in English, I might have listened to her accent and assumed that she was a French citizen of perhaps Germanic extraction. Because, outside of her manner of speaking English, there was very little about her that seemed American. Her way of walking and moving seemed—at least to me—typically French feminine: naturally balletic and confident, even a bit feline.

"If you're an American," I said, "how did you end up with the name Laurence?"

"My name is Laurie. Michel started calling me Laurence. Didn't you hear his sister calling me Laurie?"

I told her I did.

"Michel has always wanted me to be as French as possible. Hence the name." Hesitating a moment, she said, "So you're probably wondering why I invited you in."

"Of course."

"Well, first let me explain that Michel and I are not always together. We often do things separately, even spend time apart. This is probably what the newspaper picked up on. However, I just want you to know, the idea of divorce has never even once crossed our minds."

I stared at her, wondering where all this was leading.

"A few weeks ago, we took another small apartment in the Marais. It was given to us. Michel has been staying over there from time to time. He is terribly depressed these days and says he needs time alone. He's about to turn fifty."

"Fifty?" I cried out.

"Didn't you know how old he is?"

Without pinpointing his age, Michel had managed to imply that he was substantially younger. "He never really said. He certainly looks younger," I pointed out, remembering that when I'd first met Michel I'd pegged him for thirty-five.

She smiled tightly. "Are you sure he didn't actually lie to you?"

"I don't think so."

"I ask this because he holds everyone to a standard about telling the truth. He's told the girls many times that they mustn't lie and that if they lie and are caught they will always be punished severely."

"So I suppose the question is: Does he practice what he preaches?" I thought but did not say that carrying on an affair by definition has to exact a certain amount of lying.

Laurence at first seemed pained to answer. "Recently, when he started staying at the other apartment, I asked him if he was involved with anybody else. He said he wasn't. But now you show up here. And so it makes me wonder: He may not be involved with 'anybody else' but he might once again be involved with *you*."

Laurence finally compelled herself to look at me steadily, and despite my own discomfort, I felt for her and cringed. "As I said before, it's been over since he broke it off with me two months ago. I haven't seen or spoken to him. As far as anybody else is concerned, I have no idea," I said, hoping that as much as Ed wanted to assume it, Michel hadn't merely just moved on to somebody else.

At this point a lovely young girl appeared—perhaps fourteen or fifteen—dressed in stylishly tight, low-riding black jeans that showed her midriff and the developing curves of her body. Her face was a feminine replica of her father's; I nearly gasped at the uncanny resemblance. However, she was pallid like her mother. Of course she's desperate not to lose him, I thought of Laurence. Look at this exquisite child. Who can blame her?

"My dance class, *Maman,* it's time." The schoolgirl English was spoken for my benefit."

"*Un moment,*" her mother answered.

The girl threw me a look at once inquisitive but also unmistakably tinged with distrust.

"I must take my daughter now. I really should go."

"Before you do, could you take my phone number and ask Michel to call me?"

Laurence flinched with momentary vexation. "Michel already has your phone number," she said with unmistakable disdain. "You live on the rue Birague with an American poet. He told me. So I figure he knows how to find you."

Standing up, she led the way out of the library, and I followed her, staggered by the revelation that Michel had known all along where I'd been living and had never even bothered to make contact. But then, just as I was leaving the room, I happened to notice in the bookshelf a duplicate Pléiade of *Les Misérables*, just like the one that Michel had given me and that was still in my possession. He must have gone out and bought himself another copy. Perhaps Laurence had insisted.

Six

~

I MANAGE TO FALL ASLEEP HOLDING on to Ed's manuscript and awaken a few hours later to voices arguing outside my bedroom. I peek out of the door to see Marina in a
full-length turquoise bathrobe, surrounded by her brood of
mutts, disputing something with Carla, who seems to be up-
braiding her, but whose thick dialect is difficult to understand. I
finally decipher, "You should've put them on last year when it
first happened."

Marina throws up her hands and yells, "Okay, I am an imbe-
cile. Let's just go to the *carabinieri* and file the report."

I address them. "Put on *what* last year?"

"Window bars," Carla barks at me just as Marina pivots and
sees me.

"Ah, Russell, bravo. You're awake."

"I told her last year to put up window bars when we had that
other thief. But of course she never listened to me . . . the
crazy!" Carla exclaims.

"We've had a tragedy," Marina says, and then goes on to ex-

plain that just across the road at one of the villa's *dependences*,
right next door to where both Carla and Daniela live, there was
a break-in.

A man drove up to the empty house in a rickety van, climbed
up on the roof and, after jimmying a window, broke into one of
the upstairs bathrooms. He then crept downstairs, unlatched the
back door as if to load furniture and paintings, but something
made him change his mind. He got back into his vehicle and acci-
dentally backed into a neoclassical Greek statue on a pedestal and
knocked it to the ground. "He rammed a two-hundred-and-fifty-
year-old Apollo," Marina explains gravely. The collision made
such a racket that it awoke both Carla and Daniela next door.

Carla, speaking more slowly for my benefit, explains that half
asleep, with hardly a second thought, she grabbed a butcher
knife and went running outside. Apparently the man had hit his
head badly on the windshield and was sitting in his van, bleed-
ing and dazed by the collision. Carla rushed and threw open the
driver's door. "He's not such a big man," she tells me. "I stood in
front of him, waving the knife. He was too wounded to try to
drive away. The *signora*"—Daniela, she means—"called the *carabinieri,* and then she came and tied his hands. Then they showed
up and took him."

I ask if this had happened around three A.M., and Carla nods
and says it did. "I think I heard the yelling. I was actually awake."

"When you've been sleeping so much? Then it's a miracle,"
she snorts. Slapping her palms together as though she were
dusting them of filth, she says, "Such a beautiful statue. Now
he's lying on the ground. His head is next to his body. His hands
and feet have all broken off. What a shame! I've known him all
my life, ever since I was a little girl and living up the road."

"It's going to be difficult to have him repaired," Marina adds. "The statue is old enough to fall under the authority of the local museum. They will insist on overseeing every step. Such a restoration could take years."

She points out that most of the larger homes in Italy are potential targets for burglars, even those residences with elaborate alarm systems, "Which, as you may or may not know, the villa has. However, the villa itself has never been broken into. Just its *dependences*."

She goes on to say that the villa houses few objects that have more monetary rather than sentimental value. "For example, I inherited a Tiepolo. It's in the study off the library. You haven't even seen it yet, I don't think. Not one of his greater works. I seriously doubt the ordinary thief would even recognize it. But I have it insured. What I truly love, however, are the old books in my father's library—I don't think anybody would ever dream of stealing them. They are very large and heavy and probably would not be so easily resold. Up until recently I've never really worried about anybody coming into the villa at night. Because I have my dogs." She pats the large black-and-white mutt, Primo, who in turn nuzzles her affectionately. "They would certainly know if somebody was trying to break in before the motion sensors would."

I say that I've been wondering if, in light of the rumor that people wanted to harm Stefano for his political views, she isn't concerned about somebody trying to break into the villa.

She shrugs. "Of course I am. If only my friend in Intelligence could give more definite information. I called him this morning—after we discovered the break-in—and now he says the informant who told him that Stefano might be a target is not quite so certain of his information as he was a week ago. Because these people get on the Internet and do their chatter, and the chatter seems to shift like the wind. My friend is now speaking to some other informants. In the meantime, what else can we really do to protect ourselves? We do have *some* protection, however. A few years ago I and several other villa owners in the area hired a company made up of ex–military men who patrol the neighborhood in unmarked cars. Nevertheless, somebody with bad intentions doesn't even have to break in the villa. They can likely pull up in the driveway and shoot out the windows."

"God forbid, not at night," Carla points out. "We lock all the gates at night."

"But we don't lock them during the evening weddings," Marina reminds her.

Carla weighs in to say that never in all the years of Marina's family owning the villa, even when the Nazis occupied it, did anyone shoot into the house, much less break into it.

"A long history means absolutely nothing," Marina tells her. "All it takes is one weapon and a religious fanatic holding it, and *poof!* A new chapter is written. I suppose one good thing is that Stefano's bed is in an alcove away from the windows; you'd need to throw a bomb in order to kill him." Although Marina says this with matter-of-fact resignation, I can now see worry furrowing her forehead.

Remembering the amorous couple who had disregarded the DO NOT DISTURB sign on my door, I ask about the conduct of wedding guests who might wander where they shouldn't during a party and possibly do harm.

"Now, this could happen, but these days usually because there is some political figure or another who has been invited, all the wedding parties have gotten in the habit of hiring bodyguards who check the names of guests off lists and patrol the party. I must say, however, that in ten years of weddings I've never had a single incident. And not one thing stolen.

"Anyway, enough of this discussion, I will need you to come with me to the *carabinieri*."

"Why?"

"To see if you recognize anything about this thief." This takes me by surprise, and I obviously look bewildered. "Because of what happened in Paris," Marina adds.

"But I told you they were wearing masks and gloves."

"Well, then perhaps something else about this man might set him apart and spark your memory."

We are interrupted. "We need to try to find out if there is a link between what happened to you in Paris and this break-in," says a masculine voice, at once tremulous while managing also to be distinct and even authoritative.

I turn and there is Stefano, in the same blue dressing gown I spied him in previously. His eyes are rheumy yet shrewd, his face looks patrician: long and gaunt and hoary with what appears to be several days' growth of a snow-white beard. He stands perhaps twenty-five feet away from us in the main library, which unfolds beyond a doorway.

"But why would there be?" I ask him. "I'm in a totally different place now."

"Some things are difficult to explain . . . to a foreigner. And this is a unique situation," Stefano goes on. "Because so much is still speculation. I just hope that you will oblige us with your help."

Rhetorical formality, practiced among certain elderly Europeans, is clearly meant to discourage any further discussion. I can detect the noble influence of Milanese in Stefano's vowels, in his distinct pronunciation. The Milanese, after all, pride themselves on their organization and their rationality. I suddenly remember overhearing Marina discussing my sleeping for so many hours shortly after my arrival at the villa nearly two weeks ago. This is the same voice that told her that sleeping a lot after any ordeal made perfect sense.

Without another word Stefano retreats to his room and momentary silence follows his cameo appearance. Finally Carla says, *"Dio Santo!"*

Marina now explains that besides herself and Carla, I am the first individual Stefano has addressed in person for longer than they can remember. Indeed, during the last ten years she has frequently hosted dinner parties for people Stefano knows and admires, all of whom he's refused to see.

When I ask how Stefano communicates with his editors at the *Corriere*, Marina explains that he never sees them, but rather speaks to them on the phone and corresponds by e-mail. "He may seem Old World to you, but he was actually one of the first people I know who used e-mail," Marina tells me.

"Makes sense," I say. "The perfect mode of communication for a recluse. Or a misanthrope."

"He's not a misanthrope," Marina corrects me gently. "He's just a solitary, reflective man who is terribly shy. Part of it is a constant battle with depression for which he refuses all medication."

"I thought as much," I say in English. "Because he looks kind of hangdog."

"Hangdog?" Marina repeats, and the very American expression sounds farcical in the mouth of an Italian. Laughing, I try to define the idiom as best as I can. "Now, that is a good one," she remarks, and then turns momentarily philosophical. "You know, Russell, none of my Anglo friends, even writers I know, ever bother to teach me the good idioms in English or in American. But you, since you care about language, you must do so."

I promise Marina that I will teach her every familiar and obscure English and American idiom I can think of if only she'll attempt to correct my Italian—which she never bothers to do. I've already caught myself making mistakes repeatedly and she neither seems to notice nor care.

"Of course I notice, Russell. I notice every mistake you make, obviously. But I find the *bêtises* you make charming."

"Well, I don't want to be charming. I want to be correct. I want to get better. It's not a one-way street."

"Yes, sir. *Va bene,*" Marina says.

Italian is my second language, but I miss many of its nuances. I feel that it takes decades of living in a foreign country to become absolutely certain of what common phrases and expressions imply, to recognize definitive meaning. This is something that Ed and I often spoke about. For even though his French sounded perfect to my ear, he complained about it, about missing subtleties at dinner parties and in general discourse with highly educated people. Sometimes he described the experience of speaking to several foreigners at once as "grasping."

Marina turns to Carla. "And so Stefano speaks to Russell. What do you make of this?"

"He likes his story. He tells me so," Carla says.

"You think it's out of respect, then? Interesting," Marina says.

"Wait a minute," I say in English, and then force myself to switch back to Italian. "My *story?*"

Marina smiles. "He read your novella. We both did, actually."

"But . . . how did you get a copy?"

"The library in Ferrara sent it. It arrived while you were sleeping."

I'd told Marina that in light of my ancestry, the city of Ferrara had ordered a copy of my novella for its library. Assuming that my work had not been to her liking, I refrain from soliciting her opinion. Carla, however, is quite happy to act as Stefano's proxy. "He likes it. He was not expecting to. But he says that—"

"Do you see how easily he speaks to Carla?" Marina interrupts, jealous or perhaps guarding Stefano's opinion of my work being delivered to me secondhand.

Carla says defensively, "It makes sense, doesn't it? If I am the one to bring him meals, to straighten his room, to do his laundry." She bustles away to the kitchen.

Looking after her, Marina smiles dreamily. "The great intellectual and the uneducated, wise housekeeper. Have you read *Un Coeur Simple* by Flaubert?"

"Just thinking of that, actually," I tell her.

"Stefano is deeply touched by her devotion to him. It goes way beyond her paid responsibilities. They adore each other. She takes care of him like a dutiful child takes care of an ailing father. But it's more than that. I know that she's a bit in love with him, which is fine with me. Carla's husband died a few years before Stefano came to live with me. They've always gotten on extraordinarily well. I, on the other hand, just go and visit him and talk of literature and politics and the dogs and then spend the night in my own room . . ." She hesitates a moment before revealing with a bit of discomfort. "Our relationship has changed a great deal over the years. Now *they* are almost closer than he and I are."

This bolsters my hunch that Marina and Stefano's sex life is at a lull. Not only *hangdog*, he also seems quite frail. A less-than-satisfying sex life might even explain why Marina has a blooming, poised, sensual air about her.

"So, would you or would you not like to know what I thought of your work?" Marina asks me finally, with an air of impatience.

"Do I dare?"

"Oh, stop. It's good, don't worry." She laces her hands together in front of her chest, a somewhat sanctimonious gesture. "I think that the writing is, at times, strong. You've written well about the death of that child. Writing about death, that is your good suit. When you write about love"—she hesitates— "it's not so very interesting."

I'm rattled by her candid assessment and try to assure myself that it's just one person's opinion. Then again, my confidence is not exactly in tact. I'd hoped that my novella, published by a small literary journal, would attract some attention. Unfortunately, there was not a single review. Friends of mine who were readers admired my little book, and although I heard some compliments, nobody raved about it, certainly. Several people tried to remind me that one writes because one has to, not to be admired. Although I understood the wisdom in this time-worn adage, I reasoned that there needed to be some acknowledgment of several years of work, that one couldn't just release a book into a void of indifference. This was when I began to doubt my dedication, my conviction, not to mention my talent. It was hard not to assume that because the work was completely ignored that it had no merit.

Ed, who'd managed to read the novella before we met, claimed to admire the writing. But later on he told me quite pointedly that he felt that I had yet to find my real subject matter. I asked him: If writing about a harrowing event in my life wasn't my true subject matter, then what was? He shook his head and shrugged and wouldn't pursue the conversation any further. This only helped to deepen my worry that I just didn't have it.

Marina grabs hold of both my arms. "What I want to say is that you must carry on, because there is insight there and intelligence. Your best work will come when you're feeling more confident. If I hadn't liked what I read, I would have just sent it back to Ferrara without saying anything. The fact I speak of it means something."

"I appreciate your making the effort to read it."

"Oh, stop it. I wanted to, of course." She takes a step backward and looks at me appraisingly. "Look, Russell, we all want our work to be loved unconditionally. Just as *we* want to be loved, just as we want our *children* to be loved. And our *dogs,* for that matter."

"And when it's not?"

"There's always the next book."

"I don't know if the next book is ever going to happen."

"It must happen!"

"Can we just go to the *carabinieri* now?" I say in exasperation. Marina gives up. "Certainly we can go."

We wedge ourselves into Marina's tiny Renault and start down the long driveway and through the tall entry gates, then take a narrow road that follows the perimeter of a stone wall contouring the property line. We cross a small stream on a metal bridge wide enough for only one car and begin looping through backstreets, passing suburban-looking tracts of homes and apartments built since the Second World War that resemble the faux Mediterranean housing one finds in more arid regions of the United States. Still feeling a bit deflated following our brief discussion of the novella, I speak little, and Marina wisely decides to avoid pressing me into conversation.

We approach a railroad crossing that is momentarily barricaded to traffic and wait until a local train from Florence lumbers past on its way to Pisa. Teenaged passengers are hanging out the windows, grinning like monkeys, smoking cigarettes, which are now forbidden onboard. I've ridden these trains all over Tuscany and even now can conjure up their tang of cigarettes and rank body odor and motor fumes.

We are finally heading toward the city's high brick walls, which are forty feet high and more than three hundred years old. There are walls in the interior that date back to the time of the Romans, including the remnants of a small amphitheater that was once used for competitions and spectacles. Wide green lawns surround these battlements, and there are five or six portals all the way around that allow foot traffic and cars with permits to enter and leave the city. We don't venture inside the city, but rather join the throng of snarling traffic that keeps encircling ramparts that protect a core of sandalwood-colored buildings ranging in age from two hundred to eleven hundred years old.

Honking cars follow within inches of one another, motor scooters desperately weaving in and out. Most Italians seem to drive with inexplicable urgency. This is ironic in that they also seem to have written the manual on how to relax and be leisurely—so this automotive madness is at once schizophrenic and inscrutable. And it's not just the men who drive insanely. I've seen ladies leaning heavily on their horns, making the obscene two-fingered gesture for cuckold and then going on to execute perilous maneuvers. Down in the Maremma in the southern part of Tuscany, I once saw a woman who had to be at least eighty years old pass a cluster of five slower-moving cars on a two-lane straightaway. Driving in the middle of the pack, I watched her whiz past and neatly tuck herself back on the proper side of the road, barely avoiding a head-on collision with an enormous truck. Nobody this ancient relic passed honked at her. Everybody seemed to take her momentary madness in stride.

Marina, by contrast, is a more vigilant driver who suffers the constant indignity of having other cars honking and cutting in front of her. She registers displeasure but doesn't seem to care about being a slowpoke. She'll live longer with this attitude, I decide.

We finally pull up to a modern building of white stone and glass windows unadorned with the characteristic Tuscan shutters. Milling in and out of the entrance are men dressed in red-and-navy uniforms with sashes and trousers that are more militarily stylized and form-fitting than those worn by their American policemen counterparts. Several *carabinieri* seem to recognize Marina and say hello. At first I can't understand why she is so readily identifiable. Could it actually be because she is an award-winning writer? After all, she did win the Strega Prize, a dark-horse favorite who beat out the great Alberto Moravia, an upset victory that was broadcast on Italian national television. But I will soon learn there is a more pertinent reason: The local head of the *carabinieri* was her schoolmate at the *liceo,* and has remained a close friend.

She turns to me. "You know the difference between *carabinieri* and *polizie,* don't you?"

"The *carabinieri* are national police, aren't they?"

"Precisely. They are of the state."

While one of the older *carabinieri* leads us to the interrogation room where they are holding the man who broke into the *dependence,* I manage to catch the glance of a tall, muscular *carabiniere* with a deep tan and startling pale green eyes—this is the face of complete heartbreak, I think to myself. It's not a face that is totally unfamiliar to me, either. I've seen this sort of mien before in Italy, the refined features that one expects to see in a European combined with an American openness, broadness, and natural masculinity. The dazzling eyes really pierce through me. And then he actually smiles.

Marina and I are brought to the small interrogation room. Viewed through a thick glass window, it is large enough to fit a rectangular table and a small bookshelf filled with thick manuals of, I imagine, police code. Suddenly, euphoria: The handsome *carabiniere* is standing next to me, his veined masculine hands fiddling with a ring of keys to open the door. As the three of us go in, I wonder how I'm possibly going to concentrate.

The prisoner is huddled over a book that looks like a religious text, probably the Koran. He runs his fingers across columns of print, lips trembling with unintelligible words. Finally he glances up at us. From the accident he has a large purple contusion on his forehead. His complexion is dark with rough patches of acne, his hair thick and glossy and wavy black, his beard unkempt. And although we lock eyes for a moment, there is no familiar flicker of recognition on his part, no extrasensory inkling that we've come in contact in the recent past. Not that I expected there to be. He glances away quickly, a tremor of agitation knitting his features. His cowering could mean something, or it could mean nothing at all.

Taking off his official jacket, the *carabiniere* instructs us to sit down at the table. His forearms, lightly dusted with hair, are broad. His biceps swell against the conservative cut of his light blue short-sleeved shirt. He's too preoccupied with his duties, he's too unself-conscious, and I inwardly wager that he's got to be incorruptibly straight. Alas, I have found that this sort of easy-going masculinity is rarely a characteristic of a man who is sexually interested in other men.

"You *do* speak Italian, don't you?" Marina presumptively addresses the prisoner. She has already informed me that Albanian immigrants usually have a good command of the language from having watched so many Italian programs on Albanian satellite television.

The man nods.

"Good. Why don't you tell me how long you've been in Italy."

The man holds up one hand, fingers spread wide.

"Answer her!" the *carabiniere* orders him.

"Five years."

"And where do you live now?"

"In the camp by the river," the man says.

"The warehouses, you mean?"

He nods.

Marina shakes her head. "Terrible conditions there," she remarks to the *carabiniere*. Then to the prisoner, "Does the van belong to you?"

"Borrowed it."

"And have you lived in this camp since you came from Albania?"

"Yes."

"And you came to Italy by boat, presumably?"

"Yes, by boat."

"We know which dwelling is his in the camp, *Signora,*" the *carabiniere* informs her.

Marina turns to him. "So you could check and see if there is anything—"

"I was the one. I did it last year, too," says the man.

"Ah . . ." Marina glances sharply at the *carabiniere*, who calmly explains that the man has already confessed this. "That's what I came to find out for my own personal reasons." She turns to me and, seeming relieved, says in English, "Nothing to worry about now," but doesn't elaborate. Then she once again addresses the man in Italian, but sounds more lighthearted when she explains to him, "My outer buildings have been burglarized far too often—much more than the villas surrounding me. As there is hardly anything in them, it makes no sense to me."

Eyes down, the man nervously shuffles his feet back and forth under his metal chair. Finally he looks up at Marina balefully. "But they said you are rich."

"Who said?"

"People in my camp."

"Relative to them I suppose I am. But truthfully we have very few things that will resell very well."

The man shrugs.

"Shame about the statue, *Signora,*" says the *carabiniere.* "I was told—"

"Let's hope it can be repaired," Marina remarks. Then, turning back to the prisoner, she says, "Do you have a family?" The man explains there is a wife and two daughters. Shaking her head, she turns to the *carabiniere,* "If you can find out and let me know where they are, I will make sure they get food and some money." Then back to the prisoner: "And what you stole last year—"

"Sold most of it," the man says simply, looking at Marina with great solemnity.

"Of course you did. To live you sold it. I should've assumed that."

When the interview is finally concluded, we get up and file out of the cell and Marina excuses herself to say hello to her friend, the head of the *carabinieri.*

After a stretch of stiff silence the handsome *carabiniere* says to me, "She's bringing food to the family? That's kind of her. But then she comes from a family of do-gooders." He shakes his head. "Sad situation. I just wish these people could know how difficult it's going to be before they get on those overcrowded boats and cross the sea."

"They get hooked on the illusion of paradise."

"Yes, this is true." He suddenly grins, folding his arms across his chest. "So you're American, aren't you?"

The gesture, which seems flirtatious, leaves me a bit light-headed. I nod.

"Your Italian is pretty good; I wouldn't necessarily know that you were American. Except that you're built in that American way. Most Italian men are slimmer. Even the ones who go to the gym." He frowns. "And why don't I see you at the gym?"

"I need to find one." I'm having difficulty maintaining eye contact with him without blushing.

"I will take you. My gym is actually not far from where you live."

I wonder stupidly how he knows where I live and this must register on my face because he says, "Villa Guidi. Everybody knows the Villa Guidi."

He gives me the gym's address, assuring me that Marina will know it, and invites me to meet him there at five o'clock the following day. I follow him to a waiting room outside a closed office where I can hear Marina arguing vociferously. "My name is Lorenzo," he says, smiling.

"Russell," I reply. We shake hands and he walks away.

Watching him, I am reminded that here in Italy, my sexual signal-reading is consigned to a very low frequency. Body gestures, innuendos, double-meanings are cultural specifics that take years of living in a country to decipher. In America, I would know definitively if this man was trying to pick me up. In Italy, I haven't a clue, although I do have my hopes.

Moments later Marina comes storming out of the office and says haughtily, "Let's go." Once we get outside and are making our way to the car, she fumes, "I'm here because of Stefano. I am here to make sure this man is not one of those who threatened to harm him. He isn't. He's merely and only a thief. And yet he has to stay in jail. His trial won't be for at least six months. Which is a problem because his family will go hungry."

"Well, he *was* caught stealing. Aren't there social services to help his dependents?" I ask as we get into the car and Marina begins driving us home.

"Of course there are, but never enough. I don't want to be

responsible for a mother and children who starve. The problem is I expect nothing less than for this man to steal. Nobody gives these people jobs or education."

Marina gets distracted for a moment as she maneuvers to change lanes in a stream of traffic. "I suppose I should just be relieved that this was the man who robbed us last year rather than one of the people who may have threatened my husband."

After a few moments of silence, I say, "Marina, could you tell me specifically what it is that Stefano writes that puts him in danger?"

She nods and then slams her horn at an audacious Mercedes convertible. "Well, first of all, Stefano's mother died when he was ten, and his father ended up marrying a cultivated, very beautiful woman from Syria. From her, Stefano learned Arabic so that he can speak with some of the Muslims who live in Italy. And he has been warned time and again by the moderate Muslims trying to make a life here that the government should cooperate with *them* and be advised on which mosques in Italy are being used to spawn jihadists and that the government should, in fact, shut these mosques down. And Stefano has written precisely this."

"Oh," I say. "Well, that would certainly be enough to make him a target."

"Of course," Marina says. "The pity is so far the government hasn't even considered doing what he asks." She shakes her finger at me. "And the Muslims know this, too!"

We end up driving back to the villa a different way, on a more main thoroughfare. The road is passing over the *autostrada* that stretches between Florence and coastal Viareggio when Marina says, "Now, about this *carabiniere* who seems to fascinate you so much—"

"How do you know?"

She laughs. "How could you not be fascinated?"

"Okay, okay." And then I admit that he invited me to his gym.

"Ah, so I was right to bring him up." She honks at yet another car that veers dangerously in front of us. "These people are mad!" Gripping the steering wheel tightly, she instructs me, "Just beware of him."

"Beware?"

"Well, for one thing he is most assuredly married. Did you look for the wedding ring?"

I shrug and admit that I didn't.

"So, it's wishful thinking all over again. Remember, you've already gotten twisted up in a similar situation over a married man."

I certainly cannot dispute this. "That's assuming this *carabiniere* is even available. I have absolutely no idea what his sexual story is."

"If he looks at you the way I noticed and then invites you to his gym so quickly, he probably is a gay who is married. As are a majority of gay men in Italy. Which means he is not *available* as your Frenchman was not *available*. And probably even less *available* than your Frenchman."

"Thank you, Marina," I say with a bit of sarcasm, and then deliberately in English, "I guess I don't want to spin my wheels again."

"Spin?" she says. "What is this now?" I explain. "Ah," she says, "excellent, this one.

"I also want . . . I know this particular man a little better than some of the others. He has come to the villa on several occasions because the alarm has gone off. We have spoken. I find him a very intelligent fellow. In fact, he told me that he went to university and read philosophy and was even contemplating an advanced degree when he decided to give it all up to join the *carabinieri*."

"Did he say why he gave it up?"

"No, but I assume because it is hard to get jobs with his sort of intellectual training. He probably realized this. And then having a family to support." Marina pauses reflectively. "A few years ago he asked me to read one of his student articles, which I luckily avoided."

"Why did you avoid it?"

"Because I felt sure I'd be disappointed. And it would have made my response very awkward."

"That's rather arrogant of you to make that assumption."

She shakes her head and says in a slightly patronizing tone, "It's different here. You must be kind and obliging and fair. But you also know what to expect."

She seems to be suggesting that the difference between her social standing and Lorenzo's is intellectually impossible to bridge. Now, here is someone terribly concerned about civic issues and inequities and yet clearly presumptuous about class differences.

"I know what you are thinking," Marina says, broaching the silence. "But you must believe me. There are rarely any surprises. What you see and perceive here is normally what is. In America there is still this wonderful possibility of cultural paradox. I will give you an example of this, of something that I saw there that would never happen in Italy.

"Once I was invited to speak at Amherst College, and I asked to visit the Emily Dickinson house because she is my favorite American poet. The professor who taught her poetry and had written books about it was kind enough to take me. On the tour were he and I and a very fat man who, according to this professor, looked like he walked out of one of your trailer parks. He was wearing one of these sun visors that are popular in America, and was carrying a plastic drink container from, I believe, Disneyland that we suspected had a beer in it. He looked very rough and ill-bred.

"Well, the professor, who, mind you, seemed quite kind, whispered to me with very distinct disdain that perhaps this other fellow was drunk and that he might be looking for the Basketball Hall of Fame, which apparently is only ten miles away from this place, this poet's house. The professor kept apologizing for this man's presence on the tour. But I didn't mind. I found him a curiosity.

"The woman who led us around the Emily Dickinson house was a sylph of a graduate student, one of the professor's former protégées. As we went along, she addressed everything she said to her former tutor and to myself, of course. She completely ignored this so-called basketball fan, this 'trailer-park trash,'" Marina says in English. "Is this how you say it?"

I nod, embarrassed by the existence of such a horrible expression.

"Perhaps ten minutes into the tour, this strange man who had been completely silent finally spoke up. And he did it to kindly correct something that the graduate student had misstated. About a certain manuscript of Emily Dickinson being at Harvard rather than at Amherst. 'He's absolutely right,' the professor told his former student. But let me tell you, that professor was stunned. And then this fat man with the beer in his cup started to speak about Emily Dickinson. He knew her life, her poetry, but his knowledge wasn't pedantic, it was profound. It seemed to me that he understood the woman's writing. Then the professor, the author of critical studies on Emily Dickinson, attempted to—dared to, I should say—argue about the woman's life, her motivation, and even about certain lines of her verse, perhaps to assert and prove his dominance in front of a foreign visitor such as myself. But this trailer-park man kept up his end of the discussion with great confidence and, in my opinion, made a complete fool out of the professor." Marina turns to me and says with great vehemence, "This, my dear friend, could never happen in Italy. And I never loved America more than I did at that very moment. It was perhaps one of the three or four high points of my entire life."

We have entered the residential road that will lead to the villa, but then Marina surprises me by making a sharp right turn onto a one-way thoroughfare. "You haven't been this way, have you?" she says.

"Don't think so."

"I want to show you."

We drive down a narrow lane barely wide enough for one car and suddenly, on either side of us, rise stone walls that are at least twenty feet high. The vaulting effect is dramatically Old World. The road narrows to a point where the Renault barely fits. Many vehicles, Marina explains, cannot venture down this thoroughfare; indeed, I can see scrape marks on some of the stones left by cars that were too wide to pass through. It occurs to me that in Europe much more than in America, the prerogatives of the past are constantly intruding upon the present.

The road spits us out directly opposite the entrance to the villa. But instead of heading through the metal grille of its gates, Marina makes a right and we drive along the property wall until we reach another driveway that is lined with fig trees and oleander bushes. The fig trees are so laden with black fruit that much of it has fallen off the boughs and is lying squashed and rotting, staining the ground like blood.

We pull up in front of a house built of stones and mortar that looks incredibly old. "This is the *dependence* that the thief broke into," Marina tells me, and goes on to explain that the building was once an active convent and is just over a thousand years old. Very little was done to it until 1950, when her father had the house updated and modernized and reconfigured into three apartments. She points out the empty pedestal that stands just to the right of the front entrance and then kills the engine. We get out of the car and approach the fallen statue that is alabaster, darkened by a quarter of a millennium of exposure to the elements. The Apollo lies on his stomach, his severed, idealized head with its tamed curls lying next to his narrow waist. His ass is perfectly globed and dimpled at the small of his back. A meter or so away from the breaks in his ankles is a neat pile of his hands and feet, which have been sheared off.

Although seeing the broken statue is disturbing, I actually expected it to be in worse shape, pulverized by the initial concussion and subsequent fall. I mention this to Marina.

"Yes, sure, we are somewhat lucky; however, even with careful restoration, he won't be the same." Sounding forlorn, she says, "I don't mind that this man steals things from me. I do mind about this piece of history being ruined."

I glance beyond the house, through the orderly-looking rows

of the villa's grapevines that are tended and cultivated by a local farmer. I notice how the road we just followed winds up to an old Romanesque church.

Marina resumes, "In a way, I understand why you attract these married men who are gays."

"Oh, and why is that?"

She picks up a shard of alabaster and lays it gently on the pile of fractured hands and feet. "You don't seem so. Your manner is rather ordinary, though of course you have the cultural refinements that many gays have. But I suppose if a married man chooses to spend time with you, then he might be able to delude himself into thinking that he is spending time with a friend rather than a lover."

Fixing my attention on the statue's beautiful yet broken limbs, I say, "I think it's a bit more complicated than that."

"No doubt it is. These thoughts are new," Marina admits and falls almost ruefully silent.

She motions me to get back into the car, and we drive the short distance around the villa's outer walls back toward the front entrance and take the turn down the long driveway. The sienna-colored building looms in the foreground; its green shutters have been opened to air out the enormous frescoed rooms. As we come to a halt, the pack of Marina's beloved mongrels gambol toward us over the wide emerald lawns.

Seven

~

*U*NA FRANCESE, A FRENCHWOMAN, called while you
were at the *carabinieri,*" Carla announces when Marina
and I enter the kitchen. The dogs are burbling and
pressing against our legs. "I don't understand her, so she tries
English," Carla laughs. "And then a miracle: Stefano actually
gets on the phone and speaks to her. He never speaks on the
phone unless it's for him," she explains as she hands me a piece
of paper with a message written in European-looking chicken
scratch: *Mme Soyer.* However, the number scribbled is not Parisian but rather a two-digit city. She is somewhere else in France,
probably Brittany.

"Phone her now," Marina suggests, and corrals Carla into the
library to explain the situation with the thief.

When the phone is answered by a young girl, I imagine I can
actually hear waves breaking in the background. Instinct urges
me to cling to English, not to venture a single word into French,
and once I identify myself, I hear her saying, *"Maman, c'est
l'americain."*

A moment later Laurence is on the line. "Hello, Russell, give me just a second. . . . Put that over there, please. And then please go out and close the door behind you." All of this is in English, as if for my benefit. During my unannounced visit to the avenue Foch, mother and daughter had enacted the same charade, when it was clear to me that their habit of conversation was primarily in French, something I would imagine Michel had insisted upon. "Hang on a bit longer, will you?"

"Sure, but can you just tell me if Michel is okay?"

"He's fine . . . as far as I know. I haven't spoken to him in a few weeks, to be quite honest."

I have no idea how expensive it is to call France and remind Laurence that I am borrowing the phone. She offers to call me straight back.

When she does, she begins by saying, "I saw the article about your friend in *Le Monde*. I just want to say how sorry I am."

I merely thank her, waiting to hear the reason why she's calling me. It cannot be because of Ed's death. The last time Laurence and I spoke was when I showed up unannounced on the avenue Foch.

"Anyway, I recently got a call from the police in Trouville. In Normandy," she qualifies.

"I know where it is. My French ain't the greatest, but I know a little geography."

"Forgive me," she says, suddenly docile.

Along a seaside road the police had found an abandoned BMW motorcycle whose license plate they traced back to Michel. They'd wanted to question him about it. When they told Laurence that the motorcycle had been irretrievably damaged, she panicked. But then they reassured her that there had been a thorough investigation of the accident scene with no indication of any kind of personal injury. Michel, or whoever had been riding his motorcycle, seemed to have walked away unharmed, leaving very expensive wreckage.

"And I haven't heard from him since the police called. I haven't heard from him in well over a month."

"And this is unusual?"

She sighs and admits, "Quite unusual, yes."

"And so why are you calling *me?*"

"Because I really need to locate him and I thought . . . you might have been in contact with him."

"You can't be serious."

There's a hesitation on the other end. "Russell . . . I'm sorry to do this." There is a noticeable plaint in her voice. "I did give him your message when you came to see me. I told him to call you."

"That was probably ten months ago. I never heard from him."

"I just figured that you had."

"It's been over a year since we've been in contact," I remind her.

"I didn't know if you'd stayed out of touch for this long. And I hope you understand. . . ." She pauses for a moment. "When the police asked me if he could've been with somebody when the accident occurred, the only person I could think of was you. I gave them the telephone number you left me, but I guess your friend, the poet, had already given up his apartment by then."

"Oh, no!" I exclaim, momentarily worrying that to the authorities it might appear odd that I could be linked to two mishaps in France: one of them a motorcycle accident, and the other, an attempted armed robbery. I mention this to Laurence.

"But if they thought you could be helpful in either case, they would've contacted you by now."

"But how would they find me?"

"Well, *I* found you."

She had a point. "I hope you're right. But now I need to ask you something." I hesitate for a moment, staring down at a fax, recently printed and waiting to be retrieved, whose address is in Sardinia. "That day I came to see you last fall, you weren't telling me the whole truth about yourself and Michel, were you?"

A short pause. "No, I wasn't. And I'm sorry," she says, going on to explain that Michel had, in fact, already moved out and was living in the other apartment.

"So then when I read that article about the two of you, the newspaper's reporting *was* accurate."

She audibly winces. "It wasn't up to me. He didn't want you to know about it. In fact, he told me that if you ever got in contact, not to give out that information. Obviously I'd go along with this."

I don't respond for a moment. Finally, I ask, "But why didn't he want me to know? I mean, was he that afraid of . . . the power I might have?"

Laurence forces a laugh. "If that were the case, it would have been . . . noble of him to ask my help. But, no, it was because he'd been in contact with the poet."

"What?" I ask, suddenly breathless.

There is a significant pause on the other end. "I thought you knew *this,* at least by now."

This can't be happening. I have to be dreaming. I manage to tell Laurence that I never knew. "I think you need to explain—"

"Fine. But, Russell, I honestly don't know how much or even when they were in contact. You have to understand that once he stopped seeing you, Michel was careful to bring up your name as little as possible. But I do know that early on, even before you came to see me, Michel tried to call you, to see how you were, or so he claimed. The poet answered the phone. Now I realize he just never gave you the message."

"Oh, Jesus!"

"Whatever the poet said strongly discouraged my husband from contacting you again," she continues. "As you know, Michel is not easily influenced. So even though I was glad that he listened to your friend, I was actually surprised that he did. And that was when he told me that if you ever called to put you off. And obviously I was happy to do it. I certainly didn't ask him why."

"God damn them!" For Michel is also culpable for not having told me anything.

"And so I've been worried about Michel because I have no idea where he is."

"But wait, how can you even know he's okay after the accident?"

Laurence lets out a sardonic chuckle. "Because a charge came through on our credit card for a new motorcycle."

"I don't understand."

She elaborates: 17,000 euros at a BMW dealer just outside Paris.

"You're saying he bought the bike but didn't even tell you?"

"Correct."

I'm still trying to assimilate the idea of Michel and Ed being in touch about me. "I wish I could help you . . . get hold of him.

But there has been absolutely no contact. I have no idea where Michel might be."

Laurence now admits that although she felt differently when we'd first discussed the idea all those months ago, she now thinks that perhaps Michel could actually be involved with somebody else.

"Did he tell you?"

"I never asked him this directly. But I plan to when I next speak to him."

I tell her, "I don't know if this will help at all, but before he started seeing me, Michel was seeing . . ." I'm not sure how to elaborate on the fact that this particular person was a beautiful transsexual.

"Yes, I know about this . . . other person," Laurence says with crisp authority in her voice. "Somebody who had a sex change, from a male to female, right?"

"Yes."

"Well, I wouldn't even know how to get in touch with her."

"I don't either . . . I never really knew her, although I met her once. She hated me for good reason," I say.

Laurence's terse response—"In case you think of something or hear about something, you have my number here"—makes me wonder if perhaps she's heard more than enough information about another of Michel's former lovers.

After I take down the telephone number of the avenue Foch apartment, I say, "Before you go, I would like to know one thing."

"Go ahead, ask," she says, almost as if she knows what the question will be.

"Did you have any idea at all about Michel before you married him?"

She quickly responds, "Of course I knew. I'm not a complete idiot! We even considered breaking off the engagement. Michel likes to joke that we got married because my father had already bought so many cases of excellent champagne, *comme il faut,* as the French say. And as my family has been coming to France every year since we were children, my father knew that you buy the best champagne you can afford for your daughter's wedding. He spent thousands upon thousands of dollars on it."

Right after all the champagne was delivered, Michel went to Laurence and made a promise that he'd never let *it* affect their life together, that he would always be discreet. That if he didn't marry Laurence, because of his family he'd be obliged to marry somebody else. Laurence discussed the situation with a wise Frenchwoman she knew "who was a dear friend of my father's. And Madame Cremieux pointed out to me that if it were not a man on the side, it could very easily—more easily, in fact—be a woman. Because mistresses are tolerated in French society . . . more than they are in America."

Laurence was told that in good families such as Michel's and Madame Cremieux's, maintaining a married lifestyle with children was far too important to ever jeopardize, so much so it was guaranteed to prevent him from being openly involved with another man.

"Madame Cremieux kept reassuring me that I was safe with him, safer than if he'd been completely straight."

This European logic will take a bit of getting used to, I decide after saying good-bye to Laurence.

So Ed's meddling was the reason why Michel never contacted me. And now that Ed has died, there is no outlet for my fury, no

way of crying foul. I'm completely powerless in my rage. In order to calm down, I try to remind myself how unhappy Ed must
have been to have tampered with my life. And yet I know that
even if I were able to confront him now, Ed would still argue
that his meddling had been for my own good. He'd regurgitate
his firm belief that if I allowed myself to get involved with
Michel once again, the pain of the inevitable second rupture
would trump the pain of the first. "This is the kind of thing that
can drive people loony," Ed had warned me on more than one
occasion, probably as firm in his conviction as wise Madame
Cremieux, whom Laurence had consulted. He felt there were too
many obstacles in Michel's life that would prevent him from
sustaining a relationship with any man.

My anxiety about Michel returns, a tsunami that has been
rolling and gathering strength across my mind. I retreat to my
bedroom, feeling as foolish as I once felt while waiting for his
phone calls when I was occupying my dreary flat in the 18th.
His calls usually came between four and six in the evening when
his office began to wind down, affording him an opportunity to
talk privately. But even then, when guaranteed solitude, he
would speak in a whisper and relied on English as a precaution.
During these late-afternoon phone calls he often told me, "*Je
t'aime bien.*" Logically, if *je t'aime* meant you loved somebody,
then *je t'aime bien* should mean that you loved someone very
well, meaning a lot. However, the literal words do not convey
their meaning in this way. For in fact, *je t'aime bien* means you
like somebody a lot and don't quite love them, whereas *Je t'aime*
means you do love them. So when Michel would say, "*Je t'aime
bien,*" I could never really trust the sentiment. There was the
odd occasion when he'd say "I love you" in English, but even

then I always suspected that it was easier for him to give lip service to a sentiment in a language that he'd adopted rather than
lived in.

And now of course, I have to wonder where Ed and Michel
had first met and what was said. I realize that my only source of
information would be the memoir. As urgent as the need is to
know more, I'm reluctant to delve into further descriptions of
Ed's unrequited love, his frustrated desires.

But at last I grab the manuscript, carefully laying its early
sections aside and finding the place where I'd last been reading.
I quickly scan descriptions of Ed's ongoing struggle to refine
several poems in his Palazzo Barbaro sequence, worrying that
they are not up to the standards of "Venice Sinking by Degrees,"
the poem about our imbalanced affection he published in *The
New Yorker*. Sandwiched between two long descriptions of back-
to-back literary dinner parties, I find a brief interlude in which
the meeting with Michel is related.

They actually met up at the same Left Bank café where Ed
and I had met for the first time. Unfortunately, Ed doesn't give a
date. He claims to have told Michel that I was still suffering
over him and that he had no business contacting me again unless he knew he was completely prepared to leave Laurence. He
then reminded Michel that his upbringing and his social class
would never allow this to happen. Then there is a short description of Michel, himself: masculine, apparently well-hung; and
that judging by his clothes, he was quite B.C.B.G.—*bon chic, bon
genre*, the French expression that is the equivalent of *yuppie*. However, it quickly seemed to become clear to Ed that Michel wasn't
going to listen to him, that he was still intent on contacting me.
"And so," he writes, "I knew then that my only alternative would

be at some point to tell Michel that Russell was sero-positive. And that it was I who had actually infected him."

His words pop and blister on the page. Stunned and whirling from this revelation, I barely manage to collate the manuscript and once again turn it over. Everything—the bookcases chock full of Pléiade, my writing desk with two Italian/English dictionaries, a stack of documents in the process of translation, an open bag of toiletries whose ingredients and directions for use are printed in several different languages—vibrates with this sense of terrible betrayal. "*You* didn't care if I got slammed," I speak to Ed aloud. "*You* just couldn't bear the idea of that relationship. So you did whatever you could to keep us apart. To keep me with you."

I read further. From Ed's revelation to Michel, he goes on to discuss a poem that he wrote that I never saw, and so I imagine he must have destroyed for not living up to his expectations. The poem, written at the end of October 2003, apparently personified my state of mind when I visited Sainte-Chapelle after my breakup with Michel, right before I went to get the result of my HIV test.

For I'd told Ed about having spent an hour meditating in this, my favorite chapel in all of Paris, a vaulting jewel box of stained glass that tells various biblical allegories, how I watched the prisms of sunlight shifting through the colored panes, reminding myself that no matter what happened, I was not going to die tomorrow. Even if I were to learn that my body was full of virus, I would, at the very least, be able to return and bask in the marquise setting of this chapel. What I didn't tell Ed was how I sat there in Sainte-Chapelle, daydreaming about Michel and all our rides through Paris. How, from the rear of his motorcycle, the architectural grandeur of the city used to fall away like a cascade of golden dominoes, blurred wonderfully by speed. I imagined myself clinging to his rib cage, nuzzling the nape of his neck that I so loved, so broad and long and covered with the faintest down of silver-blond hair. I constantly had to resist the temptation to lean forward and kiss it. And how when I did succumb to temptation, he'd squeeze his shoulders together and press back against me and say how good it felt to have me behind him. Roaring down boulevard after boulevard, he'd turn his head sideways and I'd see his blissful smile, his intimate words rattling against the wind. And I would shut my eyes and feel at once exhilarated and then desperately afraid of losing him. I'd begin my pathetic praying that somehow he'd be psychologically unable to sever the cord between us. Who would ever know that if we settled into a domestic arrangement whether or not we'd last, but the physical bond was so urgent that it seemed sacrilegious to harm it. And even though I always feared that he would eventually leave me, riding on the back of his motorcycle I just could never begin to fathom life without him.

But then in the midst of all the foreign visitors, the groups of boisterous schoolchildren who suddenly stopped their clowning and fell under Sainte-Chapelle's rapture, I imagined a pair of arms snaking around me, powerful arms gripping me the way he did when our bodies rocked together. And for a moment I actually believed that he, whom I hadn't seen in months, was there with me. Then I shook off the illusion, spooked by it.

Anxious about the test results, I decided to walk from Sainte-Chapelle, in the center of Paris, to the American hospital in Neuilly, on the outskirts of the city. The mid-October weather was breezy and glorious. I wandered along streets lined with trees whose leaves had turned a translucent golden and lent the city, already famous for its light, an added refraction. I like to imagine that, in comparison to the harsh purity of American sunlight, the light in certain European countries has an aged quality, like a candle flame burning on tallow rather than wax.

It took me an hour and a half to reach the hospital. From the sumptuous à la *Architectural Digest* waiting lounge, I was shown to a barren examining room with a school desk and chair in the middle of it, no other chairs, a few stainless-steel cabinets filled with gauze pads and knee braces and sacks of cotton balls and dark amber bottles of purgatives and antiseptic. Walls, painted gray, suggested the utilitarian tone of a way station in some far-flung country. Sitting there in the hard, uncomfortable chair, I thought to myself: This is it, the moment whose outcome I shall never forget for the rest of my life, and how rare to know that something yet to happen will become a lasting recollection.

The door unlatched, a young doctor entered, and I was astonished by dark, Latino matinee-idol looks, momentarily catapulted out of desperation only to feel foolish and shallow. He introduced himself, an American with a slight Southern drawl. I searched his face to see if he was harboring good news or bad.

"We're having a little trouble locating your test result," he said by way of explanation.

"Oh, Christ," I said. "I don't believe this!"

His handsome brow furrowed. "Don't worry. It's here somewhere. We'll find it. I just wanted to tell you." It was strange to feel so nervous and distraught in the presence of a man who normally would be rousing me in an entirely different way.

"Can I ask you something?" I said.

"What's that?"

"Are the results always positive or negative?"

"Meaning?"

"Is there any possible way that the results could be neither?"

The doctor squinted at me. "It can happen, I suppose. But why so concerned?"

Was this guy for real? What planet was *he* from? "You don't know what I've done."

His eyes narrowed as something occurred to him. "Wait, are you gay?"

I nodded.

"Oh, I'm sorry," he said, flustered. "I didn't realize."

Here is one occasion where the assumption that one might be straight was actually denying me a compassion or an understanding that otherwise would have been elicited from this doctor. At this point a knock came on the door. The man looked at me keenly. "Hang on now. This may be our answer." He got up and opened it a crack, was told something in French, and then slipped through and didn't return.

My heart sputtering, I now imagined getting the result, leaving the hospital in a daze, taking the Métro back to Ed, and watching his reaction. Then one clear thought occurred to me in the midst of this anxiety reflux: Ed, on some level, would want me to be infected also; for then we'd be in it together and there would be less chance that I'd leave him. I was feeling this so acutely when the door opened; the young doctor stuck his head in and said with mock derision, "You're fine. Now get the hell out of here. And play safe," as though I were a baseball player trotting out toward center field.

In his memoir Ed finally admits that he would have said and done whatever he could to discourage Michel—even to the point of lying about my HIV status. Reading this confession, knowing that at least Ed was aware of what he was doing, I feel completely deflated by his willingness to rob me of my happiness for the sake of his own. I want to hate him for what he's done, but it's difficult; I know how unhappy he was *au fond,* despite all the fame and validation of his career.

Putting the manuscript aside for a moment, I try to think back to the evening just after I learned the results of my blood test. It was a chilly evening, and Ed and I sat warming ourselves by a fire. I'd just finished confessing to him how the waiting had nearly done me in. He then confessed to me that his waiting period for the test result was mild in comparison to the aftermath of dismal depression over the result.

"It was very difficult because I knew just how and when it happened," he explained, "knew the precise moment I became infected, like some women know the moment they conceive."

"Really?" I said.

He nodded and smiled grimly. "It certainly wasn't romantic, the punch line of some candlelit dinner, or a thrumming fuck after a motorcycle ride through the Bois de Bologne. It was a quick pickup in the Tuileries. A manly beauty, incredibly exciting, a high moment of eroticism in my life." Ed stopped for a moment, eyes blinking rapidly in what I imagined to be his reliving some of the lurid details of the encounter. "And what's strange is that I had a choice whether or not to use protection. There was one of those great polyurethane condoms in my pocket. But the man was so hot." His face flushed. "No longer the stud I once was, I actually worried that I might not ever have the same kind of opportunity again. Being so caught up, so 'mastered by his brute blood,'" Ed paraphrased Yeats. "I just

wanted him to fuck me as he was. As I was. And what I actually
think I realized then, the burning truth was that getting caught
up in the power of that kind of sex makes everything that goes
against the grain diluted." Ed finally took off his reading glasses
and stared at me with his naked deep blue eyes. "You see, Russell, in my life I've always chased pure experience. And so I took
my moment of raw passion and it was absolutely divine. And afterward as I was walking back here to the apartment I somehow
knew in my gut that I was, at that very moment, in the earliest
stages of sero-conversion."

Disturbed, I looked away toward the fire whose flames were
suddenly roaring higher. I contemplated the idea of "sero-
conversion," a medical phrase that has become part of the general lexicon, widely known, even among the less educated, a
phrase that for many has the same far-reaching resonance as "terrorist attack." But it was an attack within the body itself, a ram-
page of an inscrutable virus that takes charge of healthy cells
and converts them to carry out a slow self-destruction. Finally I
said, "I can't believe you never told me this story."

"It's not an easy thing to speak about, or even admit to. It's in
the memoir, though. You'd have read about it at some point,
even if I hadn't told you."

"Better that you're explaining it now. Because obviously I
want to ask you things."

"Like what?" he asked in a suspicious tone.

"Like how it is dealing with such specifics. Knowing when
and who did it to you."

Surprisingly, it quickly ceased to make a difference, Ed told me.
In fact, the diagnosis itself demanded a far broader consideration.
For example, it forced him to be philosophical, to contemplate all

the terrible infirmities that could and did happen to people, to realize his viral infection was a lot that must be borne, like losing a loved one, or suffering from yet another chronic but treatable disease. How he'd had to accept that his life probably wouldn't be quite as long as he'd once hoped or imagined it would be. Yes, toward the end of his life he'd probably come down with more opportunistic illnesses than the run-of-the-mill person. Then again, can there ever be guarantees of everlasting good health or longevity for anyone? That night he'd said to me, "It also made me want to get on with it, write harder, time being more of the essence."

"You also know that you'll be leaving a substantial body of work that is respected and even taught at universities," I'd told him, thinking at the same time that I would probably never leave behind such a legacy.

"Well, yes, it's a comfort, but nothing can cheat the feeling that there is a specific time bomb ticking in your body that could go off at any moment. After all, nobody has yet been cured of this."

"Well, at least you'd lived awhile—you were in your early fifties—before you became infected. Think of all the people in their twenties and thirties who are dealing with this."

"You're too young to understand that that doesn't really make a difference!" Ed countered, getting up quickly, deftly grabbing a log and laying it crosswise on the fire. "Nobody can deal with dying *sooner,* bucko!" He sat down again next to me and looked at me crosswise over his reading glasses. "Not even octogenarians. They drum the thought out of their heads by talking about doctors and medicine and especially about everybody else who is sick and dying."

"I'm sorry," I said. "I didn't mean to minimize what it's like for you."

"Don't worry. It's all right," he said. "The interesting thing is that, being of a depressive nature, even before I knew I was HIV positive, I used to wake up, sometimes in the middle of the night, sometimes early in the morning, with this feeling of dread."

"Dread?" I asked. "What do you mean by that exactly?"

He shrugged. "Hard to explain, really. A sense that I'd lived a lot of my life, that most of it had already gone by, that I wasn't really young anymore, even though I kept trying to play at being young. Or had youthful partners around to prop myself up." He paused, allowing the remainder of his thoughts on the matter to refine themselves for a few moments. "I guess it was more that I'd reached an age where there was this constant feeling that anything could happen to me, that I could suffer and die in all manner of ways, from an illness to some freak accident. It was a terrible feeling, a constant feeling of foreboding and worry that I'd never been able to shake. And then, when I got infected, it certainly gave some meaning to that inexplicable terror."

Meditating on this for a moment, I said at last, "I wish our culture raised us to be more prepared for death."

Ed nodded. "Now, this is a truth. The idea of death is certainly not integrated into our youth-obsessed culture, which now only makes it more difficult to get older. In my lifetime I've watched how the elderly have commanded less and less veneration from the young."

A brief silence fell between us, and then he said, "I have to say, I'm surprised to see how much you *obsessed* over the results of this test, Russell. Even though you tried to hide it, you couldn't."

I said nothing in response. What, after all, could I say?

"So I was right, wasn't I? That you weren't careful with your *lover*." He said the last word mockingly.

"Please don't!"

"Why are we so foolish? Why do we blind ourselves to these risks?" Ed asked emphatically.

I tried to think about this. "I don't know. Maybe it's what you say: getting caught up in the brute passion of it all."

But Ed, unmoved by my candor, was becoming increasingly more wound up over his own insecurities. "So, you totally cut loose with him. Whereas you've been so scrupulous, so careful, so vigilant with me." This was said bitterly.

"Stop doing this!"

"Why? There are so many things in bed that you refuse to do."

I let the harsh complaint seep into me. Looking at Ed in a blousy navy-blue sweater with white piping around the cuffs and neck, I thought guiltily that his jealous scowl not only made him look poorly, it made him suddenly appear even older than his years. And this scared me in an entirely new way: Would Ed actually expect me to dedicate myself to taking care of him when the time came? "Are you actually saying you'd want me to put myself at risk?"

"No, but you've always taken that *extra* measure of precaution with me. Whereas I bet there was nothing that you wouldn't do with him."

I said nothing in response.

Ed went on. "We're talking about love here and attraction. We're talking about rejection and repulsion. No matter how accomplished or self-confident people are, they still have the basic hunger to want and be wanted by somebody else."

I now think of the young college student with whom Ed had had the affair of his life, somebody who probably loved him but who then, in an alcoholic stupor, had tragically fallen off the roof of a fraternity house.

"Let me ask you just one question," Ed resumed, raking aside some hair that had tumbled into his eyes. "What would have happened if the result was . . . if you'd found out you'd been infected. Would that have changed the way you make love to me?"

I looked at him, incredulous. He knew as well as I that it would have changed nothing. So why ask such a question? "You really want me to try to imagine that? Now?"

Was it here that I really failed to understand his great distress? Did this obvious hedging of what we both knew to be the truth end up insulting him even more profoundly? He got up again and stoked the fire violently with a black iron poker that had been leaning against the limestone fireplace. Remaining standing, he turned to face me. "It was always your excuse to avoid any real intimacy."

"Sex is just one part of any relationship," I stated the obvious.

"Yes," he said sadly, and then made a pinching gesture with his thumb and forefinger. "And a tiny part of this one. Because you don't find me attractive . . . probably because I'm not young enough."

"That's absolutely not true."

"Then what is it?"

I tried to warn him. "You'll feel terrible about this part of the conversation later on."

Now I see this as yet another remark that might have deeply offended him. Because he looked at me askance and his voice quieted into a tremulous rage. "Feel terrible about it later *on?* I feel terrible about it *now,* Russell," he hissed. "I've fallen in love with somebody who cannot return my affection. I'm aware of it constantly. Don't you understand? It's torture. If I could take a pill to reverse it, that would let me wake up tomorrow free of you, I'd swallow it in a second."

And of course I had to sympathize. Because, after all, I knew this feeling; I'd searched high and low for an antidote to Michel. And now, weeks after Ed's death, I find myself wondering if he truly realized that his feelings for me were in their own way as utopian as my feelings for Michel Soyer.

"One day," he said arrogantly, "mark my words, the same thing will happen to you. You'll understand firsthand what I'm going through now."

"Don't you think I've gone through something like this already?"

"No, I mean how it feels when you lose your power, when suddenly there's not quite enough—*quite* is the operative word here—to sustain yourself in somebody else's affections. Believe it or not, I once had a lot of power, too."

"I'm sure you could have had anybody you wanted."

As though not hearing me, he said, "At thirty-one you're at the peak of it. But that loss is inescapable, as inescapable as death. And it happens to every man, straight or gay."

"Yes and no. There are lots of younger guys who'd lust after a hot older man like you."

"Older man?"

"You're fifty-nine years old, Ed," I gently reminded him.

He forced a smile. "So it *is* true. If I *were* younger things would be different."

"I really don't believe so."

"You don't *believe* so." He stared at me, his eyes watery with emotion. He suddenly looked afraid and went on more quietly, "Russell, I realize there's nearly a thirty-year age difference between us. And in fact, whenever I used to see a much older man with a much younger guy, I was . . . well, actually disdainful. But this, what I feel for you, is something that has taken me completely by surprise. I can't believe it. I don't understand it. And yet I can't drag myself away from it. To be quite honest . . ." He sighed. "I have absolutely no idea why you're even with me." The words stumbled out.

I tried to gather my thoughts for a moment. And then I said, "Ed, I admire you enormously. But, as you well know, chemistry is chemistry. I can't help that and I can't change it, either. But leave that aside for a moment. I've never been so close to anybody whose writing is so powerful and so beautiful. Just like you say, whatever attractiveness I have will fade. But your writing, which is a huge part of your life, has only gotten stronger and greater as you've gotten older."

I remember how he looked at me with guarded fondness. "Well put," he said to me that day. "Bravo. Alas, this is why I love to be with you. And it's also why I *love* you," he'd said boldly, knowing I wouldn't be able to respond.

Now I find myself thinking of Michel and how I lived from day to day, wishing to hear such words from him.

That day, I said to Ed, "Has it ever occurred to you that maybe for me, this editing I'm doing for you *is* like making a contribution to your literary legacy? And that it helps to shield me against the thought that my own work probably won't amount to much?"

Ed smiled. "Yes, I've thought that. And I've been *afraid* that wanting to do this is all that's holding you to me."

The echo of truth in his words silenced me for a while. We both stared at the fire. Finally Ed said, "Well, you know, despite everything I say, I still want you to stay with me. That's really the problem."

I thanked him and, feeling a bit more resolute, replied, "Then I guess you'll just have to accept my limitations. And not punish me for them."

"I try not to, Russell. I really do. But . . . well, I guess punishing you is painfully compulsive on my part."

At the time I didn't understand the true meaning of Ed's feeling goaded to punish me. I believed that he was merely rebuking me for my lack of romantic involvement in his life, for my lackluster physical attraction to him. Now I realize Ed was implying he'd already done my life some serious injury by lying to ensure that Michel Soyer would steer clear of me forever.

Part Two

Eight

~

THE ONLY REQUEST that Marina has ever made about
my staying at Villa Guidi is that if I ever write anything
about it, I will fictionalize the location. "You could easily
say, for example, that it is a village quite close to a major Tuscan
town. And you certainly have your choice among those. It
might be near Volterra, for instance, or San Gimignano. It could
be near Siena, Pisa, Santo Stefano, or even San Vincenzo in the
Maremma. Besides, two contemporary works of fiction should
never take place at the same house. It would be literary redun-
dancy, not to mention that, after all, I do guard my privacy."

Ironically, her novel *Conversion*, of which I have now read the
first hundred pages, makes the location of the villa rather obvious. An account of the Nazi occupation of the villa and the story
of the Jewish family who converts to Catholicism is wonderfully
controlled, written with great elegance and imagination. However, in the midst of her virtuosity for invention, Marina never
bothers to fictionalize the surroundings. She describes, for example, the coral-colored chapel that was erected two hundred

years after the villa was built. She details the secret passageway that runs perpendicular to the villa's most southern wall and surfaces near the stone embankment that circumscribes the entire property. An afternoon's walk up to the convent where Puccini's sister lived is even described in marvelous detail. Reading this latter passage, most opera fans would easily identify the region. She has also written that the villa itself is a half-hour walk from the ramparts of an entirely walled city. There are few cities in Italy entirely enclosed by walls, and only one of them is in Tuscany.

Today I have received two letters: one from the executrix and the other from Ed's New York lawyer, with whom I'd once had dinner in Paris. Annie informs me that she has failed to locate a copy of Ed's "work-in-progress" in the pile of mail left at his rented house in the Berkshires. The letter concludes, "After our last conversation I remain unconvinced that you are completely in the dark as to where a copy of this manuscript might be. And thus I urge you either to get your hands on it or to come up with a more tolerable explanation as to why it's impossible for you to locate something that Ed was working on when he died."

Quite right. Annie, after all, is no fool.

The lawyer's letter is a shocker. He informs me that two months before he died, Ed, in front of a Parisian attorney, made a change on his life-insurance policy and had named me as the new beneficiary. The letter goes on to say that the manner of how the change was made still needs to be investigated in order to make sure that it was done with "American legality." If proper procedures were indeed followed, I will receive the benefit of $150,000, independent of probate.

Good news for somebody who lives on a modest income, and of course I can't help but be gratefully shocked. But I also realize that this bequest is only going to make things more complicated for the simple reason that before this change was made, Annie Calhoun (I'm almost certain) had been the life-insurance policy's beneficiary.

I can even imagine that Ed had a premonition of his own death and wanted to place a few wild balls in play in order to force his friends to engage in a scrambling endgame. Yes, he might have complained to me about Annie, but surely she deserved to reap some financial reward for her thirty years of dedication and support—especially since Ed had no real money to speak of to leave anybody. Annie had been his sounding board, a comfort to him when the student lover died or, for that matter, when any of his love affairs went south. So then why had Ed switched his insurance policy to name me?

I can only come up with one reason, flimsy at best: His decision was motivated by guilt for having lied to me and meddled in my affairs with Michel. So I don't know how I feel about this gift, if I should allow myself to receive this money, or if I even want it. But then I have to ask myself, would I take this money, turn around and give it to the person who really deserves it, much less donate it to some charitable organization? Probably not. And so I allow myself just one fantasy: of being able to return to New York City with solvency and give up my far-flung Gravesend flat in Brooklyn for an apartment on Manhattan's Lower East Side.

What concerns me now: Does Annie already know about his last-minute change of heart? I try to imagine the reverberating insult of having Ed disregard their thirty-year-old allegiance for a man he'd known for merely a year.

It would have to deeply stain her attitude toward me.

I return to Annie's letter and reread it. It is officiously turned out, completely correct in its tone; in short, there is nothing that immediately belies any outrage or resentment.

Disconcerted and confused, I leave my room with the idea of finding Marina and telling all. Hands clasped around a vase full of freshly cut chrysanthemums, she's standing in the library, a room substantially warmer in décor than the gilded formal dining room. The library is the only public room in the villa whose walls are wood paneled rather than stucco. The bookshelves are twenty feet high, there are comfortable wingback chairs for reading, and the sofa is upholstered in ruby-red velvet. Marina sets down the flowers and then goes to one of the bookshelves where she removes a gargantuan hardcover that appears to be some kind of Latin reference book; she places it on the table next to the vase. Here is where I interrupt to tell her about the letters I've just received.

She brightens and claps her hands together. "*Cazzo*, Russell, what a good turn for you."

"Well, after knowing how unfulfilled he was, I can't imagine why he'd be so generous."

Marina smiles sagaciously. "Maybe he thought you needed it more than this other lady. But we might also consider that he figured that if and when you actually did leave him, he'd easily be able to change the name of the beneficiary yet again." She pauses for a moment and then says, "Who knows? Perhaps he intended to hold this over your head, to let you know how generous he could be so you'd think twice before rejecting him and moving on to somebody else. People will do this to seize power in a love affair, to make the other person behave as they wish them to."

A very cynical, downgrading assessment, which, I must admit, does sound plausible. As I have yet to tell Marina about Ed's interfering with Michel and lying about my health, it makes me wonder if she has something personal against Ed that I am unaware of.

"Permit me to change the subject for a moment." She leads me across the room to an antique writing desk with a leather top upon which a coffee-table book of notable Italian villas has been opened to a photo of the Villa Guidi. She flips the page to a picture of herself perched at this very same writing desk holding a marked-up work-in-progress, a pair of elegant metal reading glasses dangling from a chain around her neck. "Look at me here," she says mockingly. "Don't I look virtuously literary? So posed . . . and so *fake?*" she emphasizes. "I can't believe the people who did the picture book convinced me to sit like this in such a pose."

"Why not?" Admiring the desk, I tell her that it must be a lovely place to work.

"But I never do . . . use this desk. It's too grand for me. I actually only write in bed."

"Seriously?"

"Surrounded by all my dog angels. This lady has strange work habits. And I write so little each day. I get distracted by everything that happens here. By the weddings, by the faxes for the weddings, by coordinating the caterers for the weddings, by the dogs and their petty dramas—their wounds, their illnesses, their disappearances, and their reappearances. I even get distracted by my television and so many old American movies, which are my favorite films of all. I try to do some work early in the morning. But it's not so easy. And I find that as I get older it becomes more and more difficult to finish a book."

"Yes, but you do finish them," I point out. "However erratic and inefficient your method, you've been publishing a book every three years or so."

"Yes, I suppose this is also true. But now I need to tell you that I have come to a conclusion." She pauses for effect. "That your deceased friend, God rest his soul, was keeping—and is still keeping—you from doing your own work."

"Maybe I don't want to do my own work," I say. "Maybe that's why I hold on to *his* . . . have you even considered that?"

Marina laughs. "Of course. To deliberately sidetrack yourself."

Both Marina and Ed, despite their assurances to the contrary, have during difficult times been able to hunker down and cleave to their work; whereas I, under any sort of duress, find myself cast adrift, unable to moor myself in a creative ritual.

Marina continues, "The problem with having some money will be that, if you choose, you can become even *more* sidetracked by this unfinished manuscript that you keep worrying about. And the more these demands and communications arrive, the more distracted you will become."

"That's a point," I concede.

"Why not get back to your own thoughts and your own fantasies?"

"And if there are none?"

"I don't believe you. You didn't just dry up."

I shake my head. "Neither you nor Ed understands that some people may not have more than one book in them."

Marina smiles winningly. "This is true; I know that you're afraid that you don't have more than one book in you. But I can tell you that I believe that you do, and now is the time to get on with building a body of your own work. Fifteen years from now, you'll be older and less ambitious and less hungry." Marina sits down in front of the picture book of Italian villas, leans back in her chair, and finally glances up at me. "I feel you should just send the manuscript back to those vultures and be done with it once and for all."

"But how can I do that? Knowing that he didn't want it published until it was finished?"

Marina rolls her eyes with impatience. "You're being dishonest, Russell. You can't possibly be worried about his reputation. His final work isn't up to his usual standards? So what? Haven't you heard the adage that a literary reputation is hard to tarnish?"

Churning and upset, I begin pacing the room in front of her. I continue in English. "Okay, then, I don't want it published because of all his criticisms of me—of my so-called vanity and my coldness and the fact that I was only with him because he was a well-known writer and I wanted to draft off his success to help myself. That I'm some kind of user." Then I go on to elaborate Ed's description of his machinations to keep Michel and me apart, his lying confession to Michel that he'd infected me without explaining (in his own narrative) that what he said was actually untrue. All of this I would hate to be read by the public.

Marina looks startled, and yet she says, "Why not? Yes, I understand how upsetting it is. But I also must say this is the risk one takes when one gets involved with a working author. Being written about, being complained about, being distorted—and it all begins innocently with the subject's self-serving daydream of inspiring the writer's work, their, shall I say, lyric." She grins. "Don't tell me you didn't imagine this!"

"Not consciously," I try to defend myself.

"Oh, come on! Look at that beautiful poem he wrote about Venice. One could only assume that he was writing about you. And the result? You've inspired literature. It is probably one of the greatest *foreigner's* poems about a city that has been written about ad infinitum. Perhaps no other Anglo has ever written so well about Venice except for the great Ruskin. Not even my darling Henry James."

Hesitating a moment, I say, "Funny, Ed happened to mention you think James didn't really understand the Italian temperament."

"*Caro mio!*" Marina exclaims. "I would never say that James *didn't* understand Italians. I probably said that his understanding of Italians was perhaps hardly as profound as some other European writers, such as . . . well, Stendhal, for instance. James's forte, after all, was writing about Americans in Europe, including those who lived in Italy. His Italians are, shall we say, his lesser creations."

We both fall ruminatively silent. "How about this," Marina says at last. "Send the book back to Annie Calhoun. Tell her when and where he lies and fabricates. And while you're at it, send them a doctor's report to negate his telling that you have the infection he claims you have and also to prove that he has lied at least once in his own memoir. Then let his longtime editors figure out how to publish the material."

"But why would *they* care if he lies? They only care about what he wrote."

"You're a living person whose reputation can be damaged. If you contact them to say something isn't true and argue that it would hurt you if it was published without at least acknowledging that the writer lies, then you will have grounds for a lawsuit."

"I would never trust Annie Calhoun to set things straight. Especially now that she's been taken off the insurance policy."

Marina looks at me with disapproval. "Not only did the man hinder you in life, he is now hindering you in death. Don't misunderstand. I think his death is a pity. But I have come to the conclusion that it wasn't a good thing for you to be with him. And nothing to do with his illness, either!" she emphasizes. "If, as you say, he was concerned that you were with him for his literary connections, it just proves my point that he was addicted to celebrity and fame. Probably he would have ultimately been too selfish to truly help the career of the person closest to him."

"That's absolutely untrue," I argue. "He loved me. It was only sexual jealousy that compelled him to misbehave."

"That's no excuse at all!"

"But I know if I'd stayed with him, he would've helped my career. He always said he wanted to."

Marina doesn't respond at first. Finally, skeptically, she says, "Then you should believe what your instinct tells you. My point here is that celebrity is known to distort and corrupt common values. It is far better for actors and politicians and maybe even contemporary painters, but it's not what a true writer should be about. I'll tell you a little story. When they were making the movie version of *The Portrait of a Lady,* they filmed it here in the region. And an American producer actually called and asked me to let him film the interiors of the Palazzo Roccanera here at the Villa Guidi—because of the large rooms. I asked how much they would pay and this man—who sounded intelligent, mind you—explained that it was an independent production. He said they didn't have a great deal of money and assured me that my villa was their first choice because of the size of the rooms. If I allowed them to make their film for a payment that turned out to be next to nothing, it would give us—the villa, he meant—a lot more prestige. I was shocked at his incredible stupidity, his audacity. And do you know what I told him? Very politely I said, 'No, thanks. We already have enough prestige in this house.' "

Marina suddenly becomes very tender. "I just wish you'd live your life apart from all this nonsense involving this celebrated poet's memoir. Look at my Stefano, also a true writer. But unlike your late friend, he shuns the limelight to live almost entirely in his thoughts. He has published three beautiful novels written in magnificent Italian. And yet no American or British publisher will touch them. Why? Because they don't hear of him. He's not a recognizable name. Not a Roberto Calasso, or an Umberto Eco. But both Calasso and Eco have come here to the villa to listen to him. They know Stefano is a great thinker. And I will tell you honestly, as much as my novel *Conversion* was a success all over the world and especially in your country, it is not up to the quality of Stefano's work."

I wonder if Marina is being disingenuous and tell her point-blank that I doubt her modesty. She surprises me not by becoming annoyed but by sounding even more disconcerted.

"I am telling you what I believe to be true, my friend. In every part of our conversation, I try to be as truthful as possible. Beyond this, I despise false modesty. It is even worse than arrogance."

"It *is* arrogance," I suggest.

She nods. "Yes, you are right. Bravo, Russell. Now, we both know I have plenty of arrogance to go around."

Marina finally stands up, crosses the room again, and sits down on the velvet sofa next to the vase of flowers and bids me to come and sit near her.

"And I'll tell you another story to illustrate my point. When *Conversion* was nominated for the Strega Prize—the same year Moravia was nominated, by the way—Stefano and I went to Rome for the dinner where the winner would be announced." For some reason she suddenly switches to English. "And I was the black horse . . . is that how you say it?"

"*Dark* horse."

Back to Italian. "Ah, yes, I must remember that one. Anyway, nobody expected me to win. And here I must make you understand the *logos* of Italian literary awards. They are not so . . . shall we say 'democratic' as they are in America. Often it leaks out who the winner is beforehand. And, in some cases, the winner has been known to be fixed by secret negotiations between the judges. In this instance Moravia was apparently told by someone he trusts that he was going to win the Strega that year and only traveled to Rome because he expected to do so. So when *my* name was announced, he just got up and stormed out in a rage without even congratulating me."

"That's shameful," I say.

"But not my point. I don't mean to scorn Moravia, not at all. Why I'm telling you this story is this: When my name was announced, Stefano turned to me and said, 'Marina, this is too much, don't you think?' And in this case it was not his jealousy speaking. I knew he was happy for me. For we both knew that my winning the Strega would mean that for the rest of my life my books would be published in Italy without hesitation and taken at least as seriously as they should be, no more, no less.

And that this was the most a writer could ever hope for. But Stefano also felt that my book was good but not *great*. In his estimation, Moravia's book was better and probably should have won the Strega. And I agreed with him then—and I agree with him now."

I object, "You can't judge your own work. And Stefano is probably too close himself to judge it, too." And also probably too jealous to judge it fairly, I think but do not say. "Maybe your peers genuinely thought your book was the best of the lot."

Marina shrugs. "I suppose I am a cynic—"

"Suppose?" I interrupt sarcastically.

"I suppose the likelihood was they wanted to cut down Moravia. There were more women voters, and even though I don't think it's at all true, many believed Moravia treated his wife, Elsa Morante, shabbily. And so, I was in the right place at the right time. I had a stroke of luck that got me a prize and gave a great boost to my career. It could've happened to the next nominee just as easily. I accepted the honor graciously; I thanked everybody involved and was home at my hotel within a half hour. Stefano remained at the awards dinner with all his literary friends and got drunk and stayed up all night, celebrating my good fortune."

Several moments pass, and the dogs, from some far place on the villa's property, begin an earnest baying. "May I ask you who you believe is the greatest living American writer?" Marina asks at last.

"There are many candidates," I respond. "But I guess I'd have to say Philip Roth."

She smiles. "I love him. A great mind. I hear from a friend that Roth has a bad back and that the constant pain actually, though terribly aggravating, inspires him. Which makes sense. And I adore Updike, too, his elegant prose. And of course, the greatest narrative writer in America today is, in my opinion, John Irving."

"No women?" I ask.

Marina grimaces. "Sorry, you must realize by now that I am not a feminist." She reflects for a moment. "But maybe there is somebody right now in America, somebody like yourself working in obscurity who, in one hundred years, will emerge as the great one. Maybe the books of Updike and Roth will still be widely read, but people will come to find their work no more relevant than this unknown person writing a great novel in a garret or even a villa somewhere in total obscurity. It's anybody's guess who or what might be considered great a hundred years from now. And so, my friend, I beg you to leave off this concern with the final work of a dead writer and focus instead on what *you*, as a living writer, plan to do next."

Nine

~

MASTER CLUB IS QUITE CROWDED, but Lorenzo has not yet arrived. Approaching the sign-in desk, I inquire about temporary memberships. A thin, overly tan woman looks at me appraisingly and then says, "Are you Lorenzo's friend, the American?"

I tell her I am and she informs me that he has arranged for me to have a two-week guest pass. How kind of him.

While giving me a lift, Marina ended up teasing me about working out and told me that as well as my body, I should exercise my brain by learning Latin, which would certainly help my Italian. Now, as I go to get changed, I wish I'd informed her how I maintain a jaded attitude toward gym culture and that the routines and the attitudes are hardly different between Europe and America. There is the same feeling of competition, the same rampant narcissism, the same faux macho, the same cliquishness.

The one noticeable difference between Italian and American gyms is that Italian men are far more openly affectionate with one another. An Italian man might, for example, rest an arm on a friend's shoulder during a conversation, his head mere inches away from the other person—all in all, more intimate than two Americans who have a similar rapport. An unschooled American might even wonder if the two Italians are lovers. In America I notice that people tend to keep a much greater physical distance from one another. And of course all Italians double-kiss hello.

Once when I was spending a few months doing English translations for an American art foundation in Venice, I went to a gym and found myself standing in the shower talking to a sexy built blond man whose grin was dazzled by a few gold teeth. He was explaining how he made his living as a boatman, ferrying goods into Venice through the lagoons and canals. At one point I asked if I could borrow some soap. He shrugged and held up an empty plastic container of body wash. He then scooped some of the lather off himself, approached me, and rubbed it on my chest, my shoulders, my arms, and my back in the most caring, affectionate way. There wasn't a hint of sexuality to his gesture, just his casual response. I was stunned. I felt that no American stranger would dare such an intimate gesture without some sort of sexual motivation.

I've changed into workout clothes by the time Lorenzo arrives—out of uniform, dressed in a black T-shirt and snug faded blue jeans. He smiles coolly at me and invites me to accompany him into the locker room. Afraid that I might get turned on, I tell him I'd rather meet in the gym, that I need to do some stretching. I think I may have offended him, because once he emerges in his workout clothes, he ignores me and begins weight training with two other people.

I do a quick weight workout. Finishing before Lorenzo, worrying about having to shower at the same time, I return to the locker room, undress, and enter one of the shower stalls. Moments later, much to my embarrassment, he appears naked and enters the stall opposite me. He soaps his body generously, seeming very confident and relaxed. I try not to glance at him but can't help noticing that the dusting of hair on his chest weaves a train down his ribbed stomach. From time to time, I also feel his eyes appraising me. The obvious scrutiny is stirring and I try not to let it visibly affect me.

Once we get dressed and are standing outside the establishment, I boldly say, "Ever think of doing porno? You certainly have the physique for it."

He looks horrified. "Are you crazy?"

He then asks how I arrived at the gym and I explain that Marina dropped me off. The villa is a mere two kilometers away, and I'd planned to walk home.

"You don't need to," Lorenzo says, "if you don't mind riding," and points to a black Ducati motorcycle.

"No big surprise," I say aloud in English.

"*Cosa?*" he says. "What did you say?"

"*Niente*. Nothing."

"But before I take you home, would you like to ride out to Torre del Lago? I've even brought along another helmet and jacket."

"Would that mean going on the *autostrada?*"

"Yes, it would."

"I make it a rule not to ride on *autostrade.*"

"Why? It's no less safe than a surface road. And a lot less dangerous because you don't have these foolish people cutting in from different directions. Trust me, I know. I am a *carabiniere*."

"One mishap at highway speed and I'm toast." I try to translate this idiom literally.

"I've ridden for fifteen years with only one small incident not even worth mentioning. Not to say there isn't, of course, a first time. I have ridden with many people behind me. My wife, for example, goes with me always. And so do my two children. I would never take them if I didn't feel completely safe."

"I'm sure I weigh a lot more than your wife or your children, so there is a lot more . . ." I can't think of the Italian word for *displacement*.

Lorenzo catches the drift. "Now, this I will not dispute," he says.

I finally relent. "Okay, let's just go." Lorenzo asks me if I am certain and I nod that I am.

"I will want to be telling you things," he informs me as I don the extra helmet and leather jacket and climb on the motorcycle behind him. "So make sure you put your chin on my shoulder so you can hear me. When I go in one direction, just look in that direction and don't, by God, lean that way and don't take your feet off the pegs."

Exactly the same things Michel said to me the first time I rode behind him.

Another man, another motorcycle, another country. But it feels the same somehow, the wind blasting my face, the oil smells of city and road, and the bittersweet smell of farmland and vineyards, all chased with nervous exhilaration. There is very little distance between where the gym is and A-11, the superhighway that runs to Torre del Lago. After the initial acceleration, my dread falls away and I begin to relax. The old riding euphoria returns. But instead of the Parisian metropolis, deco buildings and wide boulevards and amber light, I am hurtling through coastal Tuscany, drenched in marine air buffeting in from the Ligurian Sea.

As we rocket toward Torre del Lago, Lorenzo manages to point out the impressive twelfth-century castle of Nozzano, its now-ruined lookout towers once having guarded the region against the Pisani. The hillsides are dotted with villas, some of them fortified with surrounding walls and turrets. In the remnants of marble quarries that have eaten into hillsides I can glimpse the access paths stomped out by the mules that ferried rock to and from the stone hives. Silvery groves of olive trees, three months from harvesting, finally feather back to a fertile plain that runs toward the sea, ending in stands of umbrella pines, which in Italian have the very euphonious-sounding name *pini marittimi*.

Lorenzo brings me to a seaside restaurant shack built right in the dunes. The place is run by his family friends, who make a great commotion when we come in the door. Elbowing me, he introduces, "My American friend, a journalist writing an article about the region." A sloe-eyed teenaged girl working at the restaurant says smartly, "He doesn't look like it," assuming that I don't speak Italian.

"Oh, really?" I say. "And what exactly *do* I look like? A rhinoceros?"

She is stunned to know that I have understood her, and the restaurateurs burst into uproarious laughter.

We earmark a small table where we can speak confidentially. Although Lorenzo claims he's not particularly hungry, he ends up ordering a fish course that becomes one of those endless Italian seafood antipasti: scallops followed by mussels followed by sautéed tiny squid called *totanini* followed by three other small but delicious crustacean courses.

"They all know your wife?" I say during the second course.

He nods, but then frowns. "Is there a problem with that?" I shake my head and fall silent.

He looks concerned. "No, really, tell me. I want to understand."

"It's just different in America," I say.

"How? How is it different in *America*."

"It's not often that two male *friends* ride behind one another on a motorcycle."

"And why is this?"

I decide to be bold. "Just something that is done by men and women who are usually a couple. Or two men who are together. Or two women."

Lorenzo frowns and seems genuinely bewildered by my explanation. "So, you are saying if you and I went riding in America, they would assume I was gay?"

Suddenly nervous that both Marina and I might have misread his signals altogether, I blurt out, "I don't know what they'd assume. Forget it. Closed."

"Don't presume!" Lorenzo suddenly sounds peevish. I say nothing, wishing we could get past the awkwardness. "They would never think that about me," he resumes. "I am happily married with two children," he tells me discreetly after a conspicuous pause.

I force myself to say, "So then what's going on here? Just a friendly motorcycle ride to the sea?"

Lorenzo leans forward and surprises me by saying within possible earshot of the restaurant owners, "What I'm saying doesn't mean that I don't want you, too."

Now more assured of where this all might be heading, I say, "Well, your intentions are hard to read."

"Wait a few minutes, will you please?" He is up and swaggering in a clomp of motorcycle boots toward the restaurant owners. I can't help noticing how his legs completely fill out his jeans. He chats with them briefly, then embraces them. Once they bid me a gracious good-bye, I follow him outside the restaurant over to the motorcycle. Picking up his helmet and giving me mine he says, "So . . . what's to finish?"

Donning the riding jacket, I ask, "I'd like to know if your wife is aware that you'd play around with somebody like me."

He jams his helmet down over his head, begins fastening the chin strap. "No. Of course she doesn't know."

"Nothing at all? Not even that—"

"Nothing, I tell you. Nothing."

So Marina was right that Lorenzo might be even more closeted than Michel. Lorenzo suddenly appears impatient. He closes the plastic face shield and his next words are muffled by it. "So are we going?"

I hold my ground. "But isn't keeping this secret difficult? Especially over time?"

Lorenzo falls silent for a moment and I see the sadness my question provokes and how it also manages to dissolve his impatience. He throws open the face shield. "Of course it is," he admits, suddenly docile. "I've even been to a doctor. To try and change it. To get it out of my system."

"You mean, to a psychiatrist?"

He nods.

I tell him that in the United States it's now considered absurd, pointless, even shameful in some quarters, to try to reprogram oneself.

"Well, because there you can at least live openly. In Italy you really can't live as you do in America, especially if you have a job like mine. I've even confessed to my priest," Lorenzo goes on. "Finally. Two years ago I broke down and told him. And since then he and I have prayed. And he has prayed alone for my conversion as well."

A wheel-spinning waste of time, I think but obviously do not say.

Before following the *autostrada* back to the Villa Guidi, Lorenzo and I take a swing along the beach area. Outdoor restaurants with glass fronts are sandwiched side by side, one after another, and swarm with tourists dressed in ostentatious colors wearing lots of gold jewelry. "Milanese bourgeois," he comments over his shoulder. I keep glancing toward the sea, hoping to see glints of water, but the tall dunes and the inkblotlike umbrella pines block the view.

We finally turn off down a quieter road lined with two- and three-story residences, driving slowly so that it becomes quite easy for me to hear Lorenzo when he speaks to me. Dusk is falling and I see a line of parked cars, all with their headlamps on. Beyond them a tall woman with an amazing figure saunters along with an exaggerated yet rhythmic gait, her matching gold lamé halter and shorts catching the last rays of daylight.

"That's a transsexual," Lorenzo informs me. "Beautiful, isn't she?"

I say nothing because I am flabbergasted. The outfit, the figure, and especially her dreamy, sauntering gait are all eerily familiar. I tell Lorenzo she resembles somebody I once saw in Paris.

He continues, "A lot of men complain that there are nowadays so few female prostitutes in Italy. But that doesn't seem to stop them, either. All these cars, they are watching the trans. They are her fans. Like fans of an opera diva waiting outside the stage door to throw their roses at the great talent. All of them are probably married with children. I happen to know that this one lives in one of these apartments by the sea. My colleague, Paolo, visits her quite often. He says she is a wonderful fuck and that her rent is paid by a wealthy Milanese man who sees her when he can. That for the pleasure of her company you must call and make an appointment with her service. However, few or none of these guys who are waiting to see her now would ever make love to another man."

"But they all know her story, right?"

"Of course. They would not admit it, but they like trans even better than they like women."

I force myself to say, "Do *you* like trans?" the way I once asked Michel.

Lorenzo shakes his head and says, "No, I like men to be men."

A bit more secure about Lorenzo's intentions toward me, I squeeze my knees against him and put my lips on the back of his neck and breathe in the scent of sun-toasted skin. He shudders—with pleasure, it seems.

The motorcycle moseys on a half block or so, and then Lorenzo throws the gear into neutral, brakes to a halt, and anchors both legs on the pavement. He turns around, raises his helmet, and, wagging a gloved finger, says, "I bet you must've had her, this trans you know from Paris?"

"No, I actually didn't."

He grins mischievously, his lovely eyes twinkling. "I don't believe you."

And then I explain that she'd been involved with my former lover in a brief affair that ended when I came on the scene.

"Let's hope he was telling you the truth," Lorenzo says. "That it ended when he said it did."

"Doesn't really matter anymore," I say, even though of course it does matter. "She was a Moroccan, I believe."

"Ah, and so is this one."

On the ride back from the sea, the evening air has cooled substantially, the hillsides darkening in twilight, and as we head back toward the walled city, I shiver in my borrowed jacket even as I hold Lorenzo tight around his midsection, trying to take warmth from him. It occurs to me that I used to wonder if Michel's transsexual lover would take some sort of revenge for my having stolen him. And in fact, after the hotel room was broken into, I found myself imaging that she somehow had been involved. The men, after all, were wearing masks and loose clothing, and the one that held the knife to my throat was of slight build. The mystery of their identity remains, and sometimes I find myself grasping at the most far-fetched explanations in an attempt to unravel it.

The moment Lorenzo makes the turn into the long gravel driveway that leads to the villa, I tap him on the shoulder and motion him to stop for a moment. He steers the motorcycle over to a small parking area, kills the engine, puts the kickstand down, and we both get off. Villa Guidi is looming in the distance

with its squared five-story shape and the tall pitch-green sen-
tinels of cypress. Dark shapes of birds swoop low over the great
lawns, and several of the dogs chase them uproariously to and
fro. As we stand there watching the activity, lights in several of
the lower rooms switch on almost simultaneously.

I now tell him the story about the hotel break-in and the
ten nerve-racking minutes that probably contributed to Ed's
fatal heart attack, and how Marina is attempting to link the
incident to the attempted robbery in the villa's outbuildings
and to a group of Muslim radicals who might be out to assassinate Stefano.

"Yes, I hear about this at headquarters. My superior, the *signora's* old friend, mentions it. And that she brought you to the
jail because she thought you might somehow recognize the
thief." He grins. "This warning, this is no small piece of shit."

"You're going to joke about this?"

He squints at me. "Absolutely not. She gets information from
an important person . . . to be taken seriously."

"But I need to ask you? How possible is it really that one of
these days somebody might drive up to the villa and try and do
something to Stefano?"

Lorenzo shrugs. "She pays for the surveillance, right?"

I nod.

He thinks out loud for a moment, his lovely eyes darting
back and forth. "So that means unmarked cars patrolling the
roads . . . *Bo*," he says, blowing out air. "An attempt like
this . . . really has not happened around here in a long time, as
far as I know." He frowns. "Does the *signora* seem very concerned?"

I explain that her worrying peaked right after the break-in on the outlying property but seems to have subsided for the time being. Lorenzo goes on to point out that for several decades now modern Italy has lived with intermittent threats of terrorism, which unfortunately have transpired from time to time, such as the horrific train bombing in Bologna in the 1980s. "And several shootings and kidnappings. However, we're not quite as hysterical or as overly vigilant about these things as you Americans are. We've accepted that it's a part of life nowadays. We know that, only if we decide, we can get concerned and paralyzed by thoughts of dangers, not just terrorism. Somehow, and I can't explain quite how, we take these threats and make them part of the day. In spite of it all, we can still enjoy a good glass of wine and a wonderful home-cooked pasta. And a great fuck!" He shrugs and the discussion comes to an end.

He offers to escort me the rest of the way to the villa. I accept nervously, and then it dawns on me that perhaps Lorenzo has a sexual motivation for keeping the conversation upbeat. But no matter what his intentions toward me might be this evening, there is really nowhere for us to meet in private. The villa's gate automatically locks at dusk and I press the four-digit code to open it. Once the metal grille swings wide, we proceed until we round a bend that gives a full frontal view of the downstairs. The shutters are closed in Marina's room, but they are open in Stefano's, and I can peer right in.

Wearing the same dressing gown I'd seen him in previously, he's standing, supporting himself on a cane. Just as we pass, Carla bustles into the room holding a tray with what I presume to be his evening meal. Without saying anything to Lorenzo, I continue to watch. Carla, whose movements normally strike me as being rushed, even abrupt, tenderly hovers as she sets the plates down and actually escorts Stefano to the table. At first I think he's ill and can't help himself, but then I realize that this is their little ritual, that she's serving him the way perhaps she once had served her husband. I see them murmuring to each other, and then she leans against the wall and watches him eat. Their mutual devotion is obvious and very touching. But then I believe I can detect a weary look on Carla's face.

Lorenzo finally says, "That's the *signora*'s husband, isn't it?" I nod. "He looks a lot older than she is."

"He's also a perfect target from where we stand."

"But the gate is locked."

I shiver. "Not always."

"I shouldn't worry," he says.

"Why not?"

"Just listen to me."

I still don't believe him.

When we finally arrive at the carved wooden side door of the villa, he says, "The ballroom is amazing, isn't it?"

I hesitate and then admit that I haven't yet been upstairs; it has been nearly in constant use for the hired weddings.

"Well, then, I will show you. May I?"

"How do *you* know it?"

"Like I say to you before, this is a historic place. We came here as schoolchildren. Like going to a museum."

Would Marina object to my inviting Lorenzo into the villa? Maybe she doesn't even need to know. After all, her rooms are pretty much removed from the staircase that leads up to the second floor. I somehow sense I'm doing the wrong thing, but I want to make love to this man.

Knowing the front door has already been locked and bolted, I lead Lorenzo through a secret side entrance where the door is always kept unlocked, then down into the subterranean zone and through a dank-smelling cavelike passage with crudely constructed stone and mortar walls. We emerge into an industrial kitchen used by the wedding caterers for food preparation. We pass the bolted wooden doors of the cantina where the wine made in the villa's vineyards is bottled by the local farmer. It's hard to imagine that Marina and her mother lived down here for four years during the Second World War and that the thick walls concealed the daily movements and activities of their Jewish friends. At one point Lorenzo rests his hands on my shoulders and gives me an urgent squeeze. I automatically pick up the pace, leading the way up a steep flight of marble steps to a landing, round a corner, and proceed to a foyer from where wide, limestone stairs ascend to the villa's upper chambers. He follows closely behind, and as we pass various portraits of royal-looking subjects in period regalia, I'm aware of his breathing. And then it dawns on me that the last person I slept with—if one could even call it "sleeping with"—was Ed. And so equal measures of sadness and anger momentarily dampen my expectation.

Lorenzo slips in front of me and opens a set of hand-painted wooden doors, revealing an enormous space that runs the entire length of the villa. The ballroom is remarkably beautiful and I gasp.

The ceilings vault up into forty-foot-high Romanesque arches. Nearly every square inch of the walls and ceilings is frescoed with scenes of villages and meadows and clusters of citizens in sixteenth-century dress. There is much painterly detail in the castles, the topiary gardens with paved pathways, the bystanders, the people promenading their dogs. At the far end of the ball-

room are perhaps fifteen round tables covered with pale green
linen tablecloths and set elaborately with silver-and-crystal ware
for a wedding that will take place within a day or so. At either
end of the room enormous gothic-shaped windows are kept wide
open and don't appear to have screens.

I feel Lorenzo draw close. He puts his powerful arms around
me, then takes my head in both his hands and gently swivels it
around to make sure I see the walled city and the deep blue
Apennines ranging behind it. His rubbing deflates all the pent-
up anxiety. Our lips touch for a moment and finally our mouths
open.

"So you've been in here before?" I say after we kiss for a few
minutes.

"Yes," he says, breathing rapidly. "But so long ago. Amazing
how much I remember."

"But your work must take you to many villas like this."

"Ah, but this is a special one to me. The first villa I ever visited. Her father was very generous about opening his home to
the public. Then again, he was a politician."

Lorenzo begins kissing me again. His lips are full and he
tastes like peppermint and wine, and now I think not of Ed, but
of Michel. And the sadness is deeper and cut with bitterness:
Why do I keep finding myself attracted to married, unavailable
men? And once again I'm overcome with the feeling that surely
Marina would condemn my bringing married Lorenzo into the
villa for an assignation. I stop him and say, "Maybe we shouldn't
do this here."

He grins. "Okay, I'll tell you the real truth. This is all part of
my job. I'm supposed to protect you. But in order to do that I
have to stick really close to you." His eyes, which one could

describe as the nearly translucent green of tropical water, are mirthful.

"Yeah, right," I say in English.

He persists. "Come on, she's in her room for the night. She won't come up here. These people never spend much time in their public rooms."

"Unless she thinks somebody's here who shouldn't be."

"Don't her dogs tell her?"

It was true, the dogs for some reason haven't barked.

"There are several bedrooms off the ballroom," Lorenzo whispers. "Come with me." He takes my hand and leads the way. It's been just too long since I've had any kind of intimate contact. Missing it, needing it, I no longer can resist him.

At another set of double wooden doors, I say to his back, "And you remember all this from long ago?"

He turns to me. "I've been here a few times since then for one reason or another. Break-in attempts, that sort of thing. Though nobody has ever managed to get inside this villa."

The bedroom he chooses is frescoed in the same style as the ballroom and has a very simple wood desk with an inlaid leather blotter angled into one of the corners. There are two twin beds separated by a small mahogany night table. Facing me, he pulls off his T-shirt with a single deft movement, revealing his chest and a gold cross that rests on a tuft of hair. I feel desire tightening my stomach muscles, slightly souring my taste buds. Something inside me collapses as Lorenzo begins unbuttoning my shirt. But then, out of the corner of my eye, I see a dark shape swooping through the air and panic.

"What's wrong?" he says.

"I saw something flying."

"It's probably—"

"There it is again. I think it's a bat."

Now Lorenzo sees it. "Ah, yes, it probably came from one of those open windows in the ballroom."

Something dark heads toward me and I duck.

Lorenzo laughs. "Don't worry. They won't collide with you." He pulls me tightly to him, runs his tongue down my neck, and then bites me gently. "But if I were you, I'd watch out for the vampires."

Ten

~

A S LORENZO STAYS LATE, I don't get to sleep until well past two A.M. and manage to doze through the villa's morning clamor: workmen, dogs baying, Carla's operatic singing. On my way to the kitchen to make myself a café mocha, I run into Marina, who remarks, "Here you are just getting out of bed, and I'm already thinking about lunch." She's holding two dusty bottles of red wine pressed from her own grapes that she has just fetched from the subterranean cantina. Setting the bottles down on the kitchen counter, she says flatly, "Well, you must've made this *carabiniere* happy because he already has called you. I told him you were still sleeping, and he says you cannot reach him until this evening. But he left you his mobile phone number." She frowns. "And I was thinking to myself, these mobile phones have been around for so long now that I almost forget what secret lovers used to do to be in touch. Can you even remember?"

"They waited until their spouse or their partner was out of the room and made a quick phone call."

"Ah, yes, of course," she says acerbically. "Or they wrote secret letters late at night and hid them until they could be posted. Before the anonymity of email." She squints at me. "So, he was here with you in the villa last night, wasn't he?"

I hesitate a moment, wishing I'd followed my gut instinct not to bring Lorenzo into the house. "Yes, he was. It probably wasn't a good idea."

Marina shakes her head. "Good or bad idea. It's just not done. You're my guest. It's not correct for a guest to bring someone else in the house uninvited by me and to make love to them. Most hosts would be insulted and would ask you to leave immediately."

Speechless, I just stare at her for a moment. "So you're angry with me?" I finally say nervously.

Marina hesitates. "I am, and I am not. It's not so bad because I happen to know the person you brought here, a *carabiniere* no less, who knows that I would never stoop to report him. If he were a complete stranger, however, I'd be really cross.

"But I'm trying to understand why you might be doing this to yourself. Carrying on with another married man. My concern is certainly not moral. But rather that you would continue to choose situations that can only bring terrible unhappiness."

I find myself absentmindedly observing a row of spices, herbs, and jars of sugar and Tuscan farro noting that all these cooking ingredients are in various languages. Finally I say, "I guess I'm afraid of long-term stability, so I just keep tying myself up in knots."

Marina cries, "But then you confess to having a fantasy about the Frenchman leaving his wife for you!"

"Probably because I know he never would." I advance this

idea, but know deep down it's a lie. Indeed, Marina looks at me with skepticism. A few uncomfortable moments pass. "So you heard us come in?"

"Not I. My dogs."

"I'm really sorry. Bad judgment on my part, I admit. But I also didn't hear any barking. If the dogs had started barking I would have sent him away."

Marina smiles tightly. "They pace my room and whine instead."

"You must feel like a mother monitoring her child's activities."

"Well, certainly I am the age to be *yours*. However, I'd prefer to think of myself as a wise older friend concerned about your well-being. Concerned, shall we say, about an incurable romanticism."

Reaching up to grab a glass canister of ground coffee, I say, "Marina, do you really believe that falling in love with somebody should, in an ideal world, be a reasoned act?"

"Were that it *could* be. Let's just say if at all humanly possible, love and admiration for a lover shouldn't sway one's better judgment. My God, don't think for a minute that I'm immune to romantic folly. I've certainly committed enough of these acts of madness in my life. But let me quote Goethe to you. 'My good young friend, love is natural; but you must love within bounds. Divide your time: Devote a portion to business, and give the hours of recreation to your lover. Calculate your fortune; and out of the superfluity you may make'—here I am substituting *him* for *her*—'him a present, only not too often—on his birthday, and such occasions.'"

"Sound thinking, that."

"Now, speaking of love, have I ever told you about the romantic history of the villa?"

"You've alluded to it."

"It has to do with a love triangle." She grins. "A different sort of love triangle than the ones you seem to get yourself involved in. Would you like to hear the story?"

I nod and say by all means.

"I'm just fixing some lunch. Rather than have it in the kitchen, let's dine in the library."

Marina, a brilliant half-hour chef, whips up a pasta sauce made of home-grown tomatoes, mint, and parmigiano. I bring the steaming plates into the library while she brings the wine. The library has become my favorite room in the house. With cozier dimensions, twenty-foot-high bookshelves, and comfy sofas, it certainly is the most congenial. The other main rooms are so cavernous that you feel like an interloper within some great institution or that you're wandering through an echoing hall in a museum.

A flood of sunlight pools on one of the huge Persian area carpets, and several of the dogs are lying on their sides, basking in its warmth. Primo, the alpha, is stretched so that his stomach bows, his flanks jerking spasmodically in response to a dog dream. His black-and-white head flicks to attention as we enter, one roving eye trained on me, and then he flops down again. I sit on the ruby velvet sofa, and Marina positions herself cattycorner to me on a worsted wool armchair. The food is delicious, its flavors extraordinarily distinct, and I eat ravenously without trying to make conversation. Marina's portion is half the size of mine, and she seems amused by how zealously I polish off my pasta.

"You really are a wolf, aren't you?" she says, but still seems delighted by my appetite.

"This is amazing," I tell her, but she bridles at the compliment and claims that I'm used to Americanized pasta, which tends to have too many ingredients and none of them fresh enough.

Once I finish, Marina proceeds to tell me the tale of Napoleon III's best friend, a Dutchman named Emilien Nieuwerkerke, who, as the minister of culture, fled France when the Prussians took Paris. To escape arrest, Emilien disguised himself as a coachman and then drove three beautiful Russian princesses out of the city. Shortly thereafter, he bought the Villa Guidi and came to live here with the princesses, who actually were three generations of the same family: a grandmother, daughter, and granddaughter, each of whom, in succession, became the man's lover. But because there was such an age difference between Emilien and the youngest of the princesses, he arranged for her to be married to a titled yet impoverished Italian nobleman who agreed to live at the villa and share his wife with the older Emilien. What made the Italian willing to do this? The fact that the villa would one day be left to him and his heirs. And so, in this highly unusual arrangement, the two men and the three princesses all lived together at the villa, and when the last of them died, the property passed into Italian ownership. The extended family is now buried in the small adjacent chapel that was built two hundred years after the villa itself was completed.

"Somebody should really write this story," I suggest.

"Actually it *has* already been written. As a novel—by Stefano, as a matter of fact." Marina pauses and then smiles cagily. "*Emilien* is the first of his three novels, all written after he turned sixty. And I would like you to read it. Because, well, Stefano and I have discussed your helping us. We think that if you could translate some sample chapters, this will make it possible for us to find the right English or American publisher."

Without reservation I tell Marina that I'd be happy to help however I can.

"You're a darling," she says, reaching over to caress my cheek just as Carla comes into the room to inform her that a workman has located a clog in one of the gutters that drain the villa's flat tiled roof. The two women hurry away to consult over the proper way to remedy the situation.

Back in my room, I scan the bookshelves and, wedged together among all Stefano's precious Pléiade, are his novels, whose dust jackets have a zebralike design theme that suggests some sort of trilogy. I am hardly surprised that Marina's generosity toward me will now exact some kind of payback; this, I suppose, is as it should be. And, I reason, if I do end up doing some speculative translation work, then I will no longer be beholden to her kindness. And so, I grab hold of the novel entitled *Emilien*, gently pry it out of the bookshelf, and after reading the simple dedication to Marina, begin the first chapter.

I expect to find dense Italian wrought with imagery and literary allusion, an Italian similar to that of an Eco or a Calasso. However, I am pleasantly surprised to discover a simple, elegant style of a writer, who, at least initially, reminds me of Italo Calvino. Then again, Stefano has worked mainly as a journalist, so it stands to reason that a novel of his would be, at the very least, accessible. And yet, navigating the first hundred pages with relative ease, I find it quite dull going. The story of Napoleon's relationship with Emilien Nieuwerkerke and Emilien's sexual intrigue with the three princesses (and the subsequent introduction of an Italian nobleman into the mix) sounded a lot more concise and livelier when Marina recounted it. She apparently could not recognize (or perhaps she just refused to) that Stefano's novel does not succeed in alchemizing anecdote into drama. In fact, contrary to the narrative drive of *Conversion*, *Emilien* is a plodding, pastiche-like book. I wonder if perhaps Stefano was influenced by the newer European literary tradition in which psychological examination trumps plotting and characterization. I will certainly finish *Emilien*, but can understand why there has been no offer of an English-language publication. It's a worry.

Yet Marina believes Stefano's novels are brilliant. I wonder about this. I wonder if her opinion of his work has been tainted by the same "romanticism" that she claims has bedeviled me. But to insist that he is the greater writer of the two of them is ludicrous. *Conversion*, in comparison to *Emilien*, is consistently captivating. The narrative never stops churning, each twist of the plot expertly wrought. There are so many astonishing set pieces, moments of great hilarity illuminating what is, for the most part, a dark tale. The ending is haunting and ambiguous and, in my opinion, perfectly executed.

And though I know it's fruitless to even consider it, I can't help but imagine what Marina might have done with the story of Emilien—now, in light of Stefano's attempt, forever off-limits to the scope of her lively intelligence.

I decide to give another of his novels a go. Selecting a volume from the bookshelf, I am initially relieved to find a more contemporary story. However, even to a foreigner such as myself, it's pretty clear that he's dealing with a rather shopworn subject: the publishing scene in Milan and, specifically, a love affair between a graphic designer and a magazine fashion editor. Once again, the novel is written in an open, accessible style. Once again, I find the reading tedious.

What will I tell Marina? How will I convey to her that in my opinion, even if I am to translate some sample chapters, that these books will have a hard time being taken on by an English-language publisher? Perhaps I should be polite and just do the work on spec and let nature take its course. Then again, Marina was honest in her assessment of my little novella and no doubt would demand the same of me. But I worry that the truth might actually insult her and even jeopardize my welcome at the villa. After all, anyone's generosity has its limits, especially now that it has become clear there will be some sort of expected quid pro quo.

Suddenly there is a knock on my door. At my bidding, Marina pokes her head in with a discomfited look on her face. "You have an unexpected visitor," she says flatly.

I gape at her, wondering if it could be Lorenzo dropping by impromptu. "It's not who you think," she warns me. "It's the Frenchman. He's in the library."

I'm mystified. "Michel?"

"Correct."

"But, I don't know how he—"

"I don't either, but we can't just leave him standing there. So do I send him away, or do I say that you'll join him?" she asks impatiently. I hesitate, now worrying that she'll be bothered by yet another unannounced guest. Luckily Marina adds, "Well, I don't see that you have much choice, really, but to go and speak to him."

"Okay, I'll be there in a few minutes."

Without even knowing what I'm doing, I kneel down next to my bed, resting my forehead against the sheets, my heart clattering, my mouth sticky and dry.

Eleven

~

ACING THE GLASS DOORS that view the villa's sweeping front lawns, he's gazing up toward the convent where
Puccini's sister was a long-term resident. He's grown his
hair longer, and the broad back of his neck, my favorite part of
him, is now totally covered by loose ringlets. He's in his
standard-issue white T-shirt and pale blue jeans that are probably new and expensive and are manufactured to look as though
they've been in circulation for years. He's become more muscular, almost too much so, and I wonder if it's because he's been
living more of a single lifestyle and feels, as do many men, that
bigger size makes him more desirable.

Sensing my arrival, he turns and without hesitation approaches and snakes his arms around me. The familiar smell of
his leather riding jacket and the open road carries no trace of
Laurence's Chanel; I have to remind myself they no longer live
together. I allow the embrace to last for a moment, battling
back the surge of all the old feelings. A fleeting thought: I'm
glad to have met Lorenzo; it takes some sting and punch out of

this unexpected reunion. When I attempt to break away, Michel begins trembling and keeps me close by holding both my elbows.

Finally, I pry myself from his embrace. "Did Laurence tell you I was here?"

He looks perplexed. "Laurence?"

I explain that she'd called me here at the villa twice since my arrival.

"Why did she call *you?*" Michel asks.

"Why? You know exactly why . . . you've been out of touch with her."

His look of anticipation now glazes over, as though with the idea that I've momentarily joined the forces that are harping at him. "I'm riding, okay? I'm trying to think. Trying to make sense, trying to make some decisions."

I'm afraid to ask what these decisions may be about.

"Look, I ride a long way just to see you."

"Why do I doubt this?"

"Well, then, why else do I come?"

Watching his eyes, I say, "You suddenly track me down and show up here? Without even calling to announce yourself? Then why couldn't you have contacted me in Paris, or even called me that time I went to see Laurence . . . when I left you that message?"

He throws up his hands in frustration. "Because the day you just show up at my apartment, I don't know what to think. I don't know if you're trying to cause difficulties with Laurence, and therefore with me."

I forgot just how annoying I used to find Michel's clinging to the present tense when he spoke in English. How I conveniently used to blame Laurence for failing to help him master the past tense.

I continue, "Well, you should have found out by calling me. I left the number. But you never did. That's why I don't trust you."

Michel shakes his head and rubs his head with his fingers. "Then *you* don't understand yet. I *try to.* I wait a few days, no, a week, and then I call you. But he answers the phone. He says you are not there and that he will give you the message. But then he tells me that you just get the result of your antibody test. That he believes he has passed the virus to you."

"So that's when he told you. In his memoir he implies that he actually told you in person."

Michel shakes his head. "No, it was on the phone."

I shake my head, hating these conflicting facts. It only makes me doubt each man's version of the truth. Who knows, they both could be lying to protect themselves. One thing is certain: Ed knew exactly what to say to make Michel stay away. "But you still should've checked to see how I was, at the very least to see how I was feeling."

Michel insists, "After he tells me your news, I ask him for you to call me back."

Ed had never told me Michel had called to begin with. "Well, when you didn't hear from me, you should have tried again."

"You are right. I am sorry."

I now explain that Ed had lied about my status. That my last test results were actually negative.

Michel jolts his head back, his eyes blazing, and then lurches forward, attempting to hug me. This time I push him away. Hands intertwining with nervousness, he cries, "My God, so all this time it's a lie? I can't believe . . . but, no, it's okay, it's obviously good because this is the best news, after all." Then his expression falls into bewilderment. "But how could he do such a thing to you?"

"Because he *supposedly* loved me. And *supposedly* believed you were truly bad for me. Which you probably are. And because he was a writer, so what do you expect? They're good at telling just the right lie."

"Well, understand that he really scares me. Tells me to protect myself from you, from your infection. To think of my wife, to think of my children."

So this was the flip side of Ed's manipulations. "He was very persuasive when he wanted to be," I manage to say in the midst of renewed anger.

"But you know, even though he tells me, I'm always hoping somehow it's not true or that you will be one of the ones who survive. But I'm really sad. I even pray for you. But you must realize what he does . . . this is terribly wrong, this kind of lie."

Unfortunately, I now explain, I hadn't known about anything—that Michel and Ed met, much less the lie that Ed had told him—until I had recently read about it in the memoir. I tell Michel I thought he never contacted me because he was finished with me. "I lived with that for months. It was awful. And now the damage is already done."

Michel begins pacing in front of me. "But what does this mean?" he asks finally.

"It means that I've gotten over you," I force myself to say. "Now I can't change it. I can't reverse it."

"I see," he says sadly. "Well, in all this time I have not gotten over you. It is the reason why I move out of the flat to my own apartment. It is the reason why I go riding and am not so much in Paris."

Carla emerges from the kitchen with a tray holding a freshly made risotto and a plate of sliced tomatoes and basil and begins walking toward the front of the villa. I glance at my watch; it's three o'clock in the afternoon—Stefano certainly dines at odd hours. As she passes us, Carla meets my eyes; with a shrewd glance, she appraises Michel, then throws me a look of dismay. And somehow I divine that, for some reason, she disapproves of him rather than the idea of two men in a relationship. Balancing the tray with one hand, she reaches to open the door leading to Stefano's wing of the villa. When I rush to help her, she says proudly, "Don't bother. I do this door twice a day."

Feeling a bit constrained, I turn to Michel. "Maybe we should take a little walk, clear the air a bit. What do you think?"

He agrees and yet, now knowing that we'll no longer be in private, looking at the pale down on his forearms, the broadened chest visible through his white T-shirt, I find myself wanting to make love to him. And this is truly distressing to me.

As we pass through the formal dining room en route to the loggia, we bump into Marina, who is coming out of the kitchen holding the most enormous key I've ever seen. "Ah," she says with cool politeness. "I just found the key to the chapel I was telling you about." She then translates this into capable French and adds, "This morning I told Russell a story about a friend of Napoleon III who lived and died here at the villa with three Russian princesses. They are all buried in our chapel." She turns to me. "Are you going out?"

"Just for a walk."

Handing me the key she says, "Well, if you'd both like to visit the chapel you may do so."

"Bien sûr," Michel says.

Key in hand, he and I cross the loggia and descend the stone steps to follow a large gravel pathway flanked with blue hydrangeas that leads to the pink stucco chapel with neoclassical columns, constructed in the early seventeenth century. Compared to the grandeur of the older villa, the chapel's architecture is ordinary and imitative. Approaching a door flaking with dark green paint, I fit the teeth of the gargantuan key into a giant lock. The key rotates only a little. I keep trying to turn it but remain unsuccessful.

"May I?" asks Michel. "I believe I have a bit more experience with ancient buildings." He struggles but finally is able to turn the key in the lock. With an explosion of dust, the door creaks open.

The chapel smells moldy and dank. Amber bands of late-afternoon light slant through the small, prisonlike windows. The main room is occupied by an altar at one end adorned with a portrait of a black Madonna and child in a braided gold frame, but the Madonna in the picture looks wilder than one would expect, almost like a Gypsy. The room itself appears strangely vacant, and I realize this is because pews have been removed; the loose terra-cotta tiles of the floor are covered by a wide gray rug placed in front of the altar, which stretches the entire length of the chapel. The ceiling is painted to look heavenly azure, Tiepoloesque, populated by trumpeting angels and putti. A ray of sun is wheeling directly in the middle of the altar, where I notice a marble miniature that looks like a model replica of the chapel itself. There are two large brass candlesticks on either side of it with thick tawny candles burned halfway down.

I wonder aloud where the tombs are. Michel divines the answer and, with a deft movement, goes to where the carpeting is turned over and twists the whole thing aside.

Beneath it, the graves of the princesses and their families are marble lozenges fitted together, each inscribed with Latin texts that give details of births in Odessa and Vienna and deaths either at the villa or in some place close by. Olga, the youngest princess, apparently died in Naples.

"Can you imagine what it must've been like to transport a dead body in the nineteenth century?" I wonder aloud.

Michel says, "They have fairly sophisticated methods. After all, this happens quite a lot, especially among the wealthier classes."

I continue reading the snatches of engraved history while Michel wanders toward one of the windows. The light in the room seems to grow more potent. "Do we ever go to Sainte-Chapelle together?" he asks me innocently, as though suddenly inspired.

I tell him no, that I always went to Sainte-Chapelle on my own and in fact visited the sanctuary quite often after we broke up, hoping to get a perspective on our love affair as an impossible arrangement. "I went there the day I got the results of my blood test. Right after Ed made a point of showing me the mention in the paper that you and Laurence were separated."

"Of course he makes sure you see that."

"He also said the two of you had a brief affair."

Michel is completely taken off guard. "He says this?"

I find myself smiling for some reason. "He called it a *flingee*."

Michel shrugs and looks up at the ceiling in horror. "This is a complete fabrication." He fixes his eyes on me. "I think we are introduced somewhere. But this is all. I never meet with him until . . ." Michel suddenly hesitates. "He asks me to find him at his café."

Do I believe him? My instinct . . . What *is* my instinct here? My confusion about these two men is getting worse. On one of the chapel's far walls I notice a very crude and very graphic crucifix presenting a nude and muscular Jesus clad only in rags tied around his waist. "Something I've been wondering, Michel. In the very beginning, who contacted whom? Was it you who contacted Ed? Or vice versa?"

"I will tell you. Here is how it was. A year ago at the end of September was six weeks after it's over between us. I'm missing you, so I go to your old apartment in the eighteenth and convince them to tell me where you move. So then I go to the rue Birague and wait until I see you coming out with this older man. I think I recognize him as the American poet who lives here in Paris. Then I ask a friend who says it is and gives me his full name and I find him on the Minitel. And when I try calling, he answers the phone and tells me you are not there. He asks who I am, and then asks me to meet with him.

"And then at the café he convinces me how depressed you are and that I have no business being in contact with you unless I am prepared to leave my wife. Obviously I don't tell him and perhaps what I should tell him is that I am missing you so much by now that I *am* already seriously thinking of living always in my own apartment. To make my life more open to you."

"And then a month later you tried to call me again?"

"Yes, and at this time he tells me you're infected."

"Which scared you away for good."

Michel spreads his arms. "Well, here I am, so obviously no."

"Oh, come on! This is way, way too late."

"But if I know I have to protect myself and you might not be well eventually—and this has to be a concern, right?"

"I suppose. But like I said, you still could've checked to see how I was."

Michel ponders this. "But if I never stop thinking about you anyway, even if believing the poet's lies, does that mean something, does that mean anything?"

I study his face, constricted with all sorts of battling emotions. I want to believe him but am afraid to because somehow I don't sense I'm getting the entire story, or even the exact chronology of events. And Ed's death means I have only what he wrote in his memoir to compare to what Michel has just told me. I backtrack a bit. "What do you mean by making your life more open to me?"

"The truth is, Russell, that I will always have to stay married to Laurence. The big reason, after all: Laurence is the one who has the money. The fabrics business, although mine, failed. I'm forced to sell it to my partner. I don't get much at all, unfortunately, so I now depend even more on her. But this has always been our arrangement. She marries my family because we have an old name. And I marry her family because she has no name but money. We grow to love each other. And this often is how it goes," he says simply but painfully. And yet I can detect how difficult it is for him to admit how dependent he is upon Laurence, that on some level he feels ashamed.

I point out, "So then Ed *was* right. No matter what, you would never leave her. And even if you say that he meddled, despite his jealousy he convinced himself he was doing me a favor by keeping me away from you. And you a favor by lying."

"But if she and I will live apart, as we are now, then I will have plenty of time to spend with you. Especially because Laurence will accept this."

"What makes you assume that?"

"Well, first of all, because this can happen—"

"You mean when a man has a mistress and keeps her separate from his family and from the rest of his life?"

"Something like this, yes."

"But *I'm* a man, so it's *not* so easily accepted. This, according to your wife!" I explain that the day I showed up at the apartment, Laurence informed me that Michel's living with a man would never be accepted by the echelons of the social world into which he was born, that it would be far more difficult than having a mistress on the side.

Michel looks down at the floor, shakes his head, and says, "With this I cannot argue. But listen to me for a moment." He gazes at me balefully. "Sometimes, all these things stand in your way and you still go forward. You know what you're doing might destroy everything that is stable in your life, but you still cannot get this other person out of your head. And eventually you do what you never think you will do. In your case, this is what happens with me. And when I read your friend's obituary in *Le Monde,* I start figuring how I can get back with you again."

Moments pass and then Michel continues. "Laurence is my wife, my companion, the mother of my children, but she has not been my lover for many years. *You*, Russell, were my lover." The final words are gratifying, but I resist them as he takes a step to-

ward me, rests his arms on my shoulders, and tilts his head for a
kiss that I studiously avoid.

Instead I tell him, "When you used to say that in English,
that you loved me, I actually almost believed you."

"You should have."

"I'm glad I didn't."

Outside the chapel a lawnmower suddenly sputters and ig-
nites; the roar of its engine is so loud it threatens to deafen any
further conversation. As we make our way out, Michel struggling to turn the rusted key in the enormous lock, the Polish
gardener comes running up and asks us to lend a hand moving
the broken statue.

He leads the way across the road, along the lane of overripe
fig trees, to a group of laborers wearing paint-spattered clothes
hovering over the fractured Apollo, now wound in rope like a
captive. Once we join the band, two of the laborers grab two
ends of the rope, while the rest of us clutch at the decapitated alabaster statue and lift. There are seven of us, and still the sculp-
ture feels incredibly heavy. We manage to hoist him onto a
dolly, and then one of the workers begins pulling our splintered
quarry back down the driveway in the direction of the villa.

"Pity that this splendid figure gets so broken," Michel murmurs to me at last.

"One's beauty is always such a fragile state," I reply as I escort
him back to the villa.

Twelve

~

THE FOLLOWING MORNING, Lorenzo calls from what
sounds like a noisy bar and asks me to meet him on the
steps of the cathedral inside the city. It takes me a half
hour of brisk walking before I reach the nearest portal built in
the four-hundred-year-old ramparts. This last day of August is
the day of the antiques market, which attracts people from all
over Tuscany. I wander through the stalls, eyeing English furniture, much of it left over from the once-thriving British colony
in Livorno; there are trays of heavy ornamental silverware,
wardrobes full of starchy linens and lace, shelves of moldering
old books, boxes filled with slightly battered postcards and
magazines. My eye catches an attractive watercolor of an island;
the stall proprietor claims it's a late-nineteenth-century depic-
tion of one of the smaller archipelagos to be found in the Venetian lagoon, somewhere beyond Torcello. Knowing Ed's taste in
art, I feel certain he would have impulsively acquired this painting; the thought that he is not here to purchase it, that it will

fall in the hands of someone who probably would appreciate it less than he, makes me curiously sad.

I know I should be furious at what he's done, or undone, as it were, but find that I just cannot sustain the anger for too long. He was certainly wrong about Michel's intentions and probably would be astonished at the lengths my former lover claims to be willing to go on my behalf. But in other ways, Ed was right to remind me that even if I started spending a lot of time with Michel, I'd still be living with somebody who was, for all intents and purposes, married, and that this after a time would have to take its toll. Ed rightly reasoned that I probably would never feel satisfied or safe unless I had Michel to myself. As far as the "mistress idea" was concerned, despite my initial desire to agree to such an arrangement, Laurence and I—Americans, after all—would most certainly find that living it out would be impossibly painful. Besides, if she loved Michel, why should she have to share him, much less agree to it? And why should *I* have to share my lover? The fact that Michel could even expect this of us makes me doubt the reliability of his feelings.

The white cathedral where Lorenzo waits was built from locally quarried marble. With its intricate carvings of delicate columns and pediments, it resembles a listing wedge of wedding cake. Perched on the steps outside, wearing a pair of teardrop Ray-Bans, he is in *carabinieri* uniform. He has taken off his jacket, and his forearms, hugging his knees, are soaking in the sun. Without a word, I walk up and sit down next to him. A strange hope goes through my head: that the poison of my attraction to him will be the antidote to my remaining longing for Michel. Lorenzo leans over and kisses me gently and ceremoniously on both cheeks and then gives my shoulder a playful squeeze.

"What took you?" he carps with another intimate nudge. However, he hardly seems irritated that I am late for our appointment. I tell him I walked to town from the villa and got distracted by the antiques mart. "Come inside with me," he says and leads the way into the church, stopping at a limestone font. He dips his fingers in holy water, then kneels and crosses himself. Feeling puckish, I reach toward the holy water, but he gently slaps my arm away with an admonishment that I am not Catholic and heads to a row of pews close to the altar. He sits down and, putting his arm around me in a collegial way, says sotto voce, "If you crossed yourself like that it'd be a sacrilege."

I tell him I always do this when I visit Catholic churches, especially when I'm alone.

"Then you'll go directly to hell," he says, shaking his head, though there's an irrepressible grin curling the edges of his lips.

"Hell is right here on earth," I tell him. "That it comes after death is organized religion's biggest misconception."

"I won't discuss this with you any further!"

"So then why bring me into a cathedral at all?" I ask, noticing a tightly knit group of Japanese tourists, each armed with a camera, gravitating toward the altar.

"To speak in private," he murmurs and then explains.

The *carabinieri* have received a communication requesting them to escort an American consular attaché to the Villa Guidi. This will be happening tomorrow. I will be served a subpoena for my computer as well as for as a manuscript thought to be in my possession.

"Oh, no," I groan.

"Luckily, I just happen to overhear this." He removes his

sunglasses and his naked eyes dazzle me. "And which manuscript is this?"

I hesitate.

"It's okay. I will help you, Russell. This I promise."

And so I manage to explain the rest of the story that he
doesn't know.

"*Madonna*," he says when I've finished. "What complications
you bring into your life. This executrix, if she can prove you're
holding on to this book when you say you don't have it, then
maybe she can also protest the fact that your friend took her
away from his life-insurance policy." He grins brilliantly.
"Maybe she thinks you coerced him with your sexiness and told
him to sign over the money."

I tell him that the insurance policy is the least of my worries,
that I hardly care whether or not I get the money. "Because I really don't deserve it."

"Well, you should care."

"I can earn my own way. And honestly, Lorenzo, I don't know if
I'd even want money from somebody who manipulated my life."

Lorenzo takes this in and then says, "What he does is very human. Hard to blame him if he was that in love with you."

Indeed, I think, this is my struggle.

"Why don't you take out the part concerning your relationship with this man and give up this unfinished work and be
done with it?"

I explain that carefully weeding out the bits of the manuscript that involve me would be impossible by tomorrow. And
surely, the editors and the executrix would quickly figure out
what I'd done. Not to mention that Ed himself felt the book was
not ready for publication.

Lorenzo makes a circular gesture with one hand. "Well, he has no say over it now. He's dead."

"But I know his intentions . . . that's the dilemma."

"And what is the *signora*'s opinion of this?" Lorenzo wonders aloud. I tell him that Marina thinks I should just give it up. "Well, then do what your hostess wants. It's only proper."

"I can't. Something in me is worried that it's the wrong thing to do."

Lorenzo grabs my shoulder. "Luckily for you, I have appointed myself to come tomorrow with this official from Florence. The *capo* almost didn't let me because he knows I take you to the gym. But then I assured him I will get what I am supposed to."

"And if you don't you'll be discredited?"

Lorenzo recoils a bit. "You say there is nothing in your computer. If that is where they think this manuscript is, then obviously I will take your computer."

"You can't!" I cry out. "I won't be able to work." I remind him that I do freelance translations for American companies and that a substantial project is due in less than a month.

Lorenzo shrugs and tells me that I must make a choice: my computer or the manuscript in my possession. He confiscates either one or the other.

"I could always just leave town."

He searches my face to see how serious I am. "You could, but then they will assume I warned you. And this would not be good. This would hurt me. You will not do this, will you?" he asks sweetly, seeming unworried.

I shake my head.

One thing I like about Lorenzo is his voice, its resonant, basso quality, slightly nasal. It's very masculine.

At that moment an elderly priest passes us and seems to recognize Lorenzo, who grows noticeably bashful. The two men nod to each other; the priest eyes me and then continues to a rectangular display where a gilded glass casement encloses the blackened, gnarled remains of a body, covered with stigmata, that arrived mysteriously by rowboat in Livorno three centuries ago and was immediately declared a holy relic. I ask Lorenzo who the priest is, and he explains that the man is his confessor and has been since childhood.

"Oh." I hesitate. "So he's the one you told about your interest in men?"

Lorenzo lowers his head and nods slowly. "Recently, yes."

"Recently," I repeat. "And before recently, what were you confessing?"

Lorenzo looks at me askance. "That's between me and my confessor."

"Right. Understood. Just tell me and I won't bother you anymore."

Shaking his head, Lorenzo admits that he confessed his desires and sexual activities with women other than his wife.

Of course, I think to myself cynically. Perfect.

Lorzeno says to me breathily, "I can be free tonight to see you. Can you be free to see me?"

So for him the thrill must be indulging in something so strictly forbidden that he would even hesitate bringing it up in confession. How pathological is that? I inform him Marina knows that I secreted him into the villa and it's perhaps ill advised to invite him back.

"I never expected this," he says, "to be invited back," and admits to having another place in mind. A friend of his owns a vacation house in the Garfagnana, a mountain region forty minutes away. Much as I find the idea appealing, I don't immediately agree to the plan. For once again I'm deeply mired in thoughts of Michel and even remember thinking, just before his impromptu visit, that the passing of time had slowly leeched away the painful bits of psychological shrapnel left over from his sudden rejection—now more than a year old. In fact, in the wake of Ed's death I found myself missing Michel less, and this, in and of itself was a relief. It occurs to me that it would be better not to miss or long for anybody at the moment. And if Lorenzo is even more tied up and unavailable than Michel, in this regard, he is a potentially perilous companion. And I have to ask myself: Why am I drawn to this sort of pain?

On the way out of the church, we pass a well-lighted painting that I recognize as a copy of Carpaccio's famous portrait of Saint Augustine. "What is this doing here?" I demand. The original, housed at a Dalmatian *scuola* in Venice, is one of my favorite paintings of all time.

"Yes, you are right," Lorenzo says, and goes on to explain that it's an early replica of the masterpiece that a nobleman had had duplicated and then brought to Tuscany.

The scene is of Augustine standing at the desk in his study, which at first glance appears to be completely in order. But the man himself looks stupefied and then you notice that there are books scattered on the floor, and everyday objects are out of place. Staring at the saint is a small dog whose watchful confusion seems to indicate that something is amiss, some sense of routine and order has been uprooted.

"I've studied this painting," I tell Lorenzo. "I've been to see it in Venice at least a dozen times. It's the only one in the *scuola* that scholars don't seem to agree on."

"Really," Lorenzo says, sounding genuinely interested.

"Do you want to hear my take on it?" I ask him.

"Of course."

Saint Augustine is having a vision of Saint Jerome's death. The vision itself brings momentary chaos. Like a wind has come into the room and knocked things to the ground, and that bewildered dog only wants things to return to normal. I imagine Saint Augustine is actually seeing a soul's conversion to the immortal.

Reflective silence follows this and finally Lorenzo wonders aloud, "I wonder what will happen to our souls?"

"Purgatory at the very best," I quip, studying the painting for a bit longer while he patiently waits. It is one of the more contemplative masterpieces that I've looked at, a far cry from Caravaggio's staged "conversions" that proclaim a religious awakening to Christianity. All is not spelled out with this Saint Augustine. The great thinker's moment of indecision, his grappling to understand what is happening to him is comforting to somebody such as myself, struggling to distinguish all the betrayal surrounding me.

At last Lorenzo leads the way out of the church into the sunlit square and we begin strolling back through the antiques market toward the main piazza. I ask if he's worried that Marina knows I brought him into the villa. He surprises me by shrugging. "She doesn't bother with people such as myself. Which is not to say that she's a snob. It's more that our lives never cross except for the times I go to the villa for one professional reason or another. She would never know anybody who knows my wife. The distance between her world and mine is great."

We walk a ways in silence, and still under the spell of the powerful painting, I say, "But you seem conflicted about seeing me."

He shakes his head. "No. If I didn't really want to see you I wouldn't," he says with great simplicity. "One day I will be able to resolve this and then live my life more peacefully."

I stop walking abruptly and face him. "But you won't resolve it," I say. "Once you get that, your life will be a lot easier. Then you don't even have to worry about getting divorced."

His expression turns quizzical. "I never plan on getting a divorce," he assures me, shifting his sunglasses from their position above his brow back down over his eyes. "But I still have to lie to my wife, and this I don't like."

Naturally I think of Michel and Laurence, of her efforts to accept his sexual nature and keep their marriage together. And yet Laurence probably still doesn't quite understand, or perhaps is just too afraid to recognize, the fact that at his very core her husband is galvanized by men.

I tell Lorenzo, "You lie only because you believe your true nature cannot be accepted by those who love you."

"Yes, this is correct."

I wait a few seconds and then say, "But if it's your nature, then it's natural."

Lorenzo sighs and seems exasperated with me. Clearly he's unused to being challenged or contradicted. I can't help wondering if giving up his philosophical studies in favor of a less intellectually demanding profession makes it easier for him to avoid examining his own beliefs, much less what drives him: his motivations, his desires. Then again, Michel wasn't so in touch with himself, either.

We continue in silence to the largest square in the city, a public space ringed by cafés and boutiques, with eyeglass stores on every corner and bantering groups of teenaged kids whose backpacks are covered with race-car logos. We pass a small bakery where in the window is a handwritten sign: BRUTTI MA BUONI, cookies that are literally "ugly but good." There's a shop that sells reasonably priced underwear and stockings for both men and women.

"Maybe we shouldn't get together tonight," I say at last. For once I think that I can be proud of myself for at least trying to avoid a potentially demoralizing situation.

"But I want to see you," he insists, grabbing my shoulder again and squeezing it just the right way to challenge my resolution. "I've spent two days arranging this." And in the crowded square, amid the clattering of dishes at the cafés and the caterwauling of Vespas racing to and fro, I realize it's impossible to resist him.

No sooner do I return to the Villa Guidi than I find myself in the midst of a commotion: Carla rushing around the place fretting and in tears. In her thick Tuscan dialect she garbles to me that Stefano is gravely ill, that Marina found him unconscious with a terrifically high fever, drove him to the hospital, and is still there waiting for news. I ask if Carla knows what's wrong, and she explains that tests are being conducted, but that meningitis has been discussed as one possibility. And as if that weren't enough, she then explains that just after I'd gone to meet Lorenzo, a rock smashed through one of the front windows in the library. Both she and Marina had heard the concussion and came running. "The rock has gone to the police. It's as big as an orange. The rock has to be lucky," Carla opines. "If it hadn't been thrown today, the *signora* might not have checked in on Stefano to make sure he was fine. I, myself, never see him before midafternoon."

"Any idea who might have done it?"

"We looked for a person, or a strange car. We found nothing."

I wait a moment and then ask, "Why didn't you go with them to the hospital?" knowing that Carla would feel a lot better if she could be near Stefano.

Unable to look at me, she says, "I didn't want to leave the house with no one in it." She hesitates. "And I'm not his wife. It would not be right."

"But you're . . . his dear friend and caretaker."

"You don't understand these things," she says sadly.

Indeed. Harkening back to my conversation with Lorenzo, I want to tell her at least I am beginning to, but I know that pressing Carla like this will make her feel even more wretched.

I walk to the library, where one pane of a huge window is completely missing. There are no shards of broken glass left on the floor; Carla must have already swept them away. Who threw the rock and why did they throw it? I sense that this might not be so easily explained, and therefore the threat of future incidents will hardly be so handily dismissed. Yet another mystery like the hotel-room break-in. I get a sudden pang: What if I learn nothing more about who the intruders were and why they threatened us? This is unfathomable to me.

Around five in the afternoon, Marina phones Carla to say that Stefano's fever has gone down somewhat but still has not broken and that in the midst of a battery of tests, he, true to form, is behaving like the ornery man he is. No matter what, he will remain in the hospital for a few days, and she has no idea when she might return home. When Carla knocks on my door to relay this information, I ask if there is any way that I might contact "the *signora*" myself; after all, I need to warn Marina of the subpoena that will be served tomorrow by Lorenzo and the American attaché. Carla goes away and returns with a shred of paper scrawled with a mobile phone number.

Marina answers after the first ring. I apologize profusely, inquire about Stefano, and once I hear the same report Carla gave me, quickly explain about the subpoena.

"I already know this," she informs me. Her friend, the *capo* of the *carabinieri,* has already contacted her. "Just before I realized that Stefano is unwell. They were to come tomorrow, but now they will not be able to."

"I'm sorry to add all this to what's already going on."

"This is *your* problem, Russell," she says tersely. "Not mine. You are my guest and you also know my feelings about this business."

I do, indeed. Before signing off, I ask Marina what she makes of the broken window.

She pauses for a moment as I hear her muffling the phone. Then she says, "I really don't know. The rock could be thrown by anyone, even by stupid kids from in town. But I can't try to figure it out now. I'm worried about Stefano. His health has always been so fragile. And seeing him like this makes me . . ." She doesn't finish the sentence. "Ah, the doctor is here," she says. "I must go now."

That evening, after spending a few hours with Lorenzo in the Garfagnana, I let myself into the house to the sounds of sobbing.

I find Carla in the kitchen, her head on the table, weeping inconsolably. Sensing I am there, she peers up at me and in a tremulous voice announces that Stefano has died. And that Marina is in her room and has asked not to be disturbed. Bleary-eyed and with a look of complete misery, Carla lays her head back on the table and stares into space. This is the true face of grief, I realize, the immediate response that comes from deep devotion to another. There is no mantle of numbness, no knee-jerk, self-protective disassociation, but rather the agony of loss, as pure as water. I can't help but think of my slow realization and acceptance of Ed's death and that I never descended to this level of inconsolable distress. I think of the painting I saw earlier in the cathedral and Saint Augustine's pitiful confusion at the news of the death of Saint Jerome. Feeling terribly awkward in the midst of Carla's grief, I offer my sincere condolences and ask her to tell me if there is anything I can do.

"Yes," she says immediately as she sits upright and swipes the tears from her eyes. "You can help."

"Tell me how."

"You can do something about his books being in English."

Baffled, I stare at her and wonder if somehow Marina has put her up to this. "I can try," I say, not very convincing.

"More than try, do something!" Carla insists. "Being in English was important to him. And he says you knew somebody who would *not* help," she emphasizes.

"Me? *I* knew somebody?"

"Yes." She is staring at me with bloodshot eyes.

"Somebody who would *not* help?" I repeat to make sure I've heard correctly.

"Don't I say this?"

"And his or her name?"

She shrugs. "I don't know. Stefano just told me one day."

Wondering who this person might be, I wander from the kitchen into the dining room; from the dining room, I cross into the library that leads to Marina's bedroom and end up standing right next to her door. I hear no keening, no conversation at all except for what is blaring from the television. And yet I can still make out Carla once again weeping in the kitchen. I glance over to the place where the rock crashed through the window. The broken pane has been replaced with a lozenge of wood. Cringing, I listen to the televised voices filtering from Marina's bedroom; she is watching a movie, an American movie. And I think: It has been quite a while since I've heard native speakers from my own country.

But then everything switches to Italian, some sort of announcement or news bulletin. I now put my ear against the door and listen to an eerie story of an Italian soldier killed by a roadside bomb in the Middle East and how his fiancée was so distraught at the news that she went and drowned herself in a lake right next to his family's home. *"Dio Santo,"* I can hear Marina saying. "This is like Shakespeare."

Thirteen

~

I T'S ALL QUITE SIMPLE, REALLY," Marina explains to me two weeks later. "You let the official come here. You give him your computer, which will be investigated and nothing found. And then it's finished. You go on with your life."

As long as they don't send it back to America to be searched, I point out. In that case I would be unable to finish my translation project.

Dressed in a thin black cashmere sweater and dark gray slacks, Marina sits on one of the sofas in the library, legs crossed, holding one temple of her reading glasses. She looks forlorn but determined, as though she's spoken for her own edification as well as mine. I'm amazed at her stoicism, at the way she carries on her life, dealing with the villa's considerable daily activities without faltering. Although grief is noticeably written on her face in a frown, in a downward cast of features, articulated in her body by a slightly forward slump, she has spoken very little about Stefano's death. This is surprising; after all, they were together for fifteen years.

She resumes, "Why would anyone bother sending a computer back to America? It's only a machine, after all. That can be scanned and diagnosed and even fixed—like a car. The modern world, for some reason, loves to lend it an animus. Stefano says that these computer experts can even tell if you've had something on your computer and then removed it." She pauses, realizing she has referred to Stefano as though still living, and is sobered into silence. Not quite gathered together, she goes on with a quavering voice, "Computers . . . may seem mysterious to somebody like me, but they are not, after all, nearly as complicated as the human psyche." At last I see a tear dripping down her cheek.

As though needing an activity to dispel her sudden melancholy, Marina strolls over to the enormous fireplace and, grabbing a poker, taps underneath. Chunks of soot spew out, and I can hear the sounds of beating wings and the dull thud of birds colliding in the chimney. "Oh, God, the *chimney swifts*!" She warbles the last two words in English, as though I won't recognize their equivalent in Italian. "But wait, it's September. They shouldn't be nesting now."

"Why are you testing the fireplace?"

She looks at me sharply and says, "Because it's supposed to be chilly tonight. Cold for September in Tuscany. The weather has certainly changed the short time we've been away."

Marina is referring to the journey that she and Carla made to Milan, the city of Stefano's birth and where he requested a burial. After making the necessary arrangements, they drove the three hours and were met by Marina's daughter, who flew in from London, and by her son, who shuttled up from Rome. Oddly, neither child returned to Tuscany.

"They seemed relieved I didn't ask them to come back," she informs me when I inquire why neither child accompanied her home. "They are used to me being a tough cookie," she says in English, which happens to be one of her favorite expressions. "They know I don't like to be taken care of."

"Well, you might need to be at some point in time."

Glowering at me, she says, "Why bring this up *now* of all times? I will cross this bridge when it comes." Continuing in English for some inexplicable reason, "As you probably figured out, I prefer taking care of people rather than vice versa."

I reflect that because Stefano had been such a recluse, so far his death doesn't seem to make all that much difference in the order of life at the Villa Guidi. The dogs roam the rooms and the grounds at whim, a chorus of barking and howling erupting several times a day. The workmen still arrive and depart, repairing pipes in far-flung bathrooms, replastering cracks in walls, unclogging roof drains, tinkering with faulty wiring. Marina deals with them with characteristic noblesse oblige; in most cases Stefano's death is not referred to.

But now, in the midst of our discussion, the plumber arrives and there's a touching commotion; he actually becomes weepy when he gives Marina his condolences. She, in turn, moved by his compassion, sheds a few more tears herself. "He is a fine fellow," she explains after the plumber leaves the room. "A very capable man. Stefano wrote about him, a very famous article that was reprinted all over Italy."

Marina further explains that there was a time, during the sixties and seventies, when many intellectuals from Italy were emigrating to America and taking up posts at universities: linguistics professors, literary theorists, contemporary philosophers. In his article, Stefano noted these various departures and then boldly claimed that Italy could spare them because the universities would always seed a new galaxy of bright stars. "But now, for example, this man you've just met is the third generation of plumbers who have worked at the villa." In his article Stefano reveres these wise old plumbers and electricians who know the old villas and palazzi, can divine the antiquated systems of energy and waste removal. Theirs is a rare knowledge passed down to them from their fathers, who, in turn, came from a long line of electricians and plumbers dating back to the advent of electricity and, before that, when modern plumbing was developed. And so once these people died off, if their understanding was not passed along, the knowledge of how to run Italy's old buildings would die with them. "Stefano said, 'Let the intellectuals go. Italy doesn't need them. She requires her plumbers and electricians.'"

After a substantial pause Marina says to me regretfully, "You wouldn't even know he was gone, would you?"

I remind her that I hardly ever saw Stefano.

"A funny man." She sighs—I imagine at a torrent of memories. "He changed a lot over the last ten years. He used to be not so removed from everyone and everything."

"You said his seclusion was a symptom of depression."

She nods. "This is true. But more important, Stefano considered himself a failure." I obviously must look skeptical because she becomes more emphatic. "Yes, he always did, which made him try harder and probably was the reason why he developed such a first-rate mind. I know you didn't really get a chance to speak to him because he was so walled in, but if you had you would have marveled at his intelligence.

"And I must say that our discussions and listening to him speak were some of the great pleasures of my life. Which only makes the fact that I was more successful than he a horrible burden." Marina pauses, swinging her eyeglasses. "You might find this surprising but often I found myself wishing it was reversed and that *he* was the more famous, the more celebrated of the two."

"I think I realized this after you told me the story of the Strega Prize, how he turned to you and made it seem as though you didn't deserve it."

Marina is startled by my observation. "I suppose you're right. I suppose I would have preferred to be on his arm and he be the winner."

"And so would *he*. It's no wonder that you have such mixed feelings about celebrities," I comment, thinking of her offbeat evaluation of Ed. "You don't seem to like being one yourself, for example."

She admits, "Well, it's different when you grow up with a well-known father."

"Still, you get what I mean," I say in English, for unassailable emphasis.

Marina nods.

"I just hope that this wanting to displace your success on Stefano doesn't have to do with your being a woman," I hazard to say.

"So what if it does?" Marina challenges me. "The feminists would cringe, but you well know I am not one of them. There is part of me that likes to be the woman courted by the man, even to be a little bit overshadowed. Beyond this, I have two children. So I'm very aware of the biological imperative. My male dogs run all over the neighborhood when they smell a bitch in heat. But my girls stay with me. No matter what, they want to stick to the house. These are the properties of the blood that cannot be ignored by the rational mind."

"So wait, what are you saying?" I ask, remarking to myself that this statement contradicts what Marina had said the morning after I brought Lorenzo into the villa when she was quoting Goethe.

"That my life changed with Stefano after I won the Strega. And certainly not for the better. The prize itself ruined our romantic life. Suddenly, no matter what I said or did to reassure him, he felt unworthy of me. That's why he actually preferred that Carla took care of him."

But then, for the same reason you don't have to feel unworthy of him, I think but cannot bring myself to say.

Marina goes on. "And that's why I've tried so hard to help his career, to keep his books in print, and especially to have them translated." She now looks at me keenly.

And so we arrive at the dreaded discussion of the man's novels, something I'd hoped, at least for the time being, to avoid. I realize too late that silence is perhaps not the best response; it might infer that I understand exactly why Stefano felt himself a failure.

"So *did* you ever get a chance to read any of his work?" Marina asks me quietly at last.

I tell her I have and without hesitating offer that finding an English-language publisher who will pay translation costs as well as an advance will, alas, be very difficult.

A bitter smile crosses her lips, and soon her expression is hard and rancorous. "And what if *I* pay for translation?"

"I still think it's going to be a challenge."

"So then I should assume you didn't like what you read?" I agonize for a moment and then she says with gentleness, "Russell, tell me what you think. You know that I always demand honesty."

That is what makes it so difficult. I *am* being honest. I continue, "What I mean is there are certain works of writing that are more, er, let's say *perishable* outside their native environment."

"You're saying they don't transplant well?"

"Exactly."

"Can you specifically tell me why you think his novels will not transplant?"

I tell her that *Emilien* has too much of an anecdotal feel. Whereas *The Garden* seems a bit incestuously literary, perhaps too *Italian* in its preoccupations to be understood by, say, an American audience.

Marina stands abruptly, making her way over to the writing desk she claims never to use, and collapses in front of the volume of Tuscan villas opened to the picture of her, something that the last wedding couple who'd rented the villa had specifically requested. She turns toward me and pale eyes bore into mine. "When did you actually read them?" she demands at last.

"Right after you asked me to."

"Then why didn't you say anything *then?*" She sounds harrowed.

"I might have had it been something *you'd* written. But I was worried because I know how much you love and admire Stefano's work." After saying this I realize it's not precisely the truth. Surely I would have balked at criticizing Marina's work as well.

Reflecting for a few moments, she says bluntly, "Well, to be honest, what you say is not so very different from what some of the others have said. And as I am sure you can understand, this lack of appreciation was very hurtful to Stefano. It contributed to his feelings of failure."

"And to your feelings of helplessness," I dare to interject.

She looks rattled for a moment and then manages to respond, "Yes, I suppose this is true."

"Then again, you think his work is great. And your opinion certainly is worth reckoning with."

Her expression grows sterner still. "You tell me this, while you don't really believe in my opinion."

"Let's put it this way: I *do* believe it because I *should* believe it. I believe it because you present yourself as being objective about these things. That you consider Stefano's novels as a reader and a fellow writer and not as somebody romantically involved with the author who feels they must love the work because they love the person."

"For then I would be as much of a romantic as you, wouldn't I?" she says with a sly smile.

"I guess you would." And then in English, I say, "You'd wear your own pair of rose-colored glasses."

"*Cosa?* What is this?" she asks and I explain.

"Ah, *caspita!*" Marina says. "I will certainly remember that one now. Bravo once again for English."

Catching a glimpse of her photo staring back, she shuts the picture book of Tuscan villas with a flicker of displeasure. When she finally glances my way, her dismay and her irascibility are gone and the pinched aspect of sadness has returned.

"Well, what about Calasso? What about Eco?" I ask.

"What about them?"

If Stefano had been long admired by these giants, perhaps they could use their literary influence to help secure an English-language publisher.

Marina nods. "They admire his work, or so they *say.*"

"Well, they came to visit and pay him homage, right?"

"Ah, but he was also a very influential critic. Perhaps they say they love his work merely to *curry favor*," she switches to English for the last two words. Then back to Italian. "We will certainly find out the truth when I ask both of them for help. If they don't come through, then it will prove that their acquaintance with Stefano, and their flattery, was purely about their own gain."

I find myself turning toward the window where the rock came through, where a new pane of glass has replaced the broken one. Noticing this, Marina says wistfully, "At least we don't have to worry anymore about threats against him."

Silent for a while, I then say, "Maybe all those threats were overstated."

She shrugs and admits, "Quite possibly. We think—Carla, my friend in Intelligence, and I—that the rock was an unrelated event; probably it was thrown by some children. It somehow doesn't seem serious. These things can happen."

"But I mean, what about your conspiracy theory? What about the break-in in Paris? What about the men who supposedly wanted to harm your husband? Do you still believe in any of it?"

Marina shrugs. "I don't know what to believe anymore. But I don't have to commit myself. Obviously it doesn't matter."

"Well, it still matters to me!" I remind her. For what had happened in Paris probably ended up causing Ed's death.

Marina crosses her arms in what I interpret as a defensive

gesture. "Yes, this is quite true, I am sorry to say." She looks at me fondly. "Unfortunately, Russell, it might have to remain a mystery. Can you live with that?"

"I don't know if I can."

"I suppose you could go back to Paris and try to find out more."

"I could, this is true. But just remember, my point has always been that one threat probably had absolutely nothing to do with the other. That Ed and I were the victims of circumstance."

"That's certainly a possibility," Marina now concedes.

I wait a moment and then say, "In fact, you might not have invited me here if you didn't think that Ed was mistaken for Stefano."

Before Marina has a chance to answer, the side door buzzes. She looks at me meaningfully and goes to answer it. From well in the distance, I can distinguish Lorenzo's unmistakably baritone voice blending in with Marina's, both speaking English— Lorenzo, albeit, haltingly. Hearing him, my stomach knots and burns. Soon she returns to the living room followed by my dashing *carabiniere* in a crisply pressed uniform and the American consular attaché, a sandy-haired man with a puffy, florid face and a small port-wine stain beginning on the left side of his mouth and ending at the bottom of his chin. He is dressed in a tight sharkskin suit and looks tired and bored. I imagine him living a life of back-to-back official functions and daily alcoholic dissipation. The conversation progresses in English.

"Russell Todaro?" he says to me with the accent on the third syllable. Correcting his pronunciation to accent the first, I identify myself. He reaches into a briefcase and hands me a document with a very official-looking United States of America seal and letterhead. Three paragraphs of legalese demand I hand over both my computer and the unfinished memoir manuscript of the late Edward J. Cannon.

I excuse myself to fetch my laptop computer enclosed in its carrying case. Returning to the library with it I say, "When can I get this back?"

"We should be able to get it to you in a few days, once we go over all your activities on it and look for hidden or deleted files."

Marina glances at me knowingly when the man mentions "deleted files."

The American official resumes, "There is also a demand for the manuscript."

"I've already told them I don't have a copy of the manuscript. As far as I know Mr. Cannon mailed it back to the United States."

Out of the corner of my eye, I can see Marina bristling. When the appointment was rescheduled, she'd tried once again to convince me to give up the manuscript, which I refused to do. She'd finally capitulated, telling me that I could say and do whatever I wanted when the official came, promising not to interfere.

Now she actually surprises me. "There are no manuscript pages in this man's possession. I know this because he was not well at all when he first came here to the villa. Because of the death of his lover."

I can't help but glance at Lorenzo when the word *lover* is uttered and can actually see him flinch.

Marina goes on, "This, of course, was a terrible shock to him, and when he arrived here he slept a great deal because of it. My housekeeper unpacked all his belongings for him. She tells me there was no manuscript among his possessions. She is here, in fact, and if you'd like I will call her. However, she speaks in a Tuscan dialect. So this man"—she points to Lorenzo—"might have to translate your questions and her responses."

It's a brilliant performance. The only problem is in light of what I've already told him, Lorenzo now knows she is lying. I search his features for a sign, but he remains poker-faced. I deeply regret having confessed anything. For how can I be sure that he's completely trustworthy? Beyond his assurances, knowing how conflicted he is about his sexuality, I can't help wondering if he might betray me out of some kind of self-denial, or maybe even self-hatred. The fact that his face looks so expressionless, eyes without any sort of luster, frightens me.

"Well, yes, that would be a good idea," says the official. "Then I will have it for the record."

There is a tremor of silence and Lorenzo finally smiles at the official and responds in Italian, "I don't think you will want this. To question a person who works for her would require approval from the central office."

Marina laughs and says in English to the official, "As you know we have a bureaucracy here in Italy that snakes endlessly through the system."

"To question the lady you might have to delay by as much as two weeks," Lorenzo amends.

"Don't be so official," Marina chafes at Lorenzo in Italian. "He can question her now."

Why is she pushing the issue? I inwardly cringe. Why can't she just leave well enough alone? Then again, maybe no approval is needed to question Carla, and Lorenzo and Marina are merely enacting a charade. Indeed, I can see a faint grin on Lorenzo's face, as though she's been able to communicate something to him. Marina barrels ahead, "And as if the fact that I was once the mayor of Genoa has any bearing on whether or not I would tell the truth. We all know that some of Italy's greatest liars were politicians. Don't we?" she says to the *carabiniere*.

"Not your father," Lorenzo says.

Marina again addresses the official in English, "He says not my father, which is true."

"I know what he's saying," the official says in a frustrated tone. "I've been following your discussion perfectly. I'm quite fluent in Italian, you know. I've been speaking English only because this man is American and I am enforcing American law. Now what is this about your father?"

"He helped write Italy's modern constitution," Lorenzo tells him. "We—the country—mourned him when he died."

Marina nods and affirms this.

Growing fidgety, as though finally realizing he's completely out of his element, the American official asks me to sign one paper that says I release the computer and then another to warrant there is no physical copy of Edward Cannon's unfinished memoir/manuscript in my possession. I hate giving an official signature to my lie, and yet I know there is no going back.

"I will try to give you a call about your laptop within a few days," the man informs me.

"You know the way out," Marina tells Lorenzo, who leads the official away.

We wait until we hear the front door close. And the moment it does Carla enters the room, dressed in a roomy two-piece floral suit. She's lost some weight during the past two weeks and looks pale as she stands before us, pressing her shoulders together as though suddenly uncomfortable in her own skin. "My goodness, but don't you look lovely," Marina tells her with great affection. "Too bad today isn't Sunday. You could go directly to church."

"And pray forgiveness for lying," Carla says humorlessly.

I can't help but compare the two women and note that Stefano's death seems to be taking a greater toll on Carla. Then it suddenly occurs to me, "Oh my God. She was all ready to go on, wasn't she?!"

Marina nods. "She takes this very seriously. Even though, as you know, I was all for your giving them the memoir, Stefano was with you . . . and completely against me. And so was . . ." She glances at Carla.

"Stefano is only reason why I help," Carla blurts out, and continues to stand there looking forlorn.

Regarding her, Marina says, "We're really missing Stefano today, Carla and me. Aren't we?"

Carla's eyes blink with tears. "We are," she affirms in a shaky voice.

"We were, Carla and I, talking about how you really come to love someone the most exquisitely when they're dying. The annoying things about them, their pettiness, the difficult parts of their nature are all washed away and they become pure again and adorable. Witnessing someone die is supposed to be the most natural thing in the world, but it becomes something truly incomprehensible, especially the very last moment when everything stops moving and there is supposed to be grace in the final stillness. No, it's actually horrible to watch."

Marina now reaches for Carla's hand. "And sadly, she and I cannot really give each other comfort about this. Because she's a believer and I am not."

"The *signora* is lapsed," Carla explains with a bit of disdain.

"Lapsed, perhaps, but I would still never enter a church wearing a pair of shorts. Out of profound respect."

"So then you don't believe in God?" I say, fixing my eyes on her.

Marina sighs and shakes her head. "Nor an afterlife. Stefano did, however, which is quite ironic if you knew him. Something else that he and Carla had in common." Marina turns to me. "I assume that you're a believer."

"In some form of divine spirit, yes," I say.

"Let's put it this way. I don't rule it out. I just don't live as though there is anything beyond the grave." Then her eyes blink rapidly with what seems to be a new thought. "Although I do think there might be something. Yes, I think I feel it sometimes when I'm out walking the dogs. Just myself and them. Especially if we're in a wide open space. At that moment it seems to me that there is no longer any hierarchy of being, that we're all just creatures inhabiting the earth, our soul visible in our eyes. I suppose if I had to say there was something divine, something godlike, it would be what is between my dogs and myself when we go for a walk in the fields."

Once Carla leaves us alone again, I mention to Marina, "I've been meaning to ask you about something Carla said to me the night Stefano died."

Marina frowns, waiting to hear.

"She said that I actually knew somebody who might have helped Stefano's books be translated into English, but refused. Who is this?"

At first Marina looks surprised, but then her brow crinkles in bewilderment. "Ah, yes? Why didn't you ask her then?"

"I did, but she didn't know the name."

"Russell, I have no idea what she means. But I certainly hope to find out."

Because the air in Tuscany is so dry, as has been predicted, the temperature does a nosedive in the evening, and the villa is beset by the first hint of autumn, whose official beginning is still a few weeks away. After a very quiet dinner, Marina and I are sitting in the library. The villa's enormous rooms ache with the early chill, and she has built a fire, which now roars before us. It almost seems that we are both separately musing that Stefano's death and my computer being seized mark a kind of turning point. Perhaps because of this—and maybe even because of the abrupt change in weather—Marina says, "So what are you planning to do now?"

Could she be suggesting that my visit should come to an end?

"You mean where do I plan to go?"

This seems to catch her unawares, which in turns surprises me. "No. I told you to stay as long as you like. That hasn't changed."

I remind her that that was before Stefano passed away.

"As if his passing would alter my invitation."

And then I realize on the contrary, Stefano's death might make her more anxious for me to remain. "It's hard to know. Nobody has ever invited me to stay anywhere this long."

"Excuse me. What about in Paris?"

"Yeah, but Ed had motivations."

"Who is to say that I don't?" Marina winks at me, looking a bit embarrassed. "In Paris when I heard that your Italian was pretty good and learned that you didn't really want to go back to America, I thought I would invite you here and perhaps at some point bring up doing our translation."

"And if Ed hadn't died?"

"Moot. You simply would've gone back to America with him."

This is certainly true.

Marina goes on, "Now that you've signed a paper saying that you don't have the manuscript and have no more obligations toward it, editorially speaking, what about your own writing?"

"Well, now I don't even have a computer."

"Don't be evasive, my friend." She smiles.

I ponder this for a moment. "I told you I don't have any ideas, good ideas I mean, for a book."

"And as I told *you*, I think you've distracted yourself from these ideas. Now you must take the risk, try to work on your own material until you can bring it to completion. To face the thing I know that frightens you the most, the terrifying prospect of something you've wrought being completely ignored by the rest of the world."

"That's easy for you to say—"

"Excuse me," Marina interrupts to inform me, "my first two novels were completely ignored. And remember that my Stefano knew this disappointment acutely. But acceptance and attention is not why we should write. To illustrate this, let me quote my kind, humble Rilke." She opens up a drawer and pulls out a piece of paper. "This is what I read to myself when I feel I cannot write another word." She reads in English.

Surely all art is the result of one's having been in danger, of having gone through an experience all the way to the end, to where no one can go any further. The further one goes, the more private, the more personal, the more singular an experience becomes, and the thing one is making is, finally, the necessary, irrepressible, and, as nearly as possible, definitive utterance of this singularity. Therein lies the enormous aid the work of art brings to the life of the one who must make it.

Without looking at me, Marina opens the desk drawer and returns the piece of paper.

"Well, I guess that clinches your point, doesn't it?" I say.

She shrugs. "I'm concerned that even though you've told them you don't have the memoir, you're still going to read and reread it, like worrying a wound, and hold on to it like some important relic." She goes quiet for a moment and then says, "My main reason for wanting you to give it up to them is I knew how afraid you were to let it go."

"That's probably accurate."

"Why not write your own memoir about the relationship . . . and be as truthful as possible. Along the way spice it up with the stories of all your ill-fated love affairs. Then your book could be compared to his. Maybe his book would create an interest in yours."

"Nobody's going to care about my memoir, much less my love affairs. I'm not anybody of note."

"It's all in the doing," Marina instructs. "Ordinary lives can often be the most beautifully rendered."

Conflicted, I fall silent, listening to the crackling fire. Maybe I should.

She gets up from her chair, comes over, and sits down next to me. "You know, Russell, this afternoon I was resting with my dogs and thinking about our conversation earlier in the day. And I actually began to wonder if Stefano's novels really aren't as good as I want to believe, and so perhaps should not be translated into English but rather left in Italian, merely footnotes to the literature of this time. And maybe I should stop trying to justify his work to feel worthy of him. Perhaps the same goes with your fascination with married men," she exclaims at last. "If you'd only choose a more distinct path for your personal life, then you more easily might make the choice to continue with your writing career."

Suddenly I make a decision. "Wait here. I'll be right back," I tell her.

I hurry into my bedroom and reach into one of Stefano's bookshelves, where, behind Italo Svevo's *La Coscienza di Zeno*, I've concealed the manuscript, whose first and last pages are now dusty with old plaster. I carry it back into the library, the ninety-page excerpt on the top. I hand everything to Marina, who dutifully reads the first page of the excerpt. She smiles, bemused, and hands it back to me. "Why are you showing me this? I told you before I don't want to read it."

"I just want you to take a look, a last look at it." I glance at the fire and then stare back at her.

"You're not going to do anything so stupid?"

"You told me that I'm holding on to it, that I'm afraid to give it up. Maybe I just need to be rid of it altogether."

"Absolutely not! Surrender it to his editors and let them do what they want with it. Let it spur you to write your own version. But no matter what, you cannot destroy another author's work."

"Even if I knew he'd want me to?"

"In his life he wanted you to!" Marina exclaims.

"Well, you don't believe in life after death," I remind her.

Looking flustered, she says, "Whatever is published about you, you can bear, Russell. You'll have to think of it as the price you pay for becoming involved with a famous author."

Marina and I stare at each other. "Unless I do this, just like you say, it *is* going to get in the way of my life."

With a resigned shrug, Marina ceases trying to persuade me. I take the manuscript and go and stand by the fireplace. She watches me with curious horror.

Hesitating, I say, "Perhaps Stefano would have even approved."

"Don't bring him into it," Marina warns me. "He's dead."

"And so is Ed."

"I think you're making a mistake, Russell," she says one last time.

"I think I have to do this," I say.

"Well, then, I wash my hands of it!"

"I take full responsibility." I divide the manuscript into approximately ten sections and begin slipping it five or ten leaves at a time into the flames.

The pages buckle immediately from the heat, turn the caramel color of toasted coconut, and then pop into conflagration. For a few moments I can understand the orgiastic glee of pyromania. But soon the sense of my purpose grows heavy, even somewhat remorseful. And when I realize there is no going back, I have a sudden aversion to what I'm doing and actually stop to agonize: What have I wrought here? But soon I'm lulled back into watching the words burning, lovely nouns and adjectives such as *lapidary, remote, binoculars, tension, recluse, steam, June, tempest;* and the delicious gerunds: *charring, blistering, pondering, demonizing, scumbling, shambling, professing, edging.*

Marina, transfixed, watches the manuscript burn and finally says, "This reminds me of once when I was on an ocean liner and threw flowers into the sea."

"Watching them disappear," I murmur.

"Yes."

And when the last of the pages have finally burned down to ashes, Marina says to me, "Well, now, I guess, there's nothing stopping you. The brace has been removed. You have no choice but to go forward on your own."

Fourteen

~

"I WOULD NEVER CONTRADICT the *signora*." Lorenzo speaks over his shoulder as the motorcycle wends its way down the Villa Guidi's driveway and begins following the curving backroad that eventually leads into the city. He drives slowly to make sure I can hear him. "Even if I was certain that she was misleading this official from America. Out of respect I would never do such a thing." When we arrive at a stop sign, he brakes and balances the bike with one leg, allowing the engine to fall into chattering idle. "And besides, you forgot to tell me s*he* knew you had this manuscript. Which, by the way, you easily could have hidden the moment you arrived so that even her housekeeper would never find it. They could have been the innocent hosts of a literary thief, after all." He grins. "Now don't forget I did promise to help you in this."

Lorenzo faces forward again, but still not engaging the gears. Softly speaking into his ear, I tell him I'd actually worried that during the meeting with the American attaché, he'd publicly unmask my deception as a perverse way of denying his attraction to me.

"What?" He raises his helmet shield, turns completely around so that his lips are inches from mine, his startling eyes boring into me. "Are you mad?" He kisses me belligerently. "Don't make me out to be so crazy/complicated. Why can't I tell you that I am unhappy because I know that there is nothing I can do, no other choice for a life other than the one I have? Don't you want honesty? Isn't this what you Americans always look for?"

Without waiting for an answer, Lorenzo faces forward again, revs the motor, and we take off toward the ramparts of the walled city. He makes a right turn at a gelateria named Gelatone. I happen to remember Marina explaining this ice cream store once was called *Benito*, a name that had to be changed to conform to the democratic climate of post World War II, when her father was helping Italy write itself a new constitution. We follow the ring road halfway around the city, passing a barracks-like train station built during Il Duce's reign, then a curving row of discount computer stores, and head diagonally down a street called Castracani. I take the name for its literal meaning, "to castrate dogs." When we pause at a traffic light, I ask Lorenzo if this name has any significance, and instead of just responding that the street actually honors a local fifteenth-century aristocrat, he asserts (as Marina had) that in Italy male dogs are seldom castrated. "Why do you ask this, anyway?"

"Because where are we headed?" I prompt, reminding him that our final destination is the apartment of his colleague, Paolo, who sometimes has sex with the transsexual we spotted out in Torre del Lago.

"Ah, of course." He picks up on the reference. "Well, the sex change isn't a castration per se. In fact they find a way to keep the nerves of the penis head and fold them into the fig, so that they still have sensation."

"How do you know all this anatomy?"

"It's common."

Squeezing the arm of his jacket: "You seem to know a lot about sex changes!"

"I said before, I have no interest in trans!" he insists. "You know, you're beginning to sound like a woman . . . for once!" which stings me momentarily into silence. And then I realize that this is perhaps the way a woman might feel when a man she's sleeping with unconvincingly denies an interest in other men. Or perhaps when a man that a man is sleeping with unconvincingly denies an interest in women. I cringe.

The light changes, curtailing any further conversation. We drive along a seemingly endless commercial thoroughfare that in its way reminds me of a generic commercial zone of hair salons and hardware stores and nurseries that one might see on the outskirts of any American urban center, although a somewhat more quaint—to my eyes anyway—equivalent of American mini-mall sprawl. But then we pass under the arch of an old Roman aqueduct, proving that we could be nowhere else but Italy. Lorenzo eventually veers off onto a side street and follows a small canal filled with oily-looking water that, in the early evening, gives off a rainbow sheen. At last we arrive at the Mediterranean-style two-level apartment complex where Paolo and his family live, but who are now on vacation in Sardinia.

I've always felt that our sex life is cheapened by the fact that Lorenzo and I have to keep borrowing different venues, that neither of us has a regular place to go. Why did I even agree to this? I wonder dispiritedly after Lorenzo and I have finished making perfunctory love. We are lying in Paolo's bed, facing a dresser that features framed photographs of the round-faced man with his wife and two small children, in a room redolent of lily-of-the-valley perfume. I feel cheap, unworthy even of myself. I suddenly think of Ed's manuscript twisting and charring in the fire, his words melting into black, reliving the sense of compulsion and regret, compulsion to break free of an obviously unhealthy pattern, but regret because, when it was all over, when I could see the ghostly outline of Ed's pages in the pile of ashes, I began to lament my impulse to destroy the writings of someone with whom I was once intimate.

Naked in his colleague's bedroom, arms cocked behind his head, Lorenzo finally breaks the silence. "You said you were afraid that I might go back on what I promised, tell that official you had the manuscript. It makes me wonder: Did you ever love somebody who betrayed you like this?"

I hesitate a moment, ever reluctant to speak of Ed's betrayal vis-à-vis Michel, or how Michel callously broke off our affair. And so instead I tell Lorenzo the story of the relationship that drove me to leave America, the Argentinean priest at Trinity Church in Manhattan's Financial District, the man whose ex-lover claimed he lied about his sero-conversion.

Lorenzo is perplexed. "But what did you do?"

"Of course I confronted him. But he denied it and said his ex-lover was delusional. He assured me I had nothing to worry about."

"But you couldn't believe him, could you?"

One Sunday morning after James left to serve mass, I

searched through his drawers and cabinets. Underneath the sink I found a cache of orange pill containers lumped together in a plastic bag; they seemed hastily stashed away. The dates were recent, however, and the address of the dispensing pharmacy was located in another part of Manhattan. I remember holding the bottles and recognizing the names of antiviral and antifungal medications I'd read about, gently shaking the contents and hearing the report of dozens of pills. It was like listening to a distant death rattle, like the clatter of rats swarming the streets below me, the streets that had been broken and fractured in the wake of a terrorist attack.

Lorenzo lies there nearly inert, listening to my story, his silence transmitting that now he's wary of me. At last he says, "I can understand how you might have gone that far with somebody, wanting to believe what you knew wasn't true. But when you finally knew . . . he was still doing something so wrong! Why didn't you get out of it?"

I didn't have to. By the time I confronted him, James had quit his job, packed his things, and left town.

Scissoring his legs free of the bed sheets, Lorenzo sits up and says, "Did you tell the church what he did to you?"

"I called them to find out where he went, but they wouldn't say. I figured he'd already told them that a crazy man might call them with accusations, just like his former lover did."

"So we can assume that he's probably out there infecting people."

"I hope he isn't."

"You hope he *isn't?*" Lorenzo repeats. And in that moment, a thought chills me: Now this man is probably done with me.

Telling the story has once again brought me to the fire, and this time it's as if I'm throwing myself in. I admit to Lorenzo, "I knew what I was getting into. There were warning signs. But I didn't listen to them."

"Why not?"

I suddenly remember the way Ed described it to me: *I just wanted him to fuck me as he was. As I was. And what I actually think I realized then, the burning truth was that getting caught up in the power of that kind of sex makes everything that goes against the grain diluted. You see, Russell, in my life I've always chased pure experience. And so I took my moment of raw passion and it was absolutely divine.*

Now I wish I had told Ed the story of my own recklessness, that back in New York, by those huge windows overlooking a devastated neighborhood, fully aware of what I was doing, I gave in to the priest and fell under the momentary fantasy of believing that everything this man had to offer me was sacred rather than contaminated. I remember how he used to whisper to me, "I'm charging you up, Russell, I'm charging you up," eventually deciphering that he wanted to pass the virus onto me, like a jolt of new life to a dying cell. And what I've been unable to admit to myself until now is that, under the delusional spell of lust that I foolishly mistook for destiny, I wanted it as much as he wanted to give it. I wanted the conversion.

Lorenzo is looking at me in horror.

"It's okay," I tell him. "I'm fine. I've been tested twice since then."

Shaking his head, he says, "But how could you make love to anyone like that . . . in such a way?"

Knowing there was no explanation that would satisfy him, I end up saying, "Sometimes death, or the idea of it, can be seductive."

Lorenzo shakes his head. "Now, this I do not understand. To me, this sounds like insanity."

Of course he's right, I think in the midst of my shame.

Tonight Marina has invited me to be her escort at one of the villa's weddings that is celebrating the second marriage of somebody very high up in the prime minister's cabinet. Many guests from as far as Rome and the Amalfi coast are in attendance; it's even rumored that the prime minister himself is slated to arrive. When Lorenzo drops me off, the villa is swarming with people, and he claims to recognize several James Bondian–looking men wearing form-fitting suits and wraparound sunglasses standing with checklists at the various entrances or milling among the well-heeled guests. "I work with these *ragazzi*," he tells me. "They must be moonlighting."

Just as I am climbing off the motorcycle, Lorenzo turns to me. "Look, I need to tell you something . . . because I may not be seeing you for some time." And of course I immediately think of how Michel so effortlessly broke off the relationship after our trip to the south of France.

"What is it?" I say without much life in my voice. I try to assure myself that this time around I will feel more relieved than rejected.

He goes on to say that the *carabinieri* have continued to interrogate the thief who broke into the villa's *dependence*. Earlier in the day they managed to extract a vital confession: that in fact, he had come to the villa not to rob it, but rather to do away with Stefano.

"What are you saying?" I cry.

"I was there when he told them," Lorenzo explains gravely.

"It seems that somebody by reading one of the *signora*'s books learned about a passageway into the villa that is accessible from that old building the thief broke into; that old building, I happen to know, has no alarm system."

I stare at him, flabbergasted.

"Remember, we found the big knife in his truck." Lorenzo pauses, adjusting his helmet. "Anyhow, he finally told us that he was planning to come in at night, cut the *signore*'s throat very quietly, and leave without being detected. But then he heard somebody, got confused, not scared—because they don't get scared, these people—and went back to his car, drove into the statue, and hit his head."

I stand there for a moment, trying to digest the news. Finally, I ask, "Has Marina been told?"

Lorenzo shakes his head. "As far as I know, not yet."

"When are you going to tell her?"

Lorenzo turns up his gloved palms. "It's certainly not for me to tell her. I assume my superior is calling her. Although probably tomorrow so as not to upset her during the party. But you must see, Russell, that if the target of the assassination is now dead, the matter is no longer urgent after all, is it?"

"I don't know, Lorenzo. I don't know what to say."

Hesitating a moment, staring at me from behind his Ray-Bans, with a glance toward some of his colleagues, Lorenzo opts to shake my hand rather than kiss me—as any two male friends in Italy would do without provoking suspicion—a clear sign that he is no longer comfortable with our "arrangement." I realize I set myself up and perhaps even curried this rejection but still feel sad, knowing that I probably won't be seeing him again. I watch Lorenzo motoring off down the driveway and, with a wave to a man in wraparound sunglasses standing by the gates, he disappears into the windy lane.

Marina is standing near the kitchen dressed in a turquoise ball gown that ruffles into two gossamer tiers near her ankles. "You're late!" she accuses as I slink in the door. She looks stern yet somehow unconcerned, and so I assume she has not learned the latest bit of news. I find her face a bit overly made up, her natural beauty masked by foundation powder and eyeliner. "You were supposed to be ready and on my arm a quarter of an hour ago."

I apologize and hurry to my bedroom to put on a navy-blue linen suit that Ed had bought me in a moment of largesse a week before he died. I'm not at leisure to ponder Lorenzo's strange news of the prisoner's confession; nor does his sudden loss of interest in me have a chance to sink in.

I've witnessed several of the hired weddings by now, and this one seems immediately more upscale than the rest. A man with a manicured beard in a starched white jacket is shucking fresh oysters, there are four huge wheels of aged parmigiano equipped with small spadelike utensils with which the guests are elegantly breaking off shards of cheese. Out on the loggia, linen-covered tables that normally are stocked with bottles of good Venetian prosecco are now chock full of Dom Pérignon. There are hors d'oeuvre–sized puffed pastries, platters of pâté and crudité arranged in the semblance of sunflowers. The wedding cake is on display: six feet high, ivory-colored, and studded with bright globes of fruit so thickly glazed with sugar it looks encased in ice. Marina whispers to me that the caterers are among the best of the Milanese companies; and because Milan is close to the Piedmont, we could expect at the sit-down dinner a fresh fettuccine prepared with shavings of prized white truffles from Alba. And the villa's proximity to the fish markets of Viareggio will guarantee an elaborate seafood antipasto.

We stroll among the guests, who, for the most part, are beautifully turned out. As is often the case at Italian weddings, there are some people dressed according to the latest fashion trend. This year, the wrinkled look is in, and several younger men with spiky hair are wearing untucked tuxedo shirts that look as though they've been washed and wadded into a ball before being allowed to dry. Marina is recognized by quite a few people, politicians and civilians alike. Someone whispers to her that the prime minister will not be in attendance and she shrugs and says, "*Meno male*"—thank goodness.

Responding to a request to fetch her a champagne cocktail, I'm slinking my way through a crowd of guests when I see Marina hurrying in my direction. "Put those glasses down for a moment and come with me," she orders and hurries out the door of the dining room and into the marbled corridor that leads to the kitchen.

"Somebody working in the kitchen took a phone message from my friend at the *carabinieri*. He says it's urgent. Since you are spending so much time with this Lorenzo, I thought you might know what this call is about."

I nod and say I do.

"Explain it to me then!" she orders.

And I elaborate on the thief's plan to enter the main house through the secret passage that was once used by the Jews.

Marina looks baffled. "No, this is impossible! How would he know this?" I look at her and I must appear doubtful because she says, "Go on, tell me how!"

"Shoot the messenger," I say with a groan. "Marina, you describe it all in *Conversion*."

Marina resolutely shakes her head; however, when she speaks she sounds more uncertain. "I describe the passageway but certainly not everywhere it goes."

"What do you mean?" I say in English. "You describe where it goes quite plainly."

"No one has ever tried to come into the house in this way . . . the Jewish way," she clarifies angrily.

"Well, now obviously somebody has. In fact, we both should have thought of this before. Especially while Stefano was alive and under threat."

Marina clasps her hands together and announces, "And now I must go back into the party. I will see you in a few minutes!"

I walk to the front of the villa and sit down on the limestone steps that Marina and I first sat on after she confessed her fear that the men who had broken into our hotel room were looking for her rather than for us, when she pointed out the convent where Puccini's sister once lived. One of the caterers has just finished lining the driveway with potted candles and is now kindling the last of them in a curving kilometer of flickering light; the sweeping scene is eerie and somehow pagan. I think back over my afternoon with Lorenzo. It certainly is not lost on me that he chose the moment we were parting to deliver the news about the man who tried to break into the villa. Obviously he elected to orchestrate such a diversion, making it easier to go off without having to intimate whether or not we'd be getting together again. I can't help wondering if I hadn't detailed the denouement of my relationship with the priest would Lorenzo have told me earlier about the thief's confession? I guess it doesn't really matter.

Soon it's one o'clock in the morning. After having dined and danced, the last straggling guests are leaving. From where we sit in the library, Marina and I can hear the sound of the departing cars crunching over the gravel that sometimes gets sprayed when somebody, probably a bit too inebriated to drive, leans heavily on the gas pedal. A few of the caterers are still completing their cleanup, packing their trucks with the hired plates, glassware, and cutlery, periodically crisscrossing, white-jacketed, in the background. Marina has decided to change into her bathrobe and bedroom slippers. She is saying, "Russell, my book has been read by many thousands of people all over the world. No has ever dared to try and come in here by that means. Ask Carla, she will tell you!" She pulls the folds of her bathrobe more tightly around herself.

And I tell her, "If you go back and look at what you've written, you'll see that it's all described very carefully."

Marina shakes her head. "I know my own work."

"I've read it a lot more recently than you. At this moment I think I probably know it better," I am bold enough to say.

Marina dismisses my statement. "You know, I find it alarming that since you've arrived, many odd and unusual things have happened. You have brought strangers into the house. A rock has come through the window. And now this crazy news."

"But neither the rock nor this news has anything to do with me."

"The villa has always been a safe place." Now she stares at me fixedly.

In the jittery silence, I begin to realize how angry she is and wonder if it has less to do with the "odd and unusual things,"

the strangers brought into the house, than the fact that I've pronounced Stefano's novels too provincial and unconvincing to
have an alternative life in another language. My honesty was
something Marina had demanded; and yet, in light of a very
pressing obligation to her dead husband's legacy, she must be
bitterly disappointed in my unwillingness to help her with the
translations. I suppose it could be argued that I've taken her
generosity for granted; or worse, still, that I'd taken a cavalier
attitude toward Stefano's work. Indeed, for she suddenly says
very simply in English, "Maybe it would be better if you went
on to your next destination."

Shocked, I feel my face flushing. I hear myself stammer,
"I . . . can do that. I can even leave tomorrow if you want me
to."

"There's no rush," she assures me with a brittle smile. "Just
figure out where you'd want to go next." With that, she gets up,
kisses me on the cheek, retires to her bedroom, and shuts the
door behind her.

Shamed and humiliated, I sit there in the beautiful library,
my favorite room in the villa, feeling like a small, insignificant
worm. I keep watching her door, thinking that Marina will
surely have second thoughts about having dismissed me in such
a way and will soon come out and capitulate. How could she be
asking me to leave when, just a few days ago, she was warmly
encouraging me to stay? Soon the bar of light showing in the
gap between her door and the floor is extinguished.

Back in my room, I lie awake for hours trying to figure out
what my next move should be and where I can go. I'm now in a
bind; just the day before I'd informed the tenants who were sub-
letting my apartment in Brooklyn that they could stay from six

to nine months longer. Although I know I might have to, it seems unfair to call back and renege on my agreement. Then I admit to myself that I'm just not ready to go back to America. Especially in such a state of rejection: first Lorenzo, and now Marina.

When the clock finally strikes six A.M., unable to restrain myself any longer, I fish out the number Michel gave me, phone Paris, and wake him up. He sounds delighted to hear from me, and I'm actually able to make mindless conversation for a few minutes without mentioning my predicament.

Michel informs me that I can take the train from Tuscany to Milan and then northward to Paris and that I'm welcome to stay with him until I figure out what to do. What other choice do I have but to accept his offer on the spot?

Yes, I'm relieved to have an alternative, but I'm still distressed and angry over Marina's directive that I move on. Needing an activity to channel this feeling of suddenly being persona non grata, I begin gathering together my belongings and packing my suitcase. When I finally finish it's close to seven A.M., and I manage to doze off until noon.

I shower and shave and find Marina in the kitchen making a champagne risotto, assiduously stirring a pan filled with arborio rice while alternately adding chicken broth and some leftover Dom Pérignon. The aromas are delicious and momentarily comforting. When I come in, she smiles warmly as though nothing untoward has happened. Looking at me fondly over a pair of pewter reading glasses, she assures me she is no longer cross with me. "I'm sorry I reacted the way I did. Of course I don't want you to go rushing off anywhere!" she exclaims. "You are more than welcome to stay as long as you like."

But now, hurt and angry, I try to convince myself that I can no longer take Marina at her word, that this great show of civility is merely her way of smoothing things over. The probability is she still wants my stay at the villa to come to an end. And so I tell her I've arranged to go back to Paris immediately.

Her eyes widen. "To be with the Frenchman?"

I look down at my feet. "I can't afford a hotel."

"So, as I told you, remain here at villa," she insists. "I apologized to you already, haven't I?" Marina now exudes infinite patience.

I look at her squarely. "I already told him I'm coming."

She nods stiffly at the news, and then, resuming her vigil over the risotto, warns, "That Frenchman is a viper. I saw him. And I can assure you he'll never leave his wife for you."

"I know he won't ever leave her," I say. "But it's going to be very different now."

Still staring down at her rice, she says, "Yes, you're going to be staying with him, that's how different it's going to be!"

"What other choice do I have, Marina?"

"Well, if you don't want to stay here, you can go back to America."

"I don't have the plane fare."

She now looks at me kindly. "I can easily lend you the money, no problem at all. I'd rather see you do that than go back to Paris."

I tell her that I'm just not ready to go back to America and that my apartment is still sublet.

She approaches me and now I can see the gloss of a tear in her eyes. She takes my hand. "I know that I've insulted you, that I made you feel unwelcome."

"But you also got me thinking, Marina. I really *can't* stay here forever. At some point I have to start considering what I'm going to do workwise, moneywise. I certainly can't count on getting any of Ed's insurance money, not that I necessarily want to."

Marina turns away for a moment to put down the wooden spoon and then faces me again. "Well, if you must, go to Paris. But once you get settled there, you should begin trying to write again. Find yourself a routine and work every day. I think that if you write your way directly into what has happened during the last year, it may even help you figure out the rest of what you don't already know."

This sounds terribly pat. And I have to refrain from saying so, from declaring it a nervy suggestion from somebody who has trouble admitting to a certain truth in her own work. Hugging me, Marina once again takes up her wooden spoon and taps my shoulder with it like a magic wand. "Lunch should be ready soon." Then something seems to occur to her. "Oh, and by the way, a courier came earlier this morning with your computer. It's in the library. You certainly couldn't have gone off without *that*."

Marina returns to stirring, her spoon moving gently, almost effortlessly in the thickening risotto. And I have the distinct impression that after apologizing for having irrevocably dismissed me, she is now at peace.

Part Three

Fifteen

~

SIX MONTHS LATER, I'm in New York City, standing at a
penthouse window, watching billowing robes of snow
swirling in the columns of air between buildings, flakes
sticking hard and fast to the frozen ground twenty-six stories
below. I'm hosting a cocktail party given at the home of a
modern-art dealer to honor a ninety-year-old doyenne, a patron
of Italian culture. Moving through the various rooms whose
walls hold Kandinskys and Mirós and De Koonings and Pol-
locks, I'm handing out glasses of champagne and making introductions. I returned to America two weeks ago to begin
working in the media department of the Italian Cultural Institute, a job for which Marina had recommended me.

Several Italians with New York City residences, having heard
that I am a friend of hers, have already asked, "What's she like?"
as though inquiring about a legendary actress. "A tough
cookie," I reply, using one of Marina's favorite American expressions, going on to say that she is frank and assured of her own
intelligence and her place in the world.

"Well, she's this way because she's from that *family*," some-body remarks, going on to say that the Vezzolis, although hardly aristocrats in noble title, rather are a political aristocracy, which in certain circles has more currency. Marina is reputed to keep her distance from almost everyone; the fact that she has allowed me to get to close to her is quite out of the ordinary. Managing to smile, I wonder if I ever really did get close to her at all.

I'm ferrying a silver tray of champagne flutes that have just been filled to the brim in the kitchen, placing them down on a linen-covered banquet table when I hear my name called. I turned to find Annie Calhoun dressed in a pinstriped business suit, a pearly-gray scarf loosely wound around her liver-spotted neck. She wears a substantially large diamond engagement ring. Last I knew she was "very single," as Ed described her. Then again, perhaps the ring is a family heirloom.

Glancing at my watch, I say, "Hello, Annie. I'm really busy at the moment. I told you I won't be able to talk to you until all this is winding down."

She glances around the party. "I actually have somewhere else to be. Can't you spare a few minutes to talk to me now?"

"I can try, but remember, this is work for me."

Interlocking her arms and grabbing one elbow with a long, veiny hand, she says with annoyance, "I didn't realize you'd be employed by the party. I thought you'd be at it!"

"Why don't you have a glass of champagne?"

"I don't drink," she informs me.

"I should have figured that."

"Don't be a wise guy, Russell."

"Then let me get one for myself."

As I fetch myself a glass of Moët, I feel Annie watching me

keenly. When I rejoin her, she says, "I used to drink along with the best of them, but I had to give it up for health reasons. In those days writers drank. Nowadays they work out like you do," she says somewhat disdainfully.

I glance around the party, figuring that I might be able to spare a few moments. "So what's on your mind?"

Just as Annie is about to tell me, my boss comes over and asks me to make a few introductions to the honored doyenne. Annie looks disgruntled; I promise to return quickly. I finish my various party obligations and grab another glass of champagne. But then I have to wait while Annie chats with the party's hostess. Finally she breaks away and faces me.

"I have a copy of a note Ed sent to Maxine Hong Kingston right before he died," she informs me. "He mentions that you, Russell, were urging him to publish a ninety-page excerpt of his memoir."

"That's correct. Go on." I begin gulping down champagne.

"And he wrote that he was going to listen to you and do so."

"I told you before that I admired parts of the memoir. This is not news."

"But if *you* thought and if *he* thought a large portion of the book was ready for publication, then where is it? It would not have just disappeared."

"Annie, I already explained to you that toward the end of his life our relationship was deteriorating. And that the more he withdrew from me, the less and less he asked for my advice about work." Cringing, I say, "I have no idea what happened to any of it."

Annie shakes her head. "I just know you're lying. And I don't believe that Marina Vezzoli's maid went through your things and found nothing. Because she"—the executrix pauses—"would have her own reasons for interfering."

"Marina has nothing to do with this!" I insist, nearly giving myself away when I say, "In fact she was actually hounding me to send the whole thing back to you," and switch gears and amend, "before she found out I didn't have it."

Annie pauses for a moment to collect her thoughts. Her inky eyes drill into me. "Unfortunately, Russell, Marina has you completely fooled here."

The words break over me like shards of ice. "What do you mean, 'completely fooled'?"

"Marina is married to another writer. Am I correct?"

"He died at the end of the summer. His name was Stefano Marzotto."

"Well, did you happen to know that this Stefano Marzotto met Ed in the South of France at a book panel discussion?"

I remember hearing something vaguely similar but couldn't pinpoint from where or whom. And then it dawns on me. During our last breakfast at the Parisian hotel the day he died, Ed had mentioned something about a man at a literary conference introducing himself as a friend of Marina's.

"Stefano tried to get Ed to help him find an English-language publisher. But Ed didn't like his novels and refused to recommend them to any of his editor friends. This apparently pissed off Marina."

Now I recall Carla mentioning somebody who might have helped Stefano get his books translated but who "wouldn't."

Totally bewildered, I reply, "But Ed and I discussed Marina at length the day he died. He never mentioned anything about this."

"I honestly don't think the man told Ed he was married to her; Ed didn't say anything to me, either." Annie pauses and then resumes. "I think this Stefano Marzotto was probably too proud to use his wife as a calling card."

"Okay, then how did you figure out he was connected to Marina?"

"After I arrived in Paris at your hotel, Marina came up to me. In the midst of everything, she actually was nervy enough to ask if I could help with this translation business. Obviously I had other things on my mind."

It was all beginning to make sense now.

"I *do* remember Ed telling me the man's books were appalling," Annie rejoins.

"Ed's Italian wasn't really good enough to judge the quality of literature in the original," I point out. "As far as I know he never read Italian for pleasure the way he read in French."

"Perhaps, but I still got the impression that Marina and her husband looked at Ed as their last resort to get the book in translation."

Before I became the last resort, I think to myself. So, when I'd asked for clarification of what Carla had said to me the night Stefano died, Marina acted as though she didn't know what I was talking about. Now I have to reconsider that all of her cynical observations of Ed may have been tainted by the fact that he stymied her hopes to get Stefano's work in translation. Perhaps Ed *was* right. Perhaps she *had* recognized him immediately in the breakfast room at the Hotel Birague and acted as though she hadn't.

We are once again interrupted. This time an elderly lady dressed in a navy-blue suit keels over onto the woman who is sitting next to her on a sofa. Even from where I stand I can see that the victim's face has turned an unnatural shade of gray and she seems to be struggling for breath.

"Choking," I hear somebody gasp. "Help her."

"Oh my God!" Annie exclaims, watching the proceedings for a moment. "Russell, I can't stand to watch this."

"Is she here with anybody?" another person asks.

My male colleagues and my boss immediately crowd around the woman. One of the men gets behind, straps his arms under her bosom, and jerks up, trying to dislodge whatever might be blocking her breathing. It doesn't work and the victim's struggling grows weaker. I'm only dimly aware of Annie saying, "I want to leave now." The scene has taken on a ghostly familiarity, bringing me back to the moment when I woke up and found Ed terrifyingly, serenely dead. I now see his death mask as clearly as I see the face of this stricken soul, and for an instant the room reels away from me and I nearly lose my balance. The disequilibrium passes just as the lady is forced to expel a tangled piece of prosciutto that goes flying across the room, the sight of it inducing a few screams.

"That was really awful!" Annie exclaims as she scurries toward the coatrack. "I'll give you a call first thing tomorrow. We'll finish our discussion then."

My apartment in Gravesend is sublet until the first of April, and I've taken a temporary share in Park Slope. During the past two weeks I've been meaning to stop by my original place to get whatever mail has accumulated. I finally made arrangements with the tenants to do so tonight after I finish working the party. However, when I leave the Upper East Side penthouse and start trudging through eight inches of fluffy snow piled up on the sidewalks, it's obvious that my decision to venture out to Gravesend is ill-timed. Sitting on the F train, crossing under the East River into Brooklyn, I notice few passengers; the weather being what it is, I seriously consider just going home, putting off my visit until the following evening.

But then I get to mulling over the conversation with Annie and, in particular, that Marina seems to have been less than honest about her dealings with Ed. I try and reconstruct the night I burned his manuscript and wonder about Marina's role in my final act of sacrilege. She'd certainly been willing to go along with the charade of pretending that I'd never brought Ed's memoir with me to Italy and had even enlisted Carla who was prepared to say that she'd gone through my things when I first arrived and had found nothing resembling a manuscript. Who knows, perhaps by helping me conceal the manuscript Marina was posthumously punishing Ed for having been so ungenerous toward Stefano. And even though she *appeared* to object to my destroying Ed's final creation, perhaps she was secretly joyful that I was doing so. Not to mention that Marina was hardly a fan of the memoir as a literary form. Suddenly, I realize I've traveled several stations past the one where I should have disembarked in order to return to my sublet. I think: Well, now I may as well continue on to Gravesend.

I stayed in Paris for several months. I spent a few weeks with Michel, who then arranged for me to borrow an apartment that a close friend of his wasn't using. He did everything he could to convince me to remain; he offered to use his connections to get me jobs teaching English, doing translations, while promising a *nearly* full-time relationship. I took Marina's advice and tried to write every day, but in general, it went very slowly and very painfully.

Anything I managed to squeeze out didn't seem to be mine, but rather something anybody could do. Part of my difficulty was remembering what Ed had written about me in his memoir, his droning doubt that I, being the sort of person who automatically puts his love life ahead of his writing life, would not go very far in my career. Not only did I find this demoralizing, I began to wonder if my anger over such a harsh assessment was yet another motivating factor in my burning the manuscript. If Ed's sentiments about my lack of commitment to the craft were brought before the world, wouldn't he be publicly damning me to a fallow creative life? And yet here I was having great difficulty writing anyway. I tried to assure myself that Ed had sworn to never publishing his book before he was completely satisfied with it. But then I found myself wondering if his dying wish might have been different, reflecting a more desperate desire to live on in any way he possibly could.

Laurence, whom I saw from time to time, had accepted my being in Paris; she even asked me to house-sit while the family went to Martinique for a vacation. The day before they left, while Michel was picking up the children at a ballet lesson, Laurence and I were sitting in the Pléiade library. She was going over a list of what I needed to know about the apartment: which plants needed to be watered when; the feeding time for the childrens' tropical fish; and when the cleaning lady would come. Facing the golden lettering on the Pléiade's green leather spine, I confided to Laurence that I had a job prospect in New York at the Italian Cultural Institute.

Laurence put her house list down on a round table next to her chair and removed her reading glasses.

"This is certainly news, isn't it?" she said.

"Well, I haven't gotten the job yet."

"Have you told him?"

I shook my head.

"He'll be very unhappy." She paused. "Could you possibly not tell him until we get back?"

"There is no point saying anything until it's definite."

She sighed and resignedly said, "And just when I thought . . . we were all getting used to one another."

"But you always knew that I wasn't going to stay here forever."

"In the beginning I did and quite honestly I was waiting for the day you'd leave."

I chuckled. "Of course you were."

"But the problem now is that when you do finally leave Paris, he will probably just find somebody else. And this I'm afraid of."

I felt for Laurence and was glad she finally was realizing what Michel was all about. "You don't have to put up with all this uncertainty," I said. "You could just divorce him and get over him and eventually meet somebody else who is straight. This way with him you'll never be safe."

Laurence raised her index finger, which struck me to be a very Gallic gesture for an American. "Ah, but there is never a guarantee that anybody will be *safe*, Russell. Yes, I could divorce Michel and marry another man. But the new man could, after a while, prove to be a terrible womanizer—as many men here are. And then I'd be right where I am now, except this new man

would not be the father of my children." There was a restless
pause, and at last Laurence said, "Russell, are you still in love
with my husband?"

After all, if I was still in love with Michel, then wouldn't I
perhaps be scheming to stay longer? "Let me put it this way.
This job in America, this job in New York, if I get it, nothing
will stop me from going back. This, I think, is really the best
way to answer your question."

The offer didn't come until early January. Ironically, I was out
on Michel's BMW, completing a revolution of the stately place
Vendôme, when a programmed wailing of bagpipes burst from
the pocket of my leather jacket. I pulled over to the side of the
road and answered the call of the man who had interviewed me
in Paris and who now offered me the job with the proviso that I
come back to America and begin work in a month's time. Peering up at the grand, spiraling obelisk that was once famously
knocked down by the Paris Communards, I accepted the position and headed over to Michel's apartment to break the news.

He greeted me at the door with a suggestive kiss, smelling
faintly of vetiver. He wore a tailored flannel shirt and a pair of
crisply pressed chinos and had a tan left over from the family
trip to Martinique. We sat adjacent to each other in his living
room, which was furnished with simple lacquered furniture,
buttery distressed leather armchairs, and tall, willowy halogen
lamps that stood sentinel in various corners and whose light lent
the room a dreamy, watery splendor. Despite his efforts to make
the place seem like a home, to me it felt cramped and temporary
in comparison to his fusty, ramshackle apartment on the avenue
Foch.

"I've been looking into the Yucatán," Michel announced to me, grinning sexily and pressing his leg against mine when I sat down next to him.

"How so?" I asked, trying to fight my feelings of immediate arousal.

"In March I think you and I should take a trip there together."

"Alone?"

Michel frowned. "Of course alone."

The sort of thing I'd dreamed about ever since I met him more than a year and a half before, the sort of idyll that even now still enticed me.

"Have you discussed it with Laurence?"

"I've mentioned it. She does not object. As long as I am going with you."

"Very understanding of her," I say, knowing that Laurence is probably assuming that I won't be able to go.

"She is a good wife."

Hesitating a moment, I told him, "Like I said before, you don't deserve her. And now that I've gotten to know her, I can say it with even more assurance."

Michel looked crestfallen; after all, it was not the first time that I'd told him this. "Well, you make it easy for me not to deserve her," he parried.

Of course he was right; for I, too, was a hypocrite. Before I'd arrived back in Paris I'd told Michel, knowing what the situation was with Laurence, knowing her feelings about it, that I'd feel like a heel if I slept with him again. But of course in the end I couldn't keep myself away from him, need and loneliness being far stronger passions than the prick of moral conscience.

"Anyway, March . . . I won't be here any longer," I said at last.
"Oh?"

Agitated, I got up and, with a clomp of motorcycle boots,
walked over to a floor-to-ceiling window that opened out onto a
side view of the Beaubourg. Looking through an angle of streets
paved in winter pallor, I could spy the cement fields of Forum
des Halles and a woman, dressed impeccably in a tailored suit,
riding a Vespa into the maze. Finally I turned around to face
him. "I was offered a job in New York," I said, watching his face
drain of color.

"From whom?"

"The Italian Cultural Institute."

"I see. And have you accepted it?"

"Today, as a matter of fact. Just before I came here."

Michel groaned and looked down at his feet. "Maybe you'll
change your mind and come anyway."

"I won't change my mind," I said gently.

He shook his head. "Well, I suppose I know this is happening
sooner or later. I hardly expect you to keep living in Paris. You
have to go back to America at some point. I don't think it will
be so soon." There was a pause, and then he inquired, "But how
soon, Russell?"

"They want me to start in a month."

He leaned forward in his armchair, the leather creaking, and
rubbed his face, his curls, bleached lighter by the Martinique
sun, spilling over his hands. I didn't go to him. I was afraid.
When he looked up at me there were tears in his eyes.

I told him to come and stay with me as much as he wanted.
"Now that you've sold the business, you'll certainly have the
time."

"It won't be the same. You know that."

"Look, Michel, I love being in Paris. But I'm nearly out of money."

"What about the insurance money?"

"No word. I think it's being contested, quite frankly. And I told you I don't want it anyway."

"Yes, you did tell me."

"Therefore all the more reason for me to find a steady, paying income."

"Well, you know you can teach English here. I can help you find more work. And of course continue with your translating. So you can write."

But Michel knew I wasn't writing. "I've been thinking that instead of doing all this freelance translation that I should pursue something a bit more challenging and with some real responsibility."

He glowered at me. "You're being so American about this."

"Wait a minute. I *am* American."

"Yes, you are. I guess I like to forget that."

"Just as you like to forget your wife is American. Take her American name away and give her a French one, instead. But she's still American in the end, isn't she?"

Michel winced. "Okay, enough!"

Beyond all this, the fact remained that I am someone who could probably never live full-time in Europe, much as I relished being there, much as I longed for it when I am back home. One disturbing thing I've noticed: The majority of Americans I've met who are living permanently in Paris for non-work-related reasons are Americans who on some level really hate their native country, embittered expats who have resolved never to cross the Atlantic again. I cannot relate to this mind-set.

At last I sat down next to him and rested my head against his shoulder. Michel resumed, "First I leave you. And now you leave me. Remember that day I broke it off? On your street in the Eighteenth?"

"You seemed so cool, so sure of yourself. That made it really hard."

"And you seemed so hurt by it."

"Well, I was."

"Now the roles are reversed," he said wistfully, managing somehow to smile.

"I guess they are."

Farther out in Brooklyn, the F train elevates to a very high van-tage point, and I can see far and wide, the winking lights of the snowbound city, the white feathering of the railings and finials of the brownstones, the sugar-coating of the lamps and the streetlights. At Avenue U, I step out into the gelid air that smells as fresh as a country hamlet, and there is even a salty hint of the not-too-distant Great South Bay. I am the only person walking down the metal steps toward the street, and once I start heading toward my destination, I find that in certain places the drifts come up past my knees. My boots aren't waterproof, I can feel snow melting inside them, and soon I begin shivering. When I reach my apartment building, I can see the entrance has been neither shoveled nor swept. Trudging up the limestone steps, heading into the warm vestibule, I am assailed by the fa-miliar smell of garlic and slow-cooking meat sauce. The build-ing is owned by a first-generation American family with

Calabrese roots; I am the only tenant who is not a relative. Despite the fact that other blood relations would love to take over my apartment, the landlords allow me to stay. They like the fact that I speak Italian and, when I was living there, had taken the liberty of knocking on my door with letters that arrived from Naples and Lecce and Palermo, asking me for an on-the-spot translation.

I walk up the rickety vinyl stairs to the second floor, where I can see several bundles of mail have been tied up by my subtenants and left outside my door. Loading everything into plastic carry bags, I notice a package wrapped in the lined brown paper used by European stationers and covered with foreign-looking decals: PAR AVION, VIA AEREA; blue stickers: 1ME CLASSE, PRIMA CLASSE. Someone has spent quite a bit of money to send me something, and at first I think Marina is forwarding me Stefano's books with yet another entreaty to have a go at translating them. But then I see the return address is the Hotel Birague, Paris. Could Ed and I have left something there?

I throw off my gloves and begin to rip into the package, which has been powerfully wrapped and gives a great deal of resistance. Finally I am able to tear a face of the outer layer away and see what is underneath.

The title page jumps out at me: *A POET'S LIFE*, in the all-too-familiar courier typewriter font. The combination of handwritten and printed pages has been carefully copied. There is a note.

Dear Russell:
I'm sending you a photostat of this just to make sure.
      Love,
      Ed

Epilogue

~

ONE YEAR LATER.

I'm browsing through the shelves of my local book-seller and notice the stack of *A Poet's Life* set out on a card table. I approach it slowly, pick up a single copy, and hold it for a few moments in cupped hands. Staring back at me from the book jacket is a thirty-year-old picture of Ed posing on the Accademia Bridge; the Grand Canal is behind him, a blur of gondolas and barges. He looks youthful and even a bit surly, the way I might look had I been blessed with such gratification so early in my career.

The moment I found Ed's memoir, the urge to delve into it once again was dead; burning the manuscript had destroyed the desire to read and reread the hurtful things that he had written about me. Unfortunately, I'd also incinerated a ten-year work-in-progress that an important writer had spent years layering with elegant language, adding and peeling away sentences and paragraphs that he deemed worthy or unworthy of a finished work of art. So much energy and worry and self-flagellation could not all be transformed to flames and smoke. Something had to remain, images of an unfinished life in words, the wisdom of the unfinished life of the author who made them. Because I was haunted by what I'd done, because I finally realized that I should never have tried to control how Ed saw me or how he wrote about me, I kept finding it impossible to write anything true of my own—until I rediscovered his manuscript.

Standing in the vestibule of my old apartment, I divined that Ed probably had some sort of premonition that he'd not live to see America again—why else would he have sent his only copy to me rather than to himself? Was he was just too egotistical to let three hundred pages lapse into obscurity? With this in mind I packed his book in the plastic bags along with the rest of my mail, trudged back out into the snowy night, and went home to my sublet. The following morning I hopped the subway into Manhattan, rang the buzzer at Annie Calhoun's apartment, and made an unannounced delivery.

Once I turned over the manuscript, I felt a sense of relief far greater than the counterfeit relief that came only fleetingly when I was burning Ed's pages. I felt fortunate to have had a chance to correct an unpardonable mistake. Somehow I knew that if I caught the subway home to Brooklyn, made my way back through the as-yet-unplowed streets of my new neighborhood, that I'd begin a long uninterrupted day of writing, the very first day I began writing a new book.

I've long since imagined the feeling of finally seeing Ed's hybrid mass of manually typed and scribbled yellow sheets translated into bold, indelible print. Although he'd had me read a substantial portion of the manuscript, I've seen only a fraction of what he's written about me. I have no idea to what extent he went in order to justify his feelings of rejection.

Frankly, I've been expecting the prose itself to have been tampered with, for many of Ed's short phrases to have been strung together, possibly linked with conjunctions in an attempt to make them fall more smoothly. However, the first thing I discover is that the sentences are published pretty much as they were composed. I feel foolish for not factoring in this distinct possibility. After all, he was a great artist whose brush-strokes should be respected and honored.

One of my early footnotes to Ed had been that he needed to fold more insight into his descriptions. Often he'd recount an anecdote but seemed neither to ponder its psychological implications nor give much attention to the reactions of the people involved in the story. And yet when I now read some of these passages, unchanged in the final version, they appear to contain just the proper amount of analysis. So what had I been thinking? Why had they bothered me before?

I'd told Ed to cut many passages in which he gave what I felt was unremarkable information about where he was when he wrote a poem as well as the circumstances surrounding the genesis of that poem. But now, as I read these depictions, they strike me to be actually vital to understanding not only how the man worked, and the emotions that drove him, but probably will help scholars fathom his state of mind: his bouts with depression, his insomnia, his ongoing struggle with his creative genius, his string of failures in love. And then, of course, there is the description of his sero-conversion, which is handled magnificently. The portrayal of that highly erotic encounter is lyrical and pitiless and may even be among the most forceful passages ever written about a disease gaining its first foothold in a human body.

I'm ashamed to realize what is actually much less compelling about the book: the story of Ed's affair with the college student that I had urged him to beef up and publish separately. Once again, outside of shifting some sentences around, he ignored my advice—luckily for him. Now the section affects me totally differently than when I first read it in Paris. It actually seems overly long and drawn out and even in some places superfluous. However, as I read further and further into the book, I keep uncovering lovely passages, filigrees of powerful insight that I seemed to have missed previously. All in all, by suggesting that he remove much of what has turned out to be important, I've proven myself to be a terrible editor. What was I thinking? Why was my judgment so off base? Were my instincts substantially different now because I was taking my own stab at some of the same material?

Finally I locate the place where the passages about mine and Ed's relationship should begin. In a matter of moments I realize that they are missing. Then I check the index, scan the alphabetized list of names, and find that mine is not among them. It's like a landscape that you have viewed so many times suddenly disappearing to become an unbending, empty horizon. How can this be? I wonder with disbelief. How did they manage to cut me out? And then I remind myself: Of course Annie Calhoun and Ed's publishers would rid the book of any allusion to me, in case I, as a defamed living person, decided to bring a lawsuit against the estate.

Trying to remain calm, I manage to digest the last fifty pages that cover the period of his life that saw the advent of me up until a few days before he died. Someone has figured out a way to present the material while whiting out any reference to a romantic interest, much less Ed's romantic obsession. I'd once deplored the idea of our relationship and Ed's dissatisfaction with it being brought before the public. Now having resigned myself to it, expecting to see it, I actually feel deflated. For I know that the reader will come away from *A Poet's Life* with the portrait of a man who was terribly lonely, who died struggling with his writing, and not of somebody tormented by his love for a younger man.

I have taken a week's vacation in Tuscany, and Marina and I are on our usual morning stroll around the grounds; the summer air is so saturated with pollen that I keep sneezing. *"Salute,"* she says as the dogs race by us on their way to the lily pond.

I look beyond Marina toward the villa and see Carla coming out onto the loggia. Sweeping the marble tiles, she catches sight of us and salutes us with her broom. "Carla seems awfully cheerful," I remark.

"That's because the farmer, the man who makes our wine, is courting her very seriously. Although she says she's too old to get married again, I do believe she enjoys his attention."

Marina picks up a soggy stick and tosses it to her pack of dogs, who chase it, gleefully yipping.

"Speaking of courtship, what about *you?*" I query. Marina blushes noticeably. "Anybody on the horizon?"

She admits to having a correspondence with a Milanese man whom she'd met years ago and who will soon come to pay her a visit. "But I am not too worried or invested in what will happen. I am like my dogs in this way," she comments. "Fine on my own, riveted to the possibilities of the present. I also have learned that the times when you are most content with your own solitude is when lovers suddenly pitch up into your path."

"I'll look forward to the day when that happens to me."

She chuckles but decides to keep her opinion about this to herself. Opting—wisely, perhaps—not to press her for it, I continue walking a few paces without further commentary.

"So what are you telling me, Russell?" She turns to me at last. "There is nobody new in your life?"

"For once I can honestly say no."

Marina grins. "I'm actually glad to hear this. And I have no doubt that it is because of this book that you are now writing."

She knows I've been working steadily for months, that the desire to set things down is stronger than it has been in years. I remember the day I went to visit Victor Hugo's house in the place des Vosges, how I grabbed the leg of his desk in desperation and prayed to be released from my obsession with Michel Soyer. Now there is no one occupying my thoughts. I am free to write my own version of my escape to Europe, my relationship with him and with Ed, and how I first came to the Villa Guidi.

"You know, Russell," Marina continues, "there is one thing about writing a book that you can be sure of."

"What's that?"

"Unlike lovers, my friend, the book will never desert you."

I, however, can desert the book, I think but do not say.

Marina has paused for a moment, leaning on her walking stick, fixing me with her pale, unnerving gaze. Her knee-high rubber boots are splattered with mud and, despite the heat, she is wearing her favorite tweed jacket. "By not being honest with you, I suppose that I am no better than some of these lovers of yours."

"But a friend—"

"A friend should be held to an even higher standard. If we put up with a lot when we're in love, accept lies when we know they're lies, then our friends should always be our allies, they should always give us the truth."

"I agree."

"You see, I tried to protect Stefano from the truth: that nobody but I considered his work very important. Meanwhile I was the one everybody thought was accomplished. Knowing how difficult this would be for him to live with, the only thing I could do was to make him greater than myself in order to make him feel like a true husband. I tried desperately hard to do this . . ." Her voice breaks. "I failed miserably!" Pausing for a moment to collect herself, she touches me on the shoulder. "And then . . . I guess I believed you were our last hope. I thought you really *could* help us." She grabs my arm for emphasis. "But, Russell, I only came to that *after* I invited you to stay here. And in the end I was too embarrassed and felt I couldn't let you know *everything*."

I decide to be gracious and refrain from telling her that I'd figured much of this out quite some time ago. "Thank you, Marina," I say. "And now that we're on apologies, I have one to make to you."

Marina begins frowning.

"For not listening."

She laughs. "How could you listen to me after all? I was so insistent about everything."

"Well, for one thing, I should not have gone back to Paris."

"Ah, yes, but you didn't *stay* in Paris. You realized what it was all about and then you went to New York."

"Luckily, the job—"

"I was afraid you wouldn't take that job, that the Frenchman would dissuade you from taking it. But when you did, I knew that you were going to be fine."

"And then, of course, Ed's manuscript. I should have sent that back just as you instructed me to. It was wrong for me to hold on to it."

Marina hesitates and then says, "Well, I've thought about this a lot myself. And I finally decided that you needed to hold on to it."

We enter a row of plane trees and she looks up into the tall matrix of branches, eyes blinking with rapid thoughts going on behind them. "I've been meaning to say I think *A Poet's Life* is a horrible title. What is your opinion of it?"

"It's not so bad. What would be better?"

Marina smiles. "How does the title *Unrequited Love* sound in English?"

I consider for a moment. "I think it's a bad title in English. In Italian it probably sounds better because of the word order: *Amore Non Richiesto*."

Marina shakes her head. "It doesn't, actually. It's wrong for the Italian, too. In fact, it sounds really ugly. Doesn't it sound ugly to you?"

"Honestly? No."

"Then again, I suppose the title is a good reflection of what the book is about."

I stop walking and look at her. "Hardly! Everything about me was taken out."

She laughs. "Russell, please, you're not the only person this man lost his head over. If you read this book it shows the unfortunate pattern of his romantic life."

"But, wait, so then you've read it, too?" Marina nods her head slowly. "You told me you'd never read it."

"Sometimes, Russell, I can be a hypocrite. But I have read this book. Rizzoli sent me an early copy in the mail. The translation will soon be available here with this horrible *Amore Non Richiesto* title that you seem to like."

"What do I know?"

Soon the pack of dogs rush by us. Marina turns to pat Primo, the black-and-white one she calls "the beneficent father," as we make the final turn back toward the villa.

The Italian version of Ed's book is lying on the dining table. The same picture of him on the Accademia Bridge glares back at me, but the photo has a sepia tint; it's more tasteful than the American edition. *Amore Non Richiesto*.

I pick it up and flip through the pages. "I guess you're right," I say. "The title's not so great."

"Of course I'm right. I'm Italian!"

"I forgot to mention to you that I got a letter from the Italians, from Rizzoli asking me to sign a form to indemnify them."

"Oh, really?"

"They must've heard that I ended up with the manuscript and were just covering themselves."

"May I have the book now, please?" Marina says. I hand it to her. Holding it against her chest, she asks with her old imperious tone, "This waiver you signed, Russell. How carefully did you read it?"

"I think I read all of it. Why?"

She grimaces. "You probably missed the fine print."

Nervous now, I say, "What are you talking about?"

"Rizzoli, apparently, was given the original manuscript *before* the Americans made their final edits." She turns to the index, flips a few pages, and then points to a name. "See . . . here you are."

Todaro, Russell, 275–320.

I grab the book and quickly find page 275, where Ed begins describing his disenchantment with me. After a few minutes I recite to Marina, "*Il fatto è che è talmente preso dal suo Francese che sarebbe capace di fare qualunque cosa. Darebbe la vita per amore. Ecco perchè non scriverà mai niente di buono.*" Then I translate, "He's so possessed by his passion for his Frenchman, he'd do anything. He'd give his life over to love. That's why he'll never write anything good."

I remember reading this for the first time in Stefano's old room. I felt so betrayed. I close the book and put it back on the table. "This really hurts me," I tell Marina. "It's as though in Italian Ed's words have been changed into something more forceful, something more emotionally true, something more beautiful."

"You idolize Italian," she points out. "In some way Italian is more real to you than English."

Could this really be why Ed's disapproval has taken on a sharper edge, wounding me unexpectedly? Or is it just that his opinion of my ability will always matter? I'm about to tell Marina how disturbing this is when a clatter of silverware in the kitchen alerts me that Carla is preparing the mint and tomato pasta she has promised me because she knows how much I love it. The sounds of domesticity silence my cry, words and recollections suddenly flooding forward, begging to reveal the story of my conversion.